Dedicated in part to

...

Kaylyn, Alex, Michael, Jason, Elizabeth, Jake, and Zach

Prologue

It doesn't matter to me if I'm being irrational. At this point, I don't see any reason to be rational. All I know is that I want to cease to be anything. Or, to correct myself, maybe I would choose to be a rock. Then at least I wouldn't feel a damn thing. Ever.

Under the sink cabinet is a fix. I fantasize, bitter slime rushing down my throat, swirling around my tongue, agonizing in cold whispers the last thing I will ever taste.

A shiver ran through my body straight to my bare feet, cold on the linoleum. In a moment's pass, I realized the empty silence of the house. What will be the last thing I hear? In all hopes, I wouldn't want it to be my parents. I need to hurry.

I rush to the medicine cabinet as it beckons. Opening the door reveals an easy solution; a present, just for me. I couldn't ask for anything more. I start picking through the bottles, letting them drop on the counter below. The impacts are like gunshots echoing in the silence, so I stop. Then I find the one. In my hand I hold Dad's sleeping pills.

Good thing for me, I have an idea of where he stores his special liquor. Double whammy. I hurry upstairs to my parent's room, trying to ignore my childhood pictures in frames on the walls. The nausea of the situation begins to set in. But I ignore it. I'm a rock for God's sake!

I saw the bottles in his wardrobe one time, I swear. That time was an accident in the game of hide and seek with Aldin. He hides them there for a reason. Me.

Aldin. I sure hope that he will be okay. Doubt was beginning to grow again. The guilt of letting down a person who looks up to me so much, or at least used to, makes me want to puke.

No. I can't do this to myself. I am determined to finish what I started.

I thrash open the doors, gritting my teeth and growling deep in my throat. I feel like tearing everything he owns apart! I grip a handful of his sweater and jackets, then I notice it.

The hell? The compartment embedded in the side threw me off. I think for a moment, the silence here gain. I have never noticed that little feature. There is no liquor here, but now my curiosity is aroused. I flip the little brass latch and pull the door flap down. My blood freezes for a breathtaking moment.

Yes.

I pull out my new deadly weapon. Goodbye world.

Chapter One

Roy

Mr. Grebb's painfully long lecture seemed to be slowing down time. I'm not much of a poet, nor am I really gifted at getting strong grades. To get to this point of the high English class, I've barely slipped by, engulfing myself in an agonizing mound of verbal garbage, vigorously polished to try and please my father. But relationships can't be polished as easily.

I was having one of those days.

"Roy, pull down your hood."

My reaction time must've irritated him, because he sighed heavily with annoyance when I finally snapped back into what was happening in the present. The past is a powerful entity. I ripped it off my head, maybe too aggressively, and the gawking heads switched their attention back to the front once a second passed. I guess it was worth it for Grebb to interrupt his lesson for me to expose my hair. I know he dislikes me.

I could see Kyle gazing at me from four desks to my right. He knew something was up. Kyle can always tell. Of course, he's used to it by now. I didn't look at him though. Instead, I sat with my fists clenched, wishing I could escape and run off to the band room early.

Grebb carried on, the speech sliding off of his tongue and piercing my ears with knives. I don't want to be in this class. AP calculus is already a burden for me. Why add on AP English as well? My older brother John somehow did it all two years ago. He took four AP classes, earned basketball and lacrosse college scholarships, came close to valedictorian, and received an honors diploma. What he didn't prepare me for was how much of a bitch senior year is. The sad thing is that I'm only a couple of weeks into school. He made it look easy.

4

"Tonight, your homework is to write an outline on what this poem's main theme is. How did Poe use diction, metaphors, and meter and rhyme to put forth the overall meaning?"

I scribbled quick notes in my notebook on what he said to write. This junk, marching band practice, and a load of brain cramping math all crunched into one evening. Great . I left the classroom in haste. Kyle caught up to me and punched my back. I kicked him in the butt. He raked a hand through his curly dark hair.

"Maybe what Poe was trying to say is kiss your teacher's ass and teacher, why don't you kiss my ass." I couldn't help but grin.

"Kiss my ass, Grebb."

Kyle has been my best friend since freshman year. I met him when I decided to get into music as a drummer. He's stuck by my side, even at times when I wasn't even sure why. He's a pretty charismatic dude. Sometimes I even think he's too cool for me.

We entered the band room and headed past all the intertwining wind instruments to the back where the percussion section resides. All of the percussion instruments were nicely organized, but shirts and shoes were scattered around, random mallets and sticks on the floor, pictures of us drummers together were on the wall, lockers were decorated, and the red fuzzy loveseat in the corner was occupied. This is home. Passing through the section was like entering my bedroom. It's our place. Call me a geek, but many can't say they have a place like that at school.

I observed the new girl with the ponytail play some fast scales on the marimba. It sounded impressive. Good technique and focus; she was better than the others in the pit last year. The "pit" consists of all percussion instruments set in the front of the production that are not marched, such as mallets and keyboards, guitars, sounds systems, tambourine, all that jazz.

Nathan and Sean, juniors, were practicing their snare parts on their practice pads. Kyle walked up to them and joined, instantly correcting Nathan's technique as well. Kyle is the center snare of the drumline, which in part, makes him section leader. He is the man.

Our high school drumline is a pretty competitive one to our region. With five tonal bass drums, four snares, two tenor players, a large pit of mallet instruments and auxiliary, and a talented percussion instructor, we put together some pretty kick-butt shows for our fall and winter competitions. I myself play the tenors with five different toned drums. These babies have been my main concern for the last three years. I can't say I've ever been more passionate about anything else, really. As I walked by, I smiled at Kyle's break of insane rudimental drumming. We're both consumed thoroughly. It's no wonder why we don't have girlfriends. I'm surprised he doesn't have one, though. He's like the lady's man of the class.

I headed straight to the drum room to bring out my tenors. We were supposed to go out on the field today and rehearse. Michael, a shy freshman and the beginning bass one player, followed behind me.

"Hey man," I said. Of course, he's intimidated by the rest of us veterans. But eventually, he'll find his place. He has the essential drumming skills and attitude for survival in the group. He slowly grabbed his drum off of the shelf, heaving a big sigh.

"That girl on bass two is showing me up. She's even taller than me. I mean, I just want to get to the good days where you are, a super cool and tall senior who plays badass tenors," Michael muttered. He blew out his chubby cheeks and sighed.

I let out a small laugh.

"Um, first of all, I'm pretty sure that's the most I've heard you talk."

Michael paused from movement. When I saw a smile appear, I grinned and continued, almost ready to laugh.

"Second of all, Krysten has been playing bass for two years. She hasn't advanced, and she probably won't because she doesn't practice anything harder."

Michael nodded, "I guess so. That still doesn't change the fact that you are twice my height," he added, giving me a once over and shaking his head.

"Psh, would you believe I was your height freshman year?"

6

He lifted the drum over his shoulder and gave me a look.

"No kidding?"

"It happened. Just ask Kyle."

He nodded, "Right."

I smiled, still pretty surprised that he just came to me and let that out. He barely knows me and he hardly talks to anyone in the group. Kyle came barging in to grab his snare followed by Nathan, Sean, Krysten, and my fellow tenor player, Preston. It became a party of attaching harnesses. The concentration of the small room broke by Preston, the jokester.

"Hey Kyle, you dropped your ear plugs," Preston noted as he brought his drums down from the shelf. Kyle frowned and set his drum down, bending over to search the floor. Unexpectedly, Preston kicked him right in the butt, almost knocking Kyle over. Krysten giggled.

"You jackass!" Kyle shouted, casting a grin.

"You bent over," Preston justified.

"What is that, a new thing?" Krysten asked, lifting her bass drum over her shoulder.

"It is now," Sean said.

Krysten rolled her eyes, "Let's all conform to Preston once again."

"Hey, sweetie," Preston said in sarcasm, "Why else are you here?" He smirked, slipping an arm around her. Krysten and Preston are seniors like Kyle and I. Preston was able convince Krysten to join drumline sophomore year, and she did. They're our drumline couple. As we walked out of the room together with our drums, Kyle spoke up,

"So drumline party at my house tonight after rehearsal?"

A response of nodding heads sparked excitement, but I glanced at Michael, who looked at the ground as he walked. I understood that we were comfortable with our group and didn't want intruders. But I knew I could change that. I caught Kyle's attention and gestured towards the freshman's direction. Kyle nodded. He slapped a hand on his back.

"You comin'?"

The freshman's smile left me feeling satisfied.

The drum majors ordered the band to head to the football field after we ran through some of the music together. I walked side by side with Kyle on the sidewalk, the sticks in our stick bags hitting the sides of our drums to our footsteps. Sun rays streaked through the overcast sky, reflecting onto the chrome of my rims. I shined it into Kyle's eyes to bug him. I wasn't expecting it, but he spoke up.

"So, what happened? You looked like crap during first period, dude. Not that you normally don't..."

The queasy feeling in the pit of my stomach began to settle again once he reminded me. Being around the drumline had numbed it. I would think that I'd be immune to it by now. I squeezed my eyes, knowing he would get it out of me no matter what. He gestured for me to speak up as I heaved a sigh.

"Just...my dad. You know."

"Hmmm, nah, you're going to be a little more specific there. C'mon, you know the drill."

"What drill?" I demanded, irritated. I dislike talking about issues dealing with my dad.

"C'mon, you know what happens when you don't talk about things. You just get all depressed and easily agitated."

I knew he was right.

"Okay, okay. I just got in another big fight with my dad this morning. It got to yelling and threatening. Just another one of those that left me feeling like I wanted to sabotage his life. Like lighting his bed on fire or throwing all of his nice business clothes out in the dog shit."

Kyle contorted his face into a grinning frown, but I knew he understood.

"Well why did he get so mad at you?"

"It's Grebb, man," I summarized. Kyle nodded. It was a mutual understanding. I had Grebb for English last year as well. Grebb

8

is a serious teacher. I've never met a bald fifty year old man with such a low tolerance of teenagers. He dislikes the sense of humor, the skater kids with long "ill-groomed" hair like mine, etc. It's not that I goof off a lot, I just don't always control what comes out of my mouth. Sometimes I'm a bit loud or rowdy in class, at least too much for Grebb. Okay, maybe you can call that "goofing off." I do my homework most of the time. It's not that I don't care about my grades. I have to. My parents are strict about it, especially since my older brother John set such high of standards. John was one of Grebb's most beloved students. It's a no-brainer why Grebb has never given me As' on papers.

"Did Grebb send an asshole email to your parents or something?" He questioned, knowing my frustration.

"You guessed it. Roy has been causing distraction in my class, blah, blah, Roy's work isn't as good as it could be, blah, blah."

Talking about it was getting me worked up.

"So what did your dad say?"

I shook my head, my chest tightening in frustration, "He went on about how I could do better in school and he doesn't like how his kid is acting like a punk in class."

"He said punk?" Kyle frowned.

"Yep. He obviously thinks so highly of me," I rolled my eyes and continued, "and no matter how much I tried to explain things from my point of view, he totally talked over me and didn't listen." There was a moment of smoldering silence.

"You should go…punch something."

Ha. Yeah. There's a reason why I cut one out on my arm this morning. I'm wearing a jacket for a reason. Of course, I wasn't about to tell him that. I bit my lip.

We walked along the turf to our opening dots after the drum major shouted out "opening set!" I sighed again and said to Kyle,

"Dude, I don't want to go home right away. Are you staying after to practice today?"

He shook his head, explaining that he had to give his little sister a ride to some birthday party. So I forced myself to relax and focus. I couldn't just suck because I had my mind wrapped around my dad. I had my drums, the line around me, and the texture of turf beneath my drill-masters. I had all that made me happy right here.

Siri

I am nervous. Why is that? Well, I just moved to this school, and I'm beginning my junior year with people I didn't know. I'm kind of a social bug admittedly, it shouldn't be hard to make some friends. I expect the anxiousness to dwindle.

I stroked the mahogany keys on this marimba with my fin-ger-tips, examining the quality and beauty. Compared to my previ-ous school, these instruments were in top-shape. They must actual-ly have money. At my old school, all of the money went to sports and dance. Therefore, I got used to mismatched mallets, banged up keys and duct-taped percussion repairs. It's even amazing that after moving here I immediately become one of two marimba players right off the bat. The other player, Fiona, is a senior and a talented player. She and a couple of others in the pit have been the only ones to break the ice since my arrival. As for the drumline? They are king. At least at my old school, being in the drumline was a big deal. Socially, if you were accepted in the drumline, you trans-formed. You were cool. Maybe I'm making the drumline sound like they're the snooty stuck-ups of the band. But in many ways, less drastically of course, it's true. It hasn't proved to be different here.

I watched as they stood in opening set. Their postures matched; feet together, straight bodies and drums level, sticks in playing position, and of course, their attention on the drum major. The tall tenor player, the long, dark- haired one who is always loud, looked like he was pissed. That's how focused he looked. One of the snare players starting talking to the one on his right when Kyle told him to hush up.

Cool, I at least know his name. Reason being, he's the section leader, but also super attractive. Yep, I just admitted it. Look at him! He looks like he could be a track star. Somehow, his sideburns and scruff complimented his curly dark hair and blue-green eyes. My question is, why isn't he taken?

Don't go there missy, like you have a chance.

I glanced at the bass drum line during my thought-processing examination of the drumline. There were two girls, one on bass two, and one on bass three. If I remember right, the one in front is Krysten, the other tenor player's girlfriend. Yeah, that's right. I'm remembering things! I guess that's what I get for missing band camp. That trip to New York with my family was great, but maybe a mistake. I was so worried I wouldn't land a good spot, but would instead be stuck playing the high-hat or something. Seriously, how did I get so lucky? Our instructor, Elliot, only needed to hear me play for ten seconds and then said, "Okay, okay, it's yours. Here's your part."

That easy. Nothing makes me happier than this thing in front of me. That's how it should be, at least in my opinion. I'm a nerd.

"Siri," Fiona hissed. She motioned for me to look at the drum major to begin our intro solo. Here goes. In just a few seconds, the melodies and harmonies of the mallets part filled the stadium air, swarming me with musical ecstasy.

Call me a band geek I guess. But music is my escape.

The field practice ended.

The band grouped in crowds and pairs, carrying their instruments back to the band room from the field. A couple of trumpet players flew past me, throwing pine cones or something at each other. It annoyed me that the skinny one bumped my marimba, which by the way, is such a pain to cart all the time. I smiled when their section leader ran after them, scolding. Glad I'm not the only one annoyed. Not only that, it's cool that the leadership of this band takes this activity seriously.

Immediately, from behind me, erupted some obnoxious laughing. Some guys were horsing around. The tall guy with the tenors ran right up next to me, sweaty in his black hoodie, looking behind him at the other tenor player chasing after him. He towered over me intimidatingly, wiping his hair from his face and shouting back at the other guy. I leaned away from him, irritated. His voice pierced my ears as he brushed past me, his left drum nicking my instrument.

C'mon!

I shook it off, glaring at him as he hastily walked off and grinned back at the other guy.

"Roy, you freakin' coward!" Called that one guy.

So Roy, that's his name. Interesting. Interesting name, weird guy. I didn't realize I was studying him like no other. He has a long face, his dark hair falling on his forehead just above his eyes. It curled at his ears and hung behind to his neck. He has an imperfect nose, but it was good for his face. I noticed that he had deep set, dark brown eyes. He's tall and slim, but he isn't skinny. He was built just right. It didn't even matter at that moment, however, if I realized he was attractive to me. I just felt he would continue to get on my nerves. He seemed like the type who has issues. Who doesn't though? That was probably too judgmental of me. I have mine as well.

Roy

I practiced in the drum room for a couple hours after school. I did it until my hands hurt and I had to stop. It's a good hurt, a satisfying type of pain that I've learned is constructive. That may sound strange…but that's being a musician. I feel good calling myself one.

I walked out of the drum room and to the parking lot feeling good.

Grabbing my keys from my pocket with my sticks in my other, I unlocked my Bronco and headed home.

Home. I didn't really want to see my dad. My hope was that he was staying longer at work today. He does that a lot. To summarize him up, he cares a lot about his image and how his family reflects him. He's strict and opinionated. Only sometimes does he actually let loose and act like an actual human being.

I cranked System of a Down on my CD player, trying to think about everything but my dad. My attempt to get lost into my music ended when I saw his sedan in the driveway. I then tried to brain-storm how I would avoid him, or just act invisible to everyone when I walked in. To be honest, I didn't want to be around my family. I knew that I could quietly come through the back door and run up to my room if I was stealthy enough.

That attempt was a fail. Aldin, my thirteen year old broth-er, greeted me with a rubber band shot to the chest as I walked through the door.

"I'm going to kill you, Al!" I reacted, shaking my head.

We've been in a rubber band battle for three days now. I told him I was tough enough to take them all, which in turn, I hoped would lead him to eventually quit the fight first. Of course, his little man syndrome kicked in.

"Sucker," he grinned. I walked up to him with a fierce face, hoping to scare him. He knew this face. Being twice his size, he knew what was coming. He backed away, concern filling his ex-pression. He stuck his fingers in his pocket and pulled out another band.

"Stay away, I'm loaded!" He warned, a defeated grin spreading across his face. He aimed it at me, but I lunged at him, ignoring the sting. He squealed, trying to escape my grasp. I lifted him up in my arms and held him upside down. He began to laugh loudly in his high, undeveloped voice, letting the defeat sink in once again.

"Hmmm, where to drop you," I teasingly contemplated, "Does the toilet sound good?"

"What? Roy, no!" He shouted. He began pounding my back.

Heh heh. I'm his tormenting big brother. I took a few steps to-wards the bathroom, and he starting flailing and shouting. Instead, I threw him on the couch. He flipped around until he stood up, patting his hair smooth.

"So what? Is this the end? I get you, and you just threaten me?"

"Pretty much," I smirked. He crossed his arms.

"Is he being mean to you, Al?" John said, coming around the corner wearing no shirt and basketball shorts that exposed his abs and bulky calves. I always have to look away. His ripped muscles make me want to flee my own body it's so perfect. I feel disgusting admitting that.

"Hey John, shut up and put on a shirt!" I boomed at him. He raised a brow.

"What? Is this too much for you, brotha?" He gestured, flexing.

"Gross," I grumbled.

"Hey John? Get him for me, please?" Aldin said. I struck a dirty look to him. I faced John and posed a fighting stance.

"Alright, let's see what you got, little brotha," John said.

He hates the irony that I'm a little taller than him. John grinned and lunged at me, grabbing my head and attempting to pull me to the floor.

He grunted in frustration, and I said, "I'm not Aldin's size anymore!"

Suddenly I felt another two hands bring me down. It was a game for me to try and stay up with the force of my brothers on me.

"Don't kill him guys!" Mom said, walking into the room with a basket full of laundry. They eased and gave up.

"When will dinner be ready, Mom? I'm starving!" Aldin said.

"I'm waiting for your dad to get home. We're going to eat together tonight," she said, putting on her slippers. Whenever possible, Mom tried to get us all to eat together. She turned her attention to me.

"Marching band tonight, right?"

I nodded.

"He better hurry then, I'm starving too," I said, patting a hand on my belly. The actual truth is that I'd rather not eat dinner with my dad and suffer through the tension.

"Isn't he home already?" John mentioned, pointing to his car.

"He's across the street at Dave's." She said, picking out a shirt and folding it.

"What the heck? Let's eat!" John said. He dug into the basket and picked a shirt to throw on. John ran out the door, letting us know he was going to get Dad. Mom sighed. It looked like she had been cleaning house all day.

"Roy, will you please set the table?" I nodded. As I walked by her, she stroked my back and paused me.

"I know that there is tension between you and Dad right now. I heard it very clearly this morning."

Of course. We were yelling.

She continued, "Just be careful about getting him angry. I absolutely cannot stand it when you two yell at each other. That means you need to really work on handling your anger and what you say."

A sigh burst from me and held back from rolling my eyes. She didn't deserve that. However, I couldn't help but feel frustrated at why she didn't validate for me that he was the unreasonable one.

I placed the forks and knives flawlessly on the table, lining everything parallel. I guess because I was in such deep thought about the fight earlier and how Dad was going to be around me, I set the table slowly. I didn't even realize it until Dad and John burst through the front door in the kitchen laughing their heads off about something. I sped up my job to finish, hoping that his laughter meant he was in a good mood.

I didn't really care what he and John were laughing about. I just noticed Dad's arm around John's shoulders. I pretended not to listen when Dad began to tell how John performed perfect cart wheels in the yard, impressing him and Dave. Apparently Dave, our overweight neighbor, tried to copy and he fell on his ass.

Once we sat down, I plopped an oversized scoop of mashed potatoes on my plate. I immediately dug in, shoving spoonful after spoonful into my mouth without a pause. I didn't want to talk. Dad asked Aldin about his day. For the next five minutes, we heard him babble about his class's pet snake and how his rowdy friend snuck it out of its cage and chased the most disliked girl in the class into the boy's bathroom. Then Aldin brought up football, which of course, Dad just eats up.

Meatloaf kept my mouth busy at a fast pace. I was eating a lot, and John seemed to notice. He looked at me and frowned. Dad began to talk about the office, and I sat with eyes downcast, hoping he would continue for a while. I dreaded the thought of him bringing up Grebb and the fight. The feeling of guilt began to rise and made me feel like I was a terrible person. At least that's how I feel when I'm around him. I reached for my cup of water and gulped as he talked.

Dad finished his sentence, and then came the blank sound of forks on plates. I was eating vigorously, but realized I may be attracting attention. Even though I was looking down at my plate, I noticed that Dad looked at me. I looked up to verify and we made awkward eye contact. He didn't say anything to me, but instead continued eating and asked John about his new apartment and his roommates. So I cleared my plate to the last nibble and gulped the rest of my water down. Everyone seemed surprised when I abruptly stood up and picked up my plate.

"Roy, we just sat down," Mon said, frowning.

"I'm going to practice early," I said shortly. I did feel kind of bad. Dad wiped his face with a napkin and anticipated to speak up as he swallowed.

"No, Roy, you're staying longer. I don't care how fast you decided to eat, but your mom worked hard for this dinner time," he ordered, using his finger to gesture at my chair. Internally, I was screaming at the top of my lungs. So I reluctantly plopped myself back down, anticipating him to either criticize me, or ask me what's wrong when he know very well what my problem is.

"Just because you are in a bad mood doesn't mean you have the right to be rude."

Here we go.

I sat with my arms crossed. When I noticed this, I straightened up so Dad wouldn't comment. Mom made eye contact with me.

16

"Roy, anything out of the ordinary at school today?"

I thought about what to say. There was only one thing.

"I practiced a lot today. Preston and I are in the middle of learning the tenors break, and it's really cool. I have this solo part Elliot wrote for me which he says is one of the most challenging pieces he's ever written for a high school line."

"Sweet," John complemented. John loves that I'm one of the top drummers in the school.

"Roy that's impressive," Mom said, sounding delighted. Dad ate his food and looked down at his plate.

"He's trying to prepare me for the drum corps. He's writing me parts that are as challenging as some of DCI's stuff. I'm—,"

"Drum corps? That summer band thing? We've talked about that. I really don't get it."

I grit my teeth, irritated once again that he proved not to know anything about drumming and marching bands even though I talk about it A LOT! Plus he interrupted me. Initially, I should have just not said anything. I tried not to hiss through my teeth,

"Dad, I've told you, I'm auditioning in November. It's what I want to do."

My hands were balled into fists. This conversation about drum corps seemed to always go in endless, ridiculous circles!

"We've talked about this. It costs lots of money, and what, you're gone all summer? What about college, Roy? Huh? You need to prepare for school, not run around all summer doing a hobby that won't get you anywhere."

"That's not fair, Dad! The drum corps is amazing. I want to be a part of it. I'm good enough. I'll make college work! I've told you that many times!"

He looked angry.

Mom spoke up, "Okay, enough, we are not discussing this right now! Richard, I don't think you're being fair to him either." I was glad she said that.

"No, he needs to understand! Roy, I don't know how I can support you if you're involved in something like that. It's…its silly!"

I threw down my fork and it bounced on the floor loudly. Aldin gasped. Dad widened his eyes as my chair flew backwards, tipping back and crashing on the back. I fled out the kitchen door without looking back, feeling the need to scream. I ran to my Bronco, holding back hot, frustrated tears. I drove off at high speed, knowing exactly where to go. Blasting angry rock music, I took a sharp turn into the road leading to the gravel river entrance. My chest was tightened with pain, and my squeezing fingers were white on the wheel.

I parked at a secluded grass clearing. Feeling my pants pocket to make sure I still had it with me, I then hopped out and starting walking hastily towards the riverbank. Glancing around at the area, I spotted the giant rock I like to sit on.

She's my friend. Kyle and I named her Brittany. I ripped off my black jacket. Gosh I had been hot all day, but it was hiding what needed hiding.

Back into my pants pocket, I pulled out my weapon, the spring assist pocket knife Dad gave me for Christmas one year. Ha, yes, if only he could've predicted its true use. The cut I created in my forearm that morning was looking pretty bad. An ugly scab crusted it over, but now I would give it a twin.

I pressed the blade tip to my skin, letting it slice. I winced, but the pain was fantastic. The red stream traveled down my arm in a trail and dripped down onto Brittany. I let out a deep breath, letting it release the rage. The hell with my untouched skin if it's not worth what's it carrying anyway. After all, I don't know who I hate worse; my father or me.

Siri

Marching band rehearsal on a Thursday night for three hours. I'm ready for this. A lot of people would complain, but I'm cool with it. I don't really have any friends to go out with yet anyways.

18

I unzipped my jacket as I entered the band room. There were a few people here, not too many yet. I guess I'm an overachiever if I show up a half an hour early. Before I went to my marimba, I felt like my bladder would burst. Had to take care of that.

I headed out to the hallway in the direction of the bathroom, but was disrupted by drumming from inside the drum room. Curiously, I decided I would just peak in. Who else would be here earlier than me practicing? I found it strange that the room was dark. Through the small window, I searched for the guy playing those advanced phrases on the tenors. Immediately, I recognized the height and hair.

Wow, whatever he was playing, it sounded very impressive. I could only see his outline because of the darkness, but my breathing froze when he stopped playing and I shifted towards the door. Embarrassed, I instantly dashed away, power walking with tip toes towards the girl's room. I hope he didn't see my face and think I was spying on him or something. That would be weird.

As I waited around, practicing new exercises on my marimba, people were slowly coming in, including the two girl bass drum players. I craved their attention, hoping at least one of them would catch my eye and say hello.

But they didn't. They just joined some other battery dudes in the red couch corner and started laughing about stuff. I sagged and sighed. Pathetic.

Why don't you just talk to them?

"Hey what's up with Roy?" Fiona mumbled to Kyle as they walked by me. She was just loud enough for me to hear. I don't think they even noticed that I stopped playing to eaves drop.

"I'm not sure. Obviously he's alienating himself. It's probably about his dad again," Kyle told her quietly. I didn't realize I was looking behind my shoulder so obviously until Kyle caught my eye with a blank expression. I snapped my head around, embarrassed. I'm just curious is all?

Roy

Kyle tapped off the warm-up for the battery and pit at Elliot's direction, and in unison, we began marking time with our feet. This is the only place where my home life gets erased from my mind, replaced by the focus I've been conditioned to. Elliot hit his sticks together to the beat, his head snapping to a bass drummer who hit a note off beat.

"It doesn't matter what is going on in your life. I don't care if your boyfriend or girlfriend breaks up with you. I don't care if... your pet bird dies. Okay, I would care, but whatever it is, when you come to drum, you focus, and stay focused. It is your responsibility to this group to leave those issues behind. We're here for music."

Those are the words Elliot drilled in our heads at the beginning of band camp. He says that every year pretty much. We are lucky to have a serious, former DCI instructor. His diligent teaching habits, intimidating looks, and exceptional percussion skill level helps us reach our potential. At the same time, he's super cool and relatable. I want to be a drum coach one day.

My arms and wrists moved in muscle memory to the warm-ups. I listened carefully to the sound, making sure I was listening in to the snares to my left. Preston seemed to be slightly lagging, and I snapped to him, "Listen!" He immediately corrected. Elliot looked my direction and walked over to listen to Preston and I. He made eye contact with me, a challenge not to glance back. He brought his sticks up to one of my one drums and played along, checking for precision. I stared straight ahead, finding a leaf on the tree to focus on. I didn't dare check his stare, feeling his breath on me. Eventually, Elliot backed away nodding with approval, and I felt myself breathe a little bit more.

Rehearsal went pretty smoothly. I made it through, sweating in my black hoodie. The pain of my new cut was beginning to seriously annoy me. As I drummed, the material brushed up against it the wounded flesh and caused me to grimace. Nobody seemed to notice. However, they did seem to notice I wasn't interacting much with them at the beginning. I felt too crummy from the arguments with my dad to say anything to anybody I suppose. I tried to cheer up at least. After all, I didn't want to be a downer at Kyle's.

"Hey Roy, your shoe is untied," Krysten noted as we walked into the band room to pack up. I stopped walking and faced her behind me.

"Oh, will you get that for me please?" I reacted, crossing my arms. I didn't bother to look down. She pretended to act confused,

"Nah, do it yourself, big boy!"

"Fine then, get in front of me."

She rolled her eyes and sighed.

"Fine! You win. Whatever," Krysten submitted, walking in front of me.

I grinned. Preston came running up.

"Did you get him, babe?"

"Nope!" I responded. Seeing her bass mallet on top of her drum, I reached over and knocked it onto the floor.

"Hey! You a-hole!" She shrieked. She reacted immediately better than I had hoped.

"Hey Chloe, grab that stick for me?"

She got a flute player to do it. Her head slowly turned back to meet me, a smug smile spread across her face. I gave her a shove forward.

"Just go, princess."

We packed up the drums on the shelves, discussing our excitement for hanging out afterwards. I dug my phone out of my jeans pocket to check the time, but noticed that I received a text from my mom. Son-of-a-bitch.

"You are grounded. Come home right after."

My body tightened. The fury was building in my throat, like I could scream at the top of my lungs until my vocal chords bled. I wanted to tear, destroy, and run. Krysten, Preston, Kyle, Michael, Gavin, Nathan, and Sean were all in the room. I had to leave.

Inconspicuously, I bolted out of the drum room, hearing their laughter and presence of each other being enjoyed. I live for these people and hanging out with them. Now it's being taken away for what? Being misunderstood by my father?

"Roy, where ya' going?" Kyle called after me in the hallway. My fists were balled, ready to punch and break something. I exhaled angry breaths rapidly, pacing the hallway. I must've looked like a maniac.

"Man, what's the matter?" He said, running down the hallway to catch up to me. Resting my hands behind my head to breathe better, I looked at Kyle.

"Just shove a stake in my chest and kill me," I said bluntly.

"Jesus, what now?"

"Apparently I'm grounded," I stared at the floor, my jaw clenched.

"Why are you grounded?"

"Well, I assume it's a combination of Grebb, and how I got pissed when my dad called me wanting to do DCI 'silly.'"

Kyle looked at the ground, unsure of what to say. There was nothing he could do.

"Sorry man."

I shoved my hands in my pockets and turned around, wishing that I could make up some believable lie. My car broke down, Elliot was giving me drum tips after practice, or that I ran into a pole and blacked out.

Ha. He doesn't think high enough of me to believe it anyway.

When I walked through the front door, I didn't even look at my family in the living room. Of course, they noticed me. My peripherals sensed that their heads turned to my hasty entrance. My mom said something. What though? It blew right past me. I didn't want anything to do with anybody, really. Instead, I headed straight for the staircase. They went back to watching the newest movie rental and I went straight to my cave.

The cut at the river only took the edge off. The other eighty percent of my anger was waiting to implode, and being at home as opposed to the people I wanted to be with agitated it to the max. I could feel it in my chest. I pounced on my bed, and before I knew it, my hands were tearing things apart. In an instant, my sheets were laying across my dresser. My sticks were laying on my practice pad and stand, screaming at me to grab them and do what I needed to do. I hopped off my bed, attempting to steer away my hot impulses, but do what I was taught and channel my anger through drumming. I tossed my practice pad off of my tenors, letting it smack as loud as possible, and began playing at loud volume the best nonsense my hands would allow. My gritting jaw suddenly began to relax as I shut my eyes. The muscle memory did the work, and I let my body slowly ease up on the tension.

Phew. This was better.

"Quit that now!" a booming voice from downstairs shouted in the most irritating manner.

What was I to expect? I wasn't allowed to play without the pads on. That's my dad's rule, at least. Inevitably, Dad's booming voice set the blood boiling back from my momentary release.

I screamed inside.

The sticks in my hands were heaved with strength. The lightweight wood was loud in its clanking noise from the impact against my bed room wall. I hate feeling out of control angry. I was careless, impossible, and maybe even possessed. Throwing myself on the floor in a ball, I sat and squeezed my knees to my chest.

I fell into a subconscious state. I could feel the tears on my face drying like scotch tape to the skin. It became heavy, similar to the stubborn lump in my throat. The smell…it became so familiar. My senses seemed to gag…a concoction of stale sweat and cheap beer. The light…it spun above me like riding a merry-go-round at night and watching the street lights wave. This ceiling light, however, had no shade. The blinding bulb sat bare, staring me in the face and laughing at my pain.

Pain. It was so identifiable. The situation was coming back to me vividly as if it was happening all over again. My little chest tightened in suppression, my stomach twisting in sickening agony. Those evil grey eyes were scum in its worst horror. I recognized them and became instantly terrified. They seared mine like darts, but that wasn't all he was tearing me apart with. A single tear leaked out of my eye. I focused as it rolled down my cheek, an attempt to distract myself momentarily. His large body overwhelmed mine, causing high shrieks to escape my mouth. My hands, the five-year-old ones just momentarily building a Lego tower across the room, were working to push him off. These weak attempts failed, leaving me feeling so defeated.

"No! No!" My feeble voice pleaded. My arms flailed at his face, but he pinned them down forcefully.

"Shut up!"

That crave for my mother at the moment became insanely intense. Every part of my young, innocent being was crying out at the moment in mortification.

He threw himself off of me, breathing quite a lot. I glanced at his forehead slimed in a shiny sweat glaze and contorted my face into a grimace. This made him shamefully frown at me. The tears rolled, but I buried my face into the bed sheets to hide from him, my fists gripping the cloth with my life.

"Stop crying," he ordered at me through a revolting breath of garlic, trying to keep his voice calm.

I felt him run his fingers along my bare leg, sending cold chills up my body. His hands began to feel further into a place I learned was forbidden for others to touch. I twitched my legs to try and shake him off.

"I want Mommy!" I cried through the sheets

I felt a pause in movement before he tore the sheets out of my fists and forced me to stare at his face. I gasped, but shut my mouth in fear.

"You're Mommy and Daddy will never know about this," he growled, shaking me by my shoulders, "If you ever, ever tell them about our little secret, you will be in big trouble. They will be very,

very mad at you. So will I."

I gulped and held back tears to prevent being scolded. I was frozen.

Confused.

Scared.

I reluctantly nodded my head in agreement, hoping he would ease up on his grip. He did by throwing me down on the bed.

"Okay. Now Roy, you be a good boy and hold still."

The fear took over. Not again.

"No, no—,"

A big hand smothered my mouth to shut me up. The other hand slid its way inappropriately towards that spot again and I became afraid.

"STOP!"

I sat straight up to a bright lit room and silenced space.

Holy crap.

The nightmare was over, the memory now fresh in my mind and settling in terribly. I observed my situation, my body covered in sweat, tangled in the sheets on my carpet floor. I was alone. He was gone. His lingering, everlasting impression, however, tormented me.

It took me a while to get to sleep that night.

Chapter Two

"Roy!" A female voice hissed at me.

I felt a shove in my back with a pencil eraser. It was a class-mate from behind me. I raised my head from my arms against my desk, the sleeve of my black hoodie damp from drool. That was when I noticed a majority of the classroom was silently looking at me as if they were waiting for an answer. Shit.

"So Sanders, did you do your homework? I want to hear what you have written."

My eyes met Grebb's up at the front, trying to register in my mind what he was saying.

NO!

How did I completely forget about my homework? I swallowed the lump in my throat and rubbed my face with my hands, groaning in frustration.

Awkward silence.

"I take that as a no," he said smugly in his terribly annoying, monotone voice. It was almost as if he was trying not to smile, like he was happy he caught me.

I hid my face in my hands, wishing I could just disappear.

"This is one thing I don't tolerate. There is never an excuse for not doing homework. You show up in my class without doing the work, I interpret that as laziness. The juxtaposition of having students who try and ones who don't easily lets me see who is going to get somewhere in life," he looks at me," and the ones who won't. Take off your hood, Roy." He then turned around and mum-bled quieter, "You can slack off and drool somewhere else." He took his attention off of me, the class slowly shifting their attention towards the front again. Slack off and go drool somewhere else? Wow. This guy is an English teacher? Sounded so lame coming from his mouth. Kyle shot me a sympathetic look.

I leap out of my desk, the old unstable piece of junk several feet towards the front. He stops, surprised with a gaping mouth, and I lunge at him with my outstretched arms. I'm too fast for him, and I grab his ridiculous bow tie and shove it down in the back of my jeans in the proximity of my ass. Next, I take hold of his shirt, squeezing his chest hair along with my grip, and throw him at his desk. He falls down, and I straddle him and shove the bow tie into his mouth and begin to strangle him...

I was shut down, hung over from the disturbing memories of last night's frenzy of a flashback. Therefore, this sent me over boiling point. I continued to stare up at the front of the room, sitting angry with fists clenched about Grebb pointing me out. Seriously, was that necessary? He doesn't go to that extent with other students. Absolutely nothing of what he was saying to the class stuck to my mind, and I didn't have my homework with me. What was I doing here?

So I stood up from my desk without a care. I was leaving. He stopped talking, shocked about me walking up to the front of the room right past him, the thought of the bow tie making me smirk in my head. My heart began to pound. In fact, I pulled my hood up just to add to my exit. He raised his finger at me with his narrow eyes widening like gumballs, his expression forming anger.

"Sanders!" He almost stuttered.

I didn't stop.

"Just go to the office, now!"

Gasps, muffled laughs, and Kyle's head shake was what I caught before leaving for good.

That was bold.

I power walked down the empty hallway, my heart still speeding in adrenaline. Maybe what I did was too drastic. The thoughts racing in my mind were crazy, trying to wrap around what I had just done. It was so stupid and impulsive.

No. Grebb is. It was better than the choking idea.

Next step? Well, what was I going to do in the office? It was quite obvious to me. I expected to enter an empty, quiet band room. I was quite surprised actually.

"What are you doing here?" I blurted. Dang. I should've just walked straight to the drum room. The petite, blondish-red pony tailed girl looked up from the marimba, looking surprised at my entrance. For a moment, I thought she wasn't going to say anything. Her freckled face contorted into a look of confusion. I continued to walk slowly towards where she was.

"Hey, umm…we've never talked before," was her response. I paused, trying to think of something to say. I didn't expect this to be awkward.

"Right. Well…you didn't answer my question."

She looked to the left, then to the right in contemplation.

"Right. Well…I could ask you the same thing."

She was interesting. I stuck my hands in my pockets and smiled slightly,

"Right."

That actually got her to chuckle a bit. She raised her brow,

"I assume you are coming in to play your tenors," she said, leaning her elbows over a stand.

"Well, you got that right. I thought that was you spying on me last night," I said, crossing my arms. I was curious to see her reaction. Her face turned into an innocent frown.

"What is there to spy on?"

"Wow, is that supposed to be like, a burn?"

She looked at the ceiling with a fake thinking-face. She was very animated.

"Dunno. You can be the judge of that. So what are you here for anyways? Get kicked out of class?"

Wow.

"Geez, who's the judge now?"

"Oh I dunno, just a curious situation. You arrive here in the middle of the period looking angry about something with no note or hall pass in your empty hands. Why else would you be turning your back on a busy, needy class like AP English?"

I frowned, "I'm sorry, we've never talked before. How do you know that I have that first period?"

She put a hand on her hip and smiled.

"Seriously, what am I, the silent nobody who knows nothing? I have ears. You rant enough about Grebb."

"Right," I responded, rocking on my heels, "So do you want to hear my real story?"

She pretended to think for a second, but nodded.

"Sure, it's not like I'm busy or anything."

I paused and gave her a look.

"You are quite sarcastic."

She sent me a smug smile,

"I know, I'm sorry. Go ahead, I'm actually curious to hear this," she assured me, smacking her hands together.

"Okay, well I walked out of class because I was angry. And let me say to you, by the way, that nobody would ever guess how talkative you are. Seriously."

She only gave a slight smile to a contemplating expression,

"Well, that was quite the story. You should write a book, Roy."

I chortled, "You know my name."

"Do you know mine?"

I stood silently, suddenly feeling terrible that I didn't. I shot her a guilty look.

"It's Siri," she said. She had light brown eyes, large in size, which looked away from me and down at the keys.

"Like the voice command on iPhones," I teased.

She paused and nodded her head, squeezing her eyes shut like what I said was expected.

"Right."

There was a pause, and I decided to act on it and head to the drum room. She suddenly spoke and I stopped in my tracks to hear her.

"Well, to answer your original question, I'm a teacher's assistant first period. He didn't need me today, so I asked if I can come in here and practice," Siri said, picking up her mallets and softly rolling on some low keys. I smiled.

"You know, it seems as though you're my new competition for biggest drumline overachiever. It's like you're married to that thing."

She exhaled a slight laugh and I rubbed my hand along the end key.

"Does he have a name? I asked. She chuckled without hesitating.

"Well, my husband Conner and I are quite intimate. I play with him, and he lets me know when I'm doing him well. See, he has a lovely voice," she said as she played a soft lullaby.

All right then.

"Well Conner is a lovely name."

She giggled,

"It appears that your love affair with your drums isn't too far off from mine. You like to bang."

Wow.

"With my stick," I added.

"In a dark room."

This got me smiling, and I nodded.

"Whelp, you covered it."

She grinned,

"Well I hope you take pleasure in the time you have to practice before band."

"Why thank you, I will," I responded, walking away, "Enjoy Conner's hard wood."

I didn't expect her to erupt in a short burst of laughter behind me as the door closed. That was an interesting conversation. Eventually, I realized, there was a smile stuck on my face. I finally noticed it when I opened the door to the drum room. Thankfully, the intriguing girl on my mind replaced the icky thoughts of Grebb and what he's going to do to me, but especially, what my dad will think when he finds out.

So I banged, letting the notes and rudiments flow in perfection until the drum room was eventually invaded by other drummers. When Kyle walked in, he gave me one look and let me know I was an idiot. In fact, he walked up in front of me and my drums, crossed his arms, and stared at me blankly in the eyes. I sighed and threw down my sticks.

"What? I'm not allowed to stick it to the man?"

Kyle shook his head and picked up my sticks, playing a lick on my drums.

"You are a dumbass."

I rolled my eyes and looked at the ceiling. I opened my mouth, but he interrupted, "A hero, no doubt about that because Grebb is a joke, but a dumbass."

"Thank you. I know."

Preston walked in loudly performing dubstep effects with his voice. The rest of us bobbed our heads to his beats.

"Drumline rave," Krysten said, grabbing her bass drum. As I bent down to detach my tenors from my stand, I aimed my butt towards the wall and away from Preston. Kyle saw this and did the same as he attached his harness to his snare. Then Kyle nudged me in the side and pointed towards Preston, who in fact, was bending over unknowingly. I took Kyle's cue and hopped up, my shoe slamming Preston's ass and sending him right to the floor. Kyle burst up laughing, and when Krysten saw, she busted up too.

"Oh my God Roy, that was heroic!" Krysten shouted, offering me a high five. I smacked her hand and Preston stood up and walked up right to my face in a threatening stance.

"What, man? You bent over," I noted, crossing my arms.

"This is war," he growled, narrowing his eyes. He pressed himself into me and squeezed me against the wall jokingly.

"Oh, oh I'm sorry am I in your way?"

I shoved him away, grinning.

"We can always settle this in a drum-off."

He raised a brow, "Oh surrrre, that's fair."

"Yeah I'd totally win!" Krysten gleamed, playing a short little bass drum phrase of sixteenth notes.

I shook my head and played a sick little phrase on my quads.

"You're a girl. You can't win."

I was totally kidding and she knew it. She stuck out her lower lip and frowned.

"Bass Mama don't like that attitude!" Krysten said, flipping back her long brown hair and sticking her nose up.

"Yeah Roy, don't insult the Bass Mama!" Kyle kidded. That nick-name just makes me laugh.

As we walked to the field in a group, Kyle brought up the get together at his house. I wish he hadn't even mentioned it. I was disappointed enough.

"We made our own Apples to Apples game. We made a special card for you."

I nodded,

"Whoop-dee-doo," I said, pretending not to care because of my frustration, "What's my description? Too cool for school? Ba-dass?"

He laughed a little, "That one really tall white guy with no life but drumming."

"Nice. Did the freshman actually come?"

"Actually, no. He probably would've felt awkward anyways."

He's right. It's the thought that counts. I just wanted to give the little guy a chance. I guess I've developed sort of a soft heart for kids who are way short for their age. Reason being? That was once me.

I noticed the sound of the rolling marimba on the asphalt coming from behind. That got my attention. I don't think Kyle or the others really know anything about Siri. I guess I don't really, either. She walked by pretending not to notice us, her short pony tail bouncing to her footsteps. I elbowed Kyle and directed his attention to her.

"I talked to her today."

Kyle slowly nodded his head, "Cool?"

"She's a spitfire, dude. I wasn't expecting it."

"She cool?"

"Yeah, her name's Siri."

He slowly nodded his head again, looking at her. Was he checking her out?

"Hey Siri!"

She turned in his direction, looking surprised, but somehow flattered. She raised her brow.

"What's up?" Kyle said, flashing her a fake wink. I grinned as she chuckled, looking down and shaking her head. Oh geez.

"Would you like that cheesiness grilled, Kyle?" Siri smirked in a sarcastic tone. Kyle raised a brow to a half smile.

"All the better. Make it extra buttery," he snickered, looking at me.

"Can you make me a sandwich too? Do you mind?" I snickered as well. Kyle nudged me in the ribs, commending me.

"The kitchen is that way," Preston barged in, pointing in the direction of the cafeteria. Wow we're jerks.

"Ha. Right. I'll get back to the kitchen…with my dinosaur," Siri said. She seemed so confident now that we were talking to her. I almost feel dumb for never even giving her the time of day.

"Ooooh," Kyle responded, shooting a grin at Preston.

"Hey now," Preston said, shooting up his index finger, "No women in kitchen jokes can get old. Don't be like that."

"Preston, you're heartless. That's offensive." Kyle shook his head.

"Yeah, what did I ever do to you?" Siri noted to Preston in exclamation.

We walked the rest of way talking as a group, including the new girl in the conversation. That was pretty cool I guess. She looked perked up at being included. As for the rest of the day, well, I avoided seeing Grebb in the halls. That included walking by his classroom. My wonder is if he actually checked that I appeared in the office. See, I really don't know. What, would he make an extension call and let them know I should be coming in? I don't know how it works. At the end of fifth, I was stopped in the hall by one of my party-crowd classmates, Cameron.

"Dude, I heard what you did. You've got balls," he grinned. One of his long arms lightly slapped me on the back. One girl approached me and asked why I did it with a smile. Her preppy friend gave me a dirty look and steered her away before I could really answer. Wow. What are most people really thinking? He's a troublemaker. He has anger issues. How can he be John's brother? Should I even give a damn? I definitely don't want to, but I can't help it.

I took a deep breath once I landed on my seat in my car. When I checked my phone, I saw that John had sent me a text: "Mom told me 2 tell you that we are going out for dinner tonight. u coming?"

I'm honestly am glad I'm missing that. John's such a family oriented guy compared to me. I typed out my reply; "no dude, got work and football game."

See, I gave up on telling my family what's going on in my life unless they ask. I haven't really figured out an actual reason. It's just that way. Maybe I'm on the path of being a complete nomad once I finally leave this house. If I keep it up this way, I'll be a millionaire some day and my family wouldn't find out. Either that, or I'll be dead and they'll never know. Most of all, in conclusion to this rant about feeling like an outsider to my family (too bad, so sad), I'm sick of hearing my dad's constant excuses for not making it to any of my performances. He's made it to two performances. One was freshman year, and he left half-way through the middle of the show at marching band finals. He couldn't stay for even the drum feature that I told him I was so excited about him hearing, or to see us win our second place trophy. He had to run to work. He totally skipped sophomore year. As for last year, he made an appearance at our hometown fundraiser show. That was good, I suppose. The problem was, he wasn't even in the gym when we performed. He completely missed the performance. Want to know the twist on the whole thing? Somehow he made time to make it to John's sports games. He continues to attend John's home games at his local university, including Aldin's as well. I just pretend to not care in order to stay out of his way.

It was going to be a long night. First, I had a three hour shift at work. Yes, Dominos Pizza. I'm the delivery guy. The tips are pretty good most of the time. I gotta earn my money somehow. How else will I pay for drum corps? Then right after work is the football game. I have to do pep band and perform the half-time show. That's right. I'll be one of those so called "geeks" in the stands instead of walking the track with friends and girls or hollering in the crowd of students dressed in school colors. But it's all good. People love the drumming. My phone vibrated and I checked John's text; "K. update me with the score at half-time and...drum your hairy ass off you nerd. make me proud."

I grinned. John gets it.

Cranking Tool on my stereo, I drove off into the student traffic with hope that I would have a decent evening with my friends.

It's been over a week since that disturbing flashback I faced that tormenting night in my room. I've learned two more pieces from The Blue Devils, went out to frozen yogurt with the group after I was relieved of being grounded, and failed to get A's on Grebb's assignments. This week has been nothing out of the usual. However, I was taken by surprise when I overheard a conversation my parents were having in their room. Actually, correction, dialogue my mom was forcing upon my dad. It wasn't meant for my ears.

"Rich, I just feel that it may be good for you and him to have a time where it's just the two of you. You spend plenty of time with John, even with him being gone half the time, and you bring Aldin along with you a lot," my mother began. I could sense my dad's reaction.

"Well, I'm not sure what to do, Cathy. I mean, you know how Roy is. He's so different from me." I heard him slap his hands on his legs.

My mom sighed, "C'mon, he's every bit like you; high-strong, won't take no for an answer, protective, serious but likes to joke around. He just needs to know that you care to relate to him as much as the other boys. You know what I mean?"

I didn't hear him reply, so I assumed he nodded his head.

"What do you want me to do?"

I paused and made sure I could hear, curious. Sometimes my mom is so in tune to things.

"What about golf? It's been years since you took the boys golfing. Take him. Just him."

It really has been a while. When we were younger, my dad searched in various garage sales over time to get us each some type of clubs so we could golf together. He took the time to work with us on our swings and forms, eventually making us competitive to himself.

"That's not a bad idea. I'll have to schedule a tee-time that doesn't conflict with my work."

"See, that wasn't hard," I heard my mom say through a smile.

"I'll take a swing at it," my dad replied. That got my mom laughing and I could hear her giving him affection of some sort. Ugh.

So there I was, leaning against the wall in secret, realizing my dad was actually going to make effort to "relate" to me. I walked away to the faint sound of them kissing through the door, ready to completely miss out on that. I'm sure my mom was planning on it being way more meaningful for me by means of my dad surprising me with the idea instead of knowing it was her idea. But whatever.

I spotted Aldin in his room texting on his bed. I decided I would walk in and be a big brother, noticing that he put up some new posters of hard rock bands.

"Since when do you like Avenged Sevenfold, shrub?"

I'm the only person he allows to call him shrub, considering I used to be as small as him. He sat back and appeared to be sleepy as he tossed his phone down onto a pillow.

"I dunno, I just do," he said, picking his phone back up after it lit and vibrated.

I raised my brow, standing still and quiet. I just stared at him until he looked up at me and gave a questioning look.

"Freak."

Pretty much. I let the creepiest smile appear on my face before he threw a pillow at me and missed. I slowly shook my head and kept the smile.

"Freeeeak," he emphasized. I chucked the pillow back at him and amazingly knocked the phone out of his hands. He gaped open his mouth.

"You texting a girl?"

"Get outta here!"

"What's her butt like?" I said jokingly to make him uncomfortable, pouncing on his bed and jumping up and down over him. He playfully shoved me away. When I saw his face turning red with a smile, I decided to stop and sit cross-legged facing him. Under brown hair almost covering his eyes, he gave an expression telling me he wasn't revealing.

"You're no fun," I said standing up, but shoving a pillow in his face before bolting and hacking out an obnoxious laugh. I felt a rubber band snap against my back before exiting his room, but acted like I didn't even feel it.

I was driving Aldin to school in fifteen minutes, then going to the worst class in existence. God it's so hard to go to school because of that reason.

I searched through the pantry and grabbed a box of cereal, realizing to my disappointment my mom bought Raisin Bran once again. It's cheap and "full of fiber," she says. I poured a heaping bowl. When I opened the fridge to grab the milk, the pudding cups in the door caught my eye, along with the bag of cheese sticks.

So I grabbed one of each, snagging a muffin from the top of the fridge as well. It all sounded so great, and my impulses dictated my hands. I ate it all in a minute, and began stuffing my mouth with cereal when I heard footsteps heading my ways. My dad entered the kitchen and gave me a glance before heading to the fridge.

I focused on my bowl of cereal, trying to catch a raisin with my spoon that sunk in the milk. Above the sounds of clanking dishes and glasses in the fridge, I caught his greet.

"You eating like crazy again?" He mumbled, bent over and searching through drawers for something to eat.

"Yeah. I'm just hungry," I replied through chewing food.

He closed the fridge, tightening his tie and then turned on the coffee maker.

"Did you sleep okay?" He asked, unwrapping leftover chicken in foil. Small talk.

"Yeah."

"Good."

He continued attending to whatever he was doing in silence, my back to him. I was just about to open my mouth to break the silence, when he blurted,

"Didn't you wear black yesterday?" He said through a sigh.

I looked down at what I was wearing, a white long sleeve with a black t-shirt over it with my black jeans and black vans. I suppose I was semi-decked out in black. It annoyed me that he brought this up.

"It's my favorite color," I responded blankly, hoping he wouldn't make a judgment. I leaped out of my seat, anxious to leave the kitchen. An argument was in the air, I could just feel it. John doesn't wear this much black and John doesn't ever grow his hair out this long. My dad was ready to indirectly accuse me of dressing like a depressed, punk teenager. I hope he noticed my sense of urgency. I wanted him to know that I wanted to get away from him.

Once I dropped Aldin off at school, I tossed him a Snickers

bar for his lunch that I had promised him for doing my laundry. I watched him walk to the entrance, monitoring a group of tall macho-like guys who seemed to look his way. I left as soon as he walked into the school, relieving me of needing to kick anybody's ass. The dread instantly sunk in as I pulled up the high school. I had to sit through over an hour of Grebb's lecturing. On top of that, I said screw it on the reading homework last night and drummed instead.

Siri

Krysten patted the space next to her on the red loveseat, her gesture for me to join her. She sent me a goofy grin and I leaped happily to her direction and plopped right down. We loudly began to talk over the crazy noise of band kids practicing.

"BOO!" We heard from behind us, Preston appearing after grabbing Krysten's shoulder. Her shriek made us both laugh, and she slapped his arm several times.

"God, I hate you!" She pouted.

"Awe, don't be like that, baby," he said, attempting to send her a sweet smile as he wrapped his arms around her.

"Gag," I blurted. Krysten grinned, and Preston dropped his curly-haired head to my comment.

"Siri...wow," he complained jokingly.

I watched Kyle and Roy walk into the percussion section, each with a pair of sticks. Roy was wearing lots of black again today, and once again, with long sleeves. It's curious, considering it's already seventy degrees out.

"It's sectionals today, guys," Kyle said, whipping out an impressive visual with his sticks. Roy went up behind him and pretended to stab him playfully with one of his sticks. Kyle turned around and pretended to pick Roy's nose with his stick.

"Here let me get that for you," Kyle grinned, getting the rest of us to laugh. Roy shoved him away.

"Let's just go outside. Now." Roy suggested, but narrowed his eyes at the rest of us to let us know it was an order.

We warmed up just a little bit, following Kyle's lead. Once we finished, we ran through the show music, Fiona and I beginning the opener with our beautiful duet. It sounded so perfect, and we both looked at each other and smiled by the end of the phrase. Twenty minutes must've gone by before Kyle told the ensemble to take a break. There are only so many times we can run through the music without Elliot to nit-pick.

Everybody but Roy put down their drums, of course. It made me roll my eyes. The rest of the battery and pit went and sat on the curb. Roy, who looked concentrated on an amazing phrase he was playing, didn't notice I was the only one still in the pit playing. As I ran through difficult exercises just because, I looked back at him, hoping he would make eye contact. I hoped that he would remember what he said about me being his threat for biggest drumline overachiever. So I continued to stare at him, a teasing smile stuck to my face.

When he finally noticed, he gave me eye contact and shot me a threatening look, narrowing his eyes and shaking his head. What I didn't expect is that suddenly he began walking over to me while he was still playing, not taking his eyes off of me until his tenors were against my back, my ears ringing from the obnoxious volume. I tried to shove him away with my hip, covering my ears with my fingers.

"Roy!" I shouted.

He stopped, a grin spread over his face.

"Be nice, Roy!" Sean yelled at him. Roy took off his drums and went to go sit with the others. It suddenly became awkward that I was the only one still playing, and I felt that I needed to go seize the opportunity of being social. I went to go sit with Krysten and Melony, the other bass drummer girl I recently began talking to as well. They were giggling at me about Roy's little act.

40

"Michael!" I heard Roy yell in the little, chubby freshman's direction. There he was, sitting over by himself, pretending to study his music. His head instantly rose to Roy, who motioned for him to come over and sit by him. He stood up, a slight smile appearing on his face.

That was really kind of Roy.

"You don't have to sit by yourself, man."

The freshman's face began to turn red, flustered at the attention suddenly put on him. He was shy.

"Who's got food?" Kyle spoke up, searching each of our faces. When Michael slowly rose his hand and pulled a Reese's out of his shorts pocket, Kyle brightened and gave him a fist pump. I smiled.

This is seriously the nicest group of people I've ever met.

Later as we wandered back into the building, my marimba giving me trouble through the doorway, Roy set down his tenors in a hasty manner to aid me.

"Such a gentleman," I commended him as he lifted the other end to make it fit.

"Nah," he shook his head, bending over to pick up his tenors. He didn't see it coming, but neither did I. So suddenly, Sean came out of nowhere from behind and kicked him in the butt. Roy almost tumbled, and I giggled.

"Oh no! No, no!" Roy said through grit teeth.

"We saw that!" I heard Preston shout from behind, laughing with Krysten, Kyle, and the others. Roy dropped the "f" bomb on Sean, who just held a smug smile on his narrow face.

"You bent over," Sean said, making eye contact with me as if he wanted approval. I just threw him a thumbs up, not sure how else to respond.

"That's for bullying Siri," Sean added. I turned my head away and secretly grimaced.

"Oh, lesson learned," Roy said dumbly, throwing his arms in the air sarcastically. Roy turned to me as he walked by my side, smiling slightly at me.

"I knew that was going to happen," he began, scratching the back of his head, "but…he just came fast and I tripped and—,"

"Oh yeah, uh huh. Totally," I rolled my eye, giving him a shove. I think that might've been interpreted as flirty. Whoops.

As we were in the hall to the band room, he leaped in front of me and propped the door.

"Thanks," I mumbled. He shrugged.

Casually, he asked me, "What's your next class?"

"History," I replied, the bell ringing simultaneously. He looked at the ground inconspicuously.

Roy

She walked along my side, her gold-red hair tied back and dancing as she walked. She swiped her bangs out of her eyes, tightened the strap on her leather, button and pin coated shoulder bag, and reached down several times to itch her leg. I didn't say anything about it, but it seemed like she was nervous and didn't know what to say to me. I don't know why. She was so talkative to me before.

"So why did you move here?" I broke out, hoping to get to know her more.

"My mom. She moved us because of advancement in her career. You know, typical. Except it sucked, because I'm halfway done with high school. Great timing, you know?" She said, looking up at me. It was almost awkward that I'm so much taller than her. We weaved through the crowd of students in the hallway until we were side to side again.

"However, my little brother was really happy we moved because he was bullied really badly at his middle school."

"No kidding?" I responded, my own memories of bullies coming back.

"It was so sad. He's just a little guy. And my older sister decided to stay back in Utah because of her boyfriend."

"So you're the middle child?" I asked, liking the similarity.

"Yep. Why?"

"So am I."

She nodded, smiling, but she was caught off guard by some commotion going on by the vending machine. Not many people around were noticing what was going on, but what I saw made me instantly feel sick. Sickly disgusted, that is.

Derek and Dion. My utterly revolting, untactful middle school tormentors who thought humiliating me was all fun and games back when I had a squeaky voice and puny arms. Humiliating goes a long way by the stunts they pulled on a daily basis. Throwing fists into me around corners was only a part of it. The other half was deliberately calling me out in false accusation, or just using me as a toy for their sadistic minds. I literally got beat up every day at school, physically and mentally. They had a weird infatuation with making me miserable. That ended once I became six foot four. In fact, I've done a pretty good job of avoiding those pricks these past few years.

"That's Michael," Siri said quietly. When I saw the sadness swell in her eyes, mine must've been reflecting fire. Derek had the little freshman pinned against the wall.

There was no time to think. My blood was to boiling point, and all I wanted to do at that moment was beat Derek. I jumped toward the corner, Siri trying to grab my arm to hold me back as she noticed my level of anger. I balled my hand into a fist and shoved Dion to the side, with a vengeance of course, and his wide face formed a frown.

"Derek, you leave him alone," I growled, forcing myself to stop before I punched him. My arms began to shake. Derek turned to look at me in the face, unfortunately at the same height level as me. His long hair hung like drapes over his shoulders, a worn out beanie with a Budweiser logo capping his head. That's not even allowed. Patches of random, disgusting hair decorated his gross, skinny face. He's such a druggie. I wanted to smack it with all my

43

might, especially when he sneered at the sight of me.

"Well look who it is," he said, shooting me a fake smile. I clenched my fists tighter, trying to hold back the urge. Instead, I gave eye contact to Michael, who looked frightened.

"You're better than these guys, Mike. Don't let them make you feel like shit just because they are."

I felt a shove from behind. Dion was attempting to pin me against the wall.

"C'mon guys, just stop!" I heard Siri call out, attempting to do something.

"Who's the girl?" Dion grinned, wrestling arms with me.

Siri had disappeared when I looked back at where she had been. I turned my attention to Derek after I gave Dion a forceful shove away. Derek ripped off Michael's back pack and began dumping the contents out. Michael gasped, but I could tell he was afraid to say "stop." Dion came forward as I reached for Derek, and I didn't expect Dion to throw a fist into my stomach. It was hard and caused me to double over, which made me angrier.

"Nothing has changed. You're still a wimpy little loser in our hearts," Dion grinned, kicking me in the leg just above my knee cap that led me to lose my balance. Just like old times. The kick was painful, but my adrenaline caused me to get right back up. That's when I noticed that an audience had formed around the fight, the mixture of concerned and grinning faces of my peers watching me rise to kick some ass. I was enraged that Dion had punched me and knocked me to the ground, but even more enraged at the sight of Derek throwing Michael into the wall.

"Roy!" Michael shouted, trying to shield himself from Derek's force. Dion made some horrendous comment about his high squeaky voice. Ha. Familiar.

At this point I wasn't thinking. My arms were reaching out for Derek's throat, which was clutched between my fingers in just a second. It felt so good. I used to dream of choking Derek to death. He fought against me, but I had him against the wall as he struggled to breathe, his face turning red. Suddenly, my buddy Josh was

44

right behind me, grabbing Dion and pushing him to the ground to protect me. Josh, at the same time, made some horrendously crude, yet satisfying sexually explicit comment to Dion that even disgusted me. Michael had grabbed his back pack and its contents and rushed out of there the second he could. Good.

I didn't want to stop. My body felt hot with that adrenaline, maybe even pumped by Josh's words, my fingers stiff against his windpipe. He was trying to rip them off.

But I had no sympathy. The anger was all back.

"Stop it right now!" Boomed an angered shout from a teacher. Then I noticed other shrill voices from the crowd yelling at me to stop. Derek looked at me in the eyes, begging me to give up.

Someone ripped me off of him, both of my arms locked behind me, but I kept my eyes locked into Derek's, sending him a death glare like no other. He stared up at me after he had fallen to the ground, gasping and coughing. I noticed that Josh had hit Dion in the nuts, because he was on the floor moaning. Geez, this escalated.

"You go near him again, and I'll kill you," I shouted at Derek.

I hope that did it. I've always wanted to own him.

At that moment, I was abruptly turned to the direction of a very angry history teacher, Siri standing a few feet behind. The two guys behind me holding me back let loose of my arms. This wasn't good.

"To the office, now!" Mr. Fraiser growled, pointing at me. I instantly began worrying that I was the only one he was sending.

"Wait a minute?" I almost yelled, "This is bullshit."

"I didn't say a minute. I said now, Sanders!" He also turned to Josh, noticing what he had done to Dion, "you too Krone!"

I looked into his wide eyes, ones I hated at the moment, and said, "But what about Derek and Dion? They completely star—,"

"Go! I've gotta get to class. So does everyone else!" He shouted among the entire area, giving a serious look to all of the student who were spectating. Kill.

"Are you kidding me?" I directly shouted at Fraiser.

"Watch it, boy!" He shouted back.

I looked at Siri, who gave me a sorrowful, apologetic look. I hope it didn't frighten her to see how angry I was.

Fraiser glanced at the defeated bullies slowly getting up from the floor.

"You two better watch it."

"Roy, I'm sorry. This is so stupid," Siri began. I could see the pleading in her eyes for me not to be mad about her getting a teacher. I knew it wasn't her fault. Fraiser just walked up to see me choking Derek.

I grit my teeth as Fraiser escorted Josh and me. It was inevitable that if I spoke, the man would not listen. I think he's a horrible person.

"Wait here," he growled, pointing to a bench outside the office entrance way. He walked in to let them know I was the criminal, the troublemaker, the bad boy who almost choked a student to death. I guessed that if Josh hadn't intervened, Fraiser would have seen the two on one and sided with me. It sucks how this world works. When he got back to me, he ordered me to wait where I was, and for Josh to wait inside until the principal came out to get me. He then impatiently powered down the hallway through the last of students walking into class rooms, and I was left sitting alone, angry and feeling bold. I was going to let them hear it.

"Cocksucker," Josh mumbled under his breath as he headed through the door.

I had done absolutely nothing wrong in my book. A few minutes went by.

"Roy!" A female voice hissed towards my direction. I turned to see who it was, and I couldn't help but smile.

"Siri, what are you doing?"

"Shh!" she said sharply, "I'm going to the bathroom."

She slid over onto the bench I was sitting on. It made me feel flattered that she was doing this for me, but I'm not sure why it was worth it to her.

"Seriously, they need a real eye witness. I had no idea he would react like that," she added.

"Siri, you are probably going to get in trouble," I told her sincerely. I was a bit overwhelmed.

"Don't worry about me. I brought the wrong teacher."

We sat in silence for a moment, thinking things over.

"It seemed that those guys have a hostile relationship with you," she said. I wanted her to understand even more than she did since she brought it up.

"That guy used to beat me up all the time in middle school. They used to shove me in a bathroom stall, soak my face in the dirty toilet, and then take my shirt," I explained bluntly, "and cornered me in the locker room, stole my food at lunch, and made sure my life was hell." Her eyes exploded, an expression of disbelief coming over her. She wasn't expecting that.

"Roy that's awful! You're not kidding?" She was seriously concerned, and even stroked my shoulder.

I shook my head.

"God why didn't you kill him?"

I chuckled, and then she mumbled that she was just kidding, even though we both knew she didn't want to be.

Her face turned to stone, "Why did they do that to you? I mean, what did you do?"

I sighed, "I was little and vulnerable. Plus I was different. I kept to myself, had my social problems. I didn't have many friends back then, so I was an easy target."

She silently shook her head.

"Well what did the teachers do? Didn't they notice?"

"They knew I was picked on by them, but had no idea to what extent. A lot of the time, I was just too afraid to tell. They threatened me quite a bit, and I didn't want to take the chance. Eventually, my mom found bruises, which was a one-time thing. Usually they didn't hit me in places where bruises could be easily seen.

47

That was smart of them. So then my mom called the school, and I was mortified. You know, nothing different than a typical middle school bully experience."

"God, that's ridiculous," she grumbled, hiding her face in her hands. She was feeling that frustration I feel. I shouldn't have said as much as I did, maybe not at all.

"There's no way in hell I'm going to let that happen to Michael. Thank God my eighth grader brother, Aldin, hasn't had those problems like I had. He got the same genes as me. I ask him about it a lot, actually. He doesn't seem to have trouble about his size. At the same time, he's a cool kid. Who would want to pick on him?"

She nodded, but gave me an unexpected shoulder bump.

"You seem to care a lot about people. I saw what you did for Michael today during band, and you were willing to risk your reputation and your pretty face for a helpless freshman against those guys. It's pretty cool."

I soaked up her words, but wasn't quite sure how to respond. Nobody really compliments me like that.

So I just smiled and said, "Did you say pretty face?"

She kind of stared at the ground.

"I said petty" She came back, grinning as she twiddled with her thumbs. I just shook my head and nudged her.

"No you didn't," I said short and quick. At that moment, one of the office ladies stuck her head through the door and ordered me to head in, giving Siri a once over, but not making much of it. Siri followed me in, and I formed a lump in my throat, my heart rate increasing. Dammit.

We entered, Principal Kaye sitting in her office chair and looking to be busy sorting through folders or papers or whatever. When she made eye contact with me, I could tell it wasn't friendly. Her eyes scanned me like a printer, trying to make out what was coming through the processor. She was judging. Her hair was pulled back tight in a bun, her outfit conservative. She just looked like a strict woman. I had seen her around, but never associated with her. Not that I had never been sent to the Principal's before, but she is new this year.

"Roy, I just got off the phone with your father. Your parents were to know of your actions. Almost choking a student to death? Is that necessary?" She said sternly.

I opened my mouth, already tightening my fists with anger for the call to my dad, just wishing I could fall to my knees and break-down. He's going to be so angry at me, especially that the call had interrupted work. She spoke before I could.

"Who is this?" She raised a brow behind glasses, glaring at Siri.

"I'm Siri. Roy was defending himself and a freshman who was being bullied. Fraiser didn't see the whole thing."

She looked surprised, "Siri, I didn't ask you to be here, did I?"

Siri responded immediately,

"No Ma'am, but Roy is the hero here. I don't want to see the bullies win."

"Okay enough, you're out of here. Get to class," Principal Kaye ordered her. Siri patted my arm before turning around, like a good luck wish. Unexpectedly, she said before closing the door,

"I'm not the only witness. Roy's a hero!" She almost shouted, the door shutting a second after. Oh my God, she's incredible. I was bewildered, and almost didn't even hear Principal Kaye. In fact, I didn't even want to look at her. I could just feel she was annoyed by Siri. I was proud.

"Sit down, Roy."

I did what she said, but just stared at the edge of the desk, re-fusing to look at her.

"Now, you had another student pinned against the wall, and you were choking him. I heard you were about to kill him. You're lucky that it isn't being considered attempted murder. Do you real-ly think that's the way you handle things?"

I shook my head, but not to her question,

"He's done worse to me."

She leaned back in her chair and folded her arms.

49

"So revenge. I see. And that makes you better than him? Is this really a prudent way of handling things? It's pretty destructive to me."

I sighed and rolled my eyes to such a stupid question. It made me want to laugh that she added the word "prudent" to make it seems like she worded the same question differently.

"Then what is? Huh? What are you suggesting, verbal resolution? Cause that doesn't work!"

"Watch your mouth! You are on the verge of suspension already!"

I felt the red hot urge to begin throwing things off her desk at the walls in the heat of that smoldering silence.

"Well what about Derek and Dion?" I said under my breath, trying to keep my cool for the sake of avoiding suspension. I get suspended, I can't go to marching band. My life would be over.

The conversation went on, and she even assured me the two of them weren't going to get away clean. That relieved me. What didn't relieve me was that they weren't the offenders in the spotlight, but that I was.

I thought today was going to be a good day.

Chapter Three

When I got home from school, I spent the few hours I had drowning in dread before my dad returned home. In the meantime, I hid in my room, angry at the world. John was home this evening, and I knew I should've been spending time with him, but I just couldn't. I knew I wouldn't be good company. He would probably call me out for being grumpy. After all, I didn't feel like being the jerk again today.

Kyle had texted me. He heard the whole story. Then went on and asked me how I was doing and how it went with the principal. I think he was especially afraid that I was suspended. Luckily, that hadn't been determined yet. I told him ultimately that whatever happens to me, it was worth defending Michael. I can afford to be disposable. Inevitably, John and Aldin both barged in my room, which annoyed me to the extreme. I threw my pillow over my head and gave them the message that I wasn't interested.

"Roy, come pass the football with us," Aldin pleaded. John must've had the football with him, because he threw it and hit my back. I yelled "OW" through the stifling of my pillow.

"What's your problem, dude? Get up!" John ordered.

"John set up ping pong in the back yard," Aldin added enthusiastically. I began to feel slight guilt for not wanting to join them. They actually wanted me around.

"Do I have to make you? You're acting emo," John said, taking another one of my pillows and smacking me on the butt with it.

"I swear, he's a closet emo," John whispered loudly to Aldin, who I could hear grinning. I grit my teeth to John's comment on calling me emo. Maybe he's actually right though. I understood that even if I had a good time hanging out with my brothers, eventually, that good time would turn to suck. My overall prediction: Dad will come home, call me out, embarrass me in front of John, Aldin, and Mom, and make me feel worthless as I sulk alone in my room after a drastic fight. I began to feel sick to my stomach, and didn't know what to say to John.

"Roy, seriously, what is going on? Why are you being like this?" John asked, pausing in trying to throw me off the bed. He was actually wanting to be serious. I knew that I should probably tell him so that at least I would have someone in this house on my side before I turn into the troublemaker son. So I threw the pillow off my face, smoothing my hair to stall before revealing my story. John could usually tell when something is wrong. I stood up and took a deep breath, both John and Aldin now staring at me curiously.

"You got into trouble, didn't you?" Aldin guessed. Smart kid. I nodded slowly.

"I got in trouble because I choked the guy tormenting my little freshman friend."

Aldin widened his eyes. John was about to say something, but I continued speaking.

"They called Dad," I stared at the ground and rubbed my eye with stress, the two of them empathetic and silent at the moment. They hardly ever get in trouble.

John spoke suddenly, "The guy who used to beat you up in middle school?"

I nodded. John let out a whistle and shook his head.

"Load of bull," he said, looking at me in the eyes apologetically. The two of them became silent. It was awkward.

Then John added, "My girl is coming over later for dinner. She's a keeper. I want you to meet her, so don't run away or anything. I'm sure Dad will hold off on killing you while she's here."

I wanted to meet her. His last one cheated on him. John has a habit of picking the wrong girls, but at the same time, a lot of girls go for him. Part of me was happy about this, but at the same time, I was worried about what she would think if Dad did end up bringing up the fight. I nodded, looking at John who was really feeling for me. He put an arm around my shoulder, something I wasn't really expecting, and led me out the door with Aldin.

"C'mon, let's forget about it for now. It doesn't have to ruin your day."

Uh huh. Right. Must be nice being him. I wiped the fresh blood leaking from under my sleeve on my pants, hoping they wouldn't notice. But it was stupid, because the red was seeping through the white. Luckily, they bought my excuse of me spilling balsamic vinegar on my shirt earlier, and that I was tired of smelling like a salad. I stuck on a new bandage and put on a red long sleeved shirt that I hadn't worn in months. John said I looked weird in it, but anyhow, I got out of that one pretty clean.

I spent time with my brothers in the yard, passing the football. They laughed when I turned the other way, oblivious to Aldin throwing it to me. I got hit in the nipple, which actually kind of hurt. Either way, they both ended up ganging up on me, trying to tackle my tall self to the ground. It's almost like Aldin's way of sucking it up to John, giving me the pleasure of being the punching bag slash laughing stock. It's not like John ever really picked on me for real, but just acted like a typical older brother who had to tease me once in a while. So I went with it, accepting that they were putting me in the center of attention. After all, it was getting my mind off of the dread I felt eating me alive for a little bit.

As I laid down in the grass after John and I ordered Aldin to get us root beers, I thought about how I could escape this household tonight. It would be easy for my family to believe I had work tonight, or an extra drumline rehearsal. I could run off to Kyle's or take my drums to the river and practice. However, I knew through my darkened heart, that I couldn't escape Dad's wrath. He got interrupted at work because of me. That was it.

When John introduced me to his girlfriend just fifteen minutes later, I was honestly dazzled by her looks. She had gorgeous long hair, big lips, a petite build, bright blue eyes, and a warm smile. Dad would be impressed. Her name is Reya. She even made a comment to me about how it was "cute" that John and I look alike. We really don't. She was probably just trying to be friendly.

I was not dazzled, however, at Dad's impatient expression

53

when he entered through the front door. We were hanging out in the living room, us four and Mom. I saw her release a tense sigh when she saw he was in a bad mood. I kind of felt for her, but felt for myself especially. The lump in my throat restricted my breathing and I was beginning to feel that frustration again. I hoped that he would give me a chance to explain myself for once. I didn't want to even look at him again.

John greeted Dad, who gave a short reply of "hey son." I stared at the floor, my hands laced together. John even looked over at me sympathetically. Reya seemed confused at the tension.

"Roy," he said in a low voice, "outside, now."

I rolled my eyes and rose up, still staring at the floor. I refused to give Dad eye contact. I rushed to the door, annoyed and embarrassed that he had to use the word "now." Once he shut the door, I immediately spoke.

"Dad, I don't know what you heard, but please, let me explain, okay?"

He looked furious.

"Roy, give me a reason why. I'm sick of your anger issues. It's obvious you got pissed off and you went too far! You have no self-control!" He fired at me, raising his voice.

"Wow, seriously Dad?! Just let me explain! That's what parents are supposed to do anyways! Listen to their kid's side of the story!"

"Yeah right! My job is to make sure you don't act like a bad kid!" He said, swatting me in the shoulder with his fingertips.

"Are you serious?!" I yelled, my breath short.

"You are going to piss me off more than you already have. Now, I received a call from your principal while I was in a very important meeting at work. She told me that you were choking someone and had to be pulled off of him? I don't understand! It's embarrassing!" He said, flailing his arms.

"I was protecting my friend, who is little like I used to be by the way, and I choked the fuck out of Derek Fawman because he is such a cruel dick! That's the guy who used to torment me to no end in middle school! I bet you don't even remember that! And it was repressed anger that did it, Dad! There's no amount of punishment that will make me think otherwise that he deserved it!" I was now yelling, my face probably beet red. My heart was racing, but it felt so good to say exactly what I wanted to. I knew he would be pissed that I was cussing in his face like that with anger.

"First of all, you watch your mouth! Secondly, does it matter to you that you might be suspended? Huh?"

"Do I really look like that much of a slacker? It matters to me because I won't get to go to marching band! But what matters most to me is that Derek and Dion pay for it! Did she mention to you that I got hit first? No, I bet not."

"I'm sorry you got hit, okay? But it appears you are fine and that you went too far." He put his hands on his hips.

He's not sorry.

"Now, this is causing me a load of trouble, because I'm swarmed at work. But we need to do whatever it takes not to get you suspended. You gotta understand that choking another kid at school is incredibly stupid and destructive! It doesn't matter how angry you were at him! And not only that, but your grades are slipping in AP English! Did you think I wasn't going to notice that?"

I sighed and stared at the ground, gritting my teeth.

"Not to mention that little incident where you decided to walk out of class and defy your teacher!"

Oh God. I wasn't expecting that at the moment.

"Dad, I swear, Grebb hates me! You can't blame me for that!"

"Of course I do! You know, you gotta act decent to get teachers to like you! That's common sense!"

"Oh my God. I can't—,"

"Get it together, Roy! You got it?"

And he slammed the door with me standing there, my mouth open to shout at him back. I was furious and choked back a scream. He humiliated me, leaving me feeling lowly. Without even thinking, I grabbed my mom's potted plant on the stoop and chucked it across the yard. Then, I beat my fist on the door as if I was trying to punch a hole through it. I imagined it splitting in half, a satisfying, destructive noise.

Because of that, I ditched the front door and ran to my Bronco, foreseeing my dad getting pissed off about my behavior. But it released a bit of my adrenaline. Knowing it would be tense and awkward, I didn't want to be around any of them now. So I left and hung out with Kyle and Preston, trying not to show in expression that I was upset.

I must've done pretty well, because it felt normal. The three of us just hung around up in Kyle's room and drummed on our practice pads, eating junk food and gulping down his mom's homemade strawberry lemonade until we had to pee really bad. Homecoming came up in conversation, which made me want to cover my ears.

"Krys wants me to ask her to the dance in some extravagant, "cute," and "creative" manner. She said she'll say no if I don't impress her enough," Preston shared nonchalantly, leaning back in the bean bag chair with his hands behind his head, "It's stupid. What's the point in putting a bunch of effort in asking your girlfriend to a friggen' dance she knows you're going to with her to anyway?"

Kyle and I expressed our empathy by laughing at him. He and Krysten have been together since freshman year, yet he's such an un-romantic guy. I'm curious to see what he does.

"I don't even really want to go, but I can't tell her that. I want to ditch the dance and go do something even more extravagant," he went on. Kyle raised a brow.

"What are you talking about?" We're supposed to go in a group! That's how it's fun, man," Kyle said. Preston picked up a dart and shot it at the dartboard, a big miss.

"Well who are you asking?" He said. It was obvious.

"McKenzie Grody, duh!" Kyle said, throwing a Skittle at him. McKenzie is a hot blonde, a girl Kyle had been talking to lately in calculus class. They were a pretty fit couple in my opinion.

"Fuck. That's right," he replied, eating that Skittle. Preston turned to me.

"You gonna shake that thang, Roy? Or do we have to drag your ass there ourselves and make you shake it?"

I frowned at his wording.

"Dude, I don't go to dances. They're not my thang."

"You're going. I'm not taking this shit this year. You're asking a girl, someone hot, and you will shake that thang," Kyle demanded, kicking my bean bag chair.

Preston eventually went home, farting before he closed the two of us up in Kyle's room. It was gross. I convinced Kyle to let me sleepover even though it was a school night, but neither of us gave a crap. We decided to skip the reading homework for AP English because we both figured we would go over it in class anyway. We played his Xbox until about eleven, and I almost fell asleep right there on the bean bag chair. He threw a heavy blanket on my face, which startled me. That was when the conversation about the fight came up. I poured out to him what had happened before I came here.

"At least your dad cares about your well-being. Some parents just don't give a dang. My mom's a social worker, I know."

That was true. Dad has some heart.

"What bugs me is that he has this fixed attitude about me causing trouble or whatever. So when he hears of something I did, he's automatically pissed and completely puts me in the defense immediately. Like, what does he expect?"

Kyle just nodded, agreeing, but had nothing to say. Instead, he randomly brought up Siri as if to lighten the mood or something.

"I'm pretty sure you have a thing for her. Don't deny it, I know you do."

Oh God, "Denied." I hid under the blanket and told him to shut up and let me sleep.

For a while, I couldn't fall asleep. I stared at the dark ceiling, faint light reflecting shadows onto the wall from the half open blinds. It must've been only twenty minutes or so, and Kyle was quietly snoring. Today kept replaying in my head by the detail. I thought about Siri and how she was there for me unexpectedly. She was the last thing on my mind before I drifted off into a bright lit cafeteria.

The whole school was crowded inside, leaving a pathway of the floor open between a high platform across the room, and a very scorned, bruised me. My body ached, and my clothes were torn like I had just been beat up. I was being stared at with looks of shame and disgust throughout the crowd of peers, making me feel sick. I was hated.

My feet carried me forward automatically to the platform illuminated by spotlights. When I saw who was standing up there, I gasped. Their expensive looks and gleaming smiles had everyone cheering, including a familiar group in the front below the plat- form who looked back at me like I was dirt when they noticed me coming. Krysten's eyes were like fire as they pierced mine, Preston flipping me the bird. Sean and Nathan had their arms crossed in front of the platform like bodyguards, shooting me frowns. Kyle's face, shining in the bright light up top, grinned at the crowd, hoots and hollers returning his gesture. Melony, Fiona, and Siri were staring up at Kyle, holding their hands up and screaming. Kyle was the star of the platform, along with other popular seniors, including McKenzie, who surrounded him. It was completely far-fetched, but felt so real at the same time.

I began to understand, and slowly turned around to leave permanently. Thoughts invaded my head about living in a tent in the woods by myself, or ultimately jumping off a cliff and making everything cease to exist. The hurt was unbearable when someone shoved me, another guy in the crowd shouting "You aren't good enough to be Kyle's friend!" Another shouted, "He's too good for you!"

As I struggled to get out of the torment, my legs moving slower than real life, I caught glimpse of John and Aldin dressed in ex- pensive clothes standing in front of a back drop. Leather jackets, brand new Nike shoes, designer jeans and fresh haircuts; they looked like money. It felt like I had been stabbed when I noticed their faces plastered on humungous posters all around the cafeteria walls. Photographers were in the middle of shooting their photos, the flashes of cameras constant and irritating. Dad was standing near a photographer, looking proud and laughing with the people around him. I became angry that I was left out of the photo shoot, and that John was putting his arm around Aldin and letting all of this happen to me.

I screamed his name, "JOHN!"

He didn't hear me over all the noise. I screamed his name again. Still no turn of his head. So I ran, my sluggish legs taking me straight up to the flashing to get my brother's attention. I waved my arms at him, getting no response. A flashy grin was stuck to his face as he posed for fame.

"JOHN! IT'S ME, YOUR BROTHER!"

He still ignored me. I had to take better action. So I pushed one of the photographers straight to the ground, grabbed her camera and chucked it towards John. It hit the back drop and shattered just slightly to the right of him. The photographer was appalled, and now all eyes were on me, including Dad's enraged stare.

"John!" I called in anger, almost out of breath. He slowly turned his head as if the shattering camera hadn't even phased him. A look of anger overcame that old grin, piercing me back with annoyance.

"You're not my brother," he spat at me in a dead voice. My chest felt like it was caving in. I began to back away, still staring at John in disbelief. A quick glance at Dad showed me a distinct message that I was not his son. I swallowed a large lump that went down harshly. My throat was squeezing itself from the inside, reacting from my emotional pain. I glanced back at Kyle across the room on the platform. Unbelievably, he stood there crossing his arms, staring at me with a hateful expression.

They all knew.

I burst through the doors outside, my legs able to go faster now that I figured out the truth. Breathing hard, I bent over, trying to figure out what I was going to do with myself. My arms were bleeding like I had been cutting away, and then I was frozen.

"C'mon Roy, let's get out of here."

I stared at him with eyes of disgust, reluctance causing me to stay planted. I opened my mouth to say something, but I was powerless.

"I know a familiar place where what we do can be accepted. Just like old times," he said, grabbing my arm like I was a child again. I followed him, afraid to say no.

I couldn't speak against him. It was like my vocal chords had been cut. He led to me a room with wood panel walls, the ceiling light with no shade. I stared at the bed and began to try and scream. Nothing came out. I tried, and tried, but I was trapped. The Lego tower in the corner was knocked down, and so was I.

"Roy, dude," I heard a soft voice say in concern. My eyes were heavy, but I began to realize I was in a different place than in that horrible room. A hand was jerking my shoulder. It forced my eyes open to the sight of Kyle's shadowed face above mine. Surprisingly, I gasped from his presence after the way he had stared at me with scorn and disownment just a few moments ago. It felt strange seeing him in front of me after such a twisted, vivid dream with him in it. It relieved me instantly that that monster was gone and nowhere in sight. I pressed my hand to my forehead, now wondering why Kyle had shaken me awake (although I was thankful he did).

"You were yelling 'no,'" he explained in his low, tired voice. I suddenly realized how interesting it was that even though I couldn't yell in my dream, I had been in my body.

I rubbed my eyes and said, "God, I had a screwed up dream, man. It was unlike anything. Seriously."

I then realized I shouldn't say anything more. It would include baring my soul about my deepest fears, reflecting demons of my past and current emotional issues I hate. Yeah, deep. So I faked it and convinced him I fell off of a roller coaster and saw Jesus on the way down. He was almost too tired to care after noticing I was fine, and immediately crashed back to his pillow. So did I, but only after about a half an hour of reflecting what I had went through in my dream, and how it seemed the universe brought to me my life fears just for torment.

Siri

I felt great. Greater than ever. I was being accepted, driven into the in-crowd of the drumline. I had got what I wanted, and now here I was, sitting on the red loveseat with Krysten, Kyle, and Fiona shortly before a rehearsal. Homecoming was the conversation, of course, to the fact that it was two weeks away and I didn't even think I was going. Preston had asked Krysten by getting a cop, who just happened to be a family friend, to pull Krysten over on purpose, and write her a ticket in explanation that Preston was taking her to the dance. Then, he climbed from the cab with a bouquet of lilies, her favorite, and handed her a dance ticket after she yelled "yes." That guy has one heck of an adventurous mind, and I envied Krysten for that exciting invitation.

"I heard Sean wants to ask you, Siri. Beware."

Sean was in my grade, polite, and friendly. However, the thought of going with him didn't excite me too much, even though I feel bad admitting it. I think the three of them caught my expression, and they even chuckled.

"Sean's a dork," Kyle said.

"Hey, but he's our drumline brother!" Krysten corrected him.

"No duh. Therefore I have to have the right to call him a dork," he said, shoving her arm.

"Roy doesn't have a date," Fiona said in surprise. There came a moment of silence, which at the same time, was when Roy walked in from the other side with his drums to practice a little bit. He was wearing that black jacket again, hair in his face, and pretended not to notice us in the corner. He was trying to mind his own business. That day when he had stood up against the jerks bullying Michael came to me every time I saw him. He didn't end up being suspended, which was a relief, especially to the group. He got away with just a referral. His bold, risky behavior in handling that whole deal probably went too far. He could have restrained himself more than he did. However, I couldn't help to admire him for other reasons.

"Good luck. He doesn't want to go," Kyle revealed.

"He's never gone to a dance, has he?" Krysten said. I frowned.

"Why not? Haven't you guys ever tried to force him?" I asked. Kyle shrugged.

"For sure. Never worked."

Now this had me curious with other questions.

"Well, hasn't he dated anyone at all?"

The three of them thought for a moment, and Kyle said, "One girl, like sophomore year?" He said, looking at Fiona for reassurance.

She nodded, "Sophie Ross. She was a year older, actually," Fiona added. I had curious thoughts about what she was like. I didn't have to ask. Kyle elaborated anyway,

"She was actually pretty attractive and funny, just….not necessarily that desirable in other ways."

"Not to be mean, but slutty bitch is what he means," Krysten said. I was taken back for a moment, surprised by Krysten, but when the rest of them nodded in agreement, it must be somewhat true. I turned my gaze over to Roy, wondering why he would be with a girl like that unless he thought low of himself.

"It lasted only a couple weeks," Fiona said.

"Yeah, and just to let you know, she was a closet slut. Suddenly she wanted to have sex with him and was really adamant, and shortly after that, he ended it," said Krysten.

"She was really embarrassed, and she made up a rumor that he was incapable of handling a girl. Then some people were accusing him of being gay," Fiona added.

"Did you guys believe it?" I asked, my heart sinking in disappointment of his horrible dating history.

"He didn't tell us much about what happened, but only that she was lying. Some people didn't care about the truth, but chose to believe her rumors. I felt really bad for him, but at the same time, he's the one who go got involved with a girl like that, you know?" Kyle explained. I nodded, and turned to Fiona,

"So what, you're thinking we should be paired up for homecoming?" I asked, curious after her suggesting he was available.

Kyle nodded, "He seems to like you. He'd probably strongly consider it."

I paused, my blood feeling like it froze inside me briefly.

"What? You think he likes me? I seriously doubt that," I said under a surprised breath.

I didn't necessarily believe Kyle. Roy is an attractive guy to me, but seems hard-to-get. It overwhelmed be a bit. I felt the urge to ask how he knows for evidence. But Krysten asked before I did.

"C'mon, you think I would know? He acts differently around you than other girls, Siri," Kyle said.

"Yeah, even Fiona had a crush on him at one point, but she didn't even bother because she knew it wouldn't happen," Krysten exposed. I looked at Fiona, expecting her to react somehow. But she didn't. It's obvious that was old news.

"He's picky," Fiona validated, "Quite frankly, I can see you two together."

I glanced back at Roy, his expression focused on his crazy good drumming, wondering if that was even accurate. I guess maybe I had the right to feel flattered, but still unsure.

"You're turning red," Fiona giggled.

I hid my face and muttered, "Whatever."

"You would have to ask him probably, that's the downfall," Krysten said. That made me feel more unsure. A part of me was up for the challenge.

"Good luck with that," Krysten said.

Roy

Dad still hasn't asked to me to go golfing with him yet. Ha. It could be because I have been purposely avoiding him for the past four days. I've considered making some kind of snide, sarcastic comment to him about it to make myself feel better. I've even noticed that he hasn't asked at all about when my marching band competitions are, or who I am asking to homecoming with any curiosity. Those are questions a father with a normal father-son relationship would ask his son. Not him. Not us. He's got his two other perfect boys.

My birthday is in a week, October fifth. I'll be eighteen, which supposedly, will give me more freedom. My dad has joked about kicking me out on the streets the day I do, which deep down in his restricted soul, he is probably a little bit serious. I've been his pain in the ass kid since long ago. I had issues as child, but now I'm a stupid, reckless teenager. Staring at him on the opposite side of the dinner table, I began to wonder if he and I would ever see eye to eye until the day he dies. He ruffled Aldin's hair to tease him, knowing he hates it when his hair gets messy. I was stabbed with envy at that moment. It came to me then that the thought of craving my dad's attention being the independent man I am seemed so absurd. In the next moment, I was then caught off guard by the overwhelming stench of my enemy from Mother Nature's making. I winced, but tried not to be dramatic.

"Mom, how much garlic did you put in this Alfredo sauce?" I asked as she hovered the pan of sauce over the table, placing a hot pad down. It was too strong for the recipe.

"I think I did add too much. It's the first time I've made this," she explained. She knows I can't stand garlic. I pictured swirls of green steam making its way into my nose, just like the cartoons. It was the stench of evil to my gagging system. We've gone through this before. I smelled strong garlic, and then I've had to leave because I couldn't handle it.

"Mom, I'm really sorry, but I can't eat this. It's too much," I said calmly, trying not to hurt her feelings. She looked disappointed.

"Roy, really? It's not that bad. Can you just try it?" She asked, placing a hand on my shoulder.

"Garlic is delicious," Aldin said, scooping noodles onto his plate.

"Not to me, little man," I said to him. Dad was looking at me questionably.

"I thought you were over your garlic phobia," he said. At that moment when Mom scooped the strong smelling garlic sauce onto my plate, I squeezed my eyes shut to the horrifying explosion to my senses, a breath of revolting garlic blasting my small little face.

I stood up out of my chair, turning my head away from my family while my hands covered my mouth and nose. I walked away to hide.

"Roy, what is going on?!" My dad asked with an irritated tone. I was embarrassed, so I ignored them. I ran straight up stairs, gripping the rail harder than normal, to get away, unsure why I had just acted like that. I felt like such a freak, and I could sense my father judging my actions back at the table. Laying on my bed curled up, I could barely make out their conversation.

"He's such a strange kid. He's so inconsiderate. That is not normal, Cathy," I heard him say.

"Well, it's just the way he is. He's always been this way."

I stood up and began to drum, attempting to calm myself down. The garlic smell seemed to linger upstairs as well, so I opened my window up, hoping it would help.

That Friday was a football game, followed by our first competition on that Saturday. I've been through many of these my last three years, but they don't seem to ever lose that special vibe. Everyone is there for the joy of music and performing. I get that I'm kind of a geek about it, but mainly because it's basically my life, and the idea of what I want to do later, playing with the big guys in DCI. It's the only thing I really have.

We lined up, following the tempo of Elliot's sticks, and played through the show music in the lot before our turn to perform. I played my solo flawlessly and received a quick smile when Elliot looked my way. A couple of instructors and snare players from another line were walking past at that moment, cheering and woo-ing at my lick. Elliot acknowledged me, sending me a nod. I felt amazing at that moment.

Once we got to the end of our phrase and it was just the pit continuing, I found myself looking Siri's way, observing her play fast notes through the melody. She was so into it, and it sounded great. Of course, she had that little golden pony tail that followed her movements. I smiled to the fact that we all look ridiculous in our uniform bibs, but she looked adorable in hers.

All eighty six of us stared up at the stadium crowd as the drum major cued the end of the production, and a pause swept through the crowds before they hooted and hollered at us. I was smiling under the shadow of my shako. Kyle began the tap of his drum to march the band off the field. A memory, one that seemed so ancient, filled my head at that very moment. When I was in sixth grade, I wanted to be like John. I wanted to play football, basket-ball, and lacrosse to impress Dad. I tried, but eventually quit. Der-ek and Dion forced me into my lowest low, and the desire to strive burnt itself out of me. Now here I am on a field. I'm not doing what my Dad wants, but I sure like it.

I lead Preston and me from behind the snare line, the basses in the back. As we all stepped to Kyle's taps with our feet in unison, I continued to think about Dad. It seemed odd to do so at such a moment, but I couldn't ignore the fact; I wished he would un-derstand what this was like for me. Instantly, I began to feel that resentment. I knew I had to shake it off before it ruined my good mood. Therefore, I stared straight ahead and continued to soak in the performance.

We took off our drums back in the lot, my shoulders and back aching from the duration of the weight. Everyone began tearing off their uniforms, sweaty and relieved to be ready to relax for a while. All of us snares and tenor players gathered together briefly and discussed the cleanliness of the beats we played. Elliot approached us and gave us feedback.

The smell of lunch greeted our hungry selves, and we gathered all together in our drumline flock and waited for the food to be served. We sat at the gate of the loading truck before some of the pit girls headed over to join us. Siri was carrying a giant bag of gummy bears.

"Well, look at this cool girl?" I said, reaching for the bag. Preston hopped down and looked at Fiona.

"She's got a bribe, where's yours?" He glared, causing her to cross her arms.

"Krys, your boyfriend is a bully," Fiona said.

"He thinks he gets some?" I said.

Siri sat right by me. I was kind of surprised by her straightforwardness, observing the way she squeezed herself boldly between my leg and Kyle's. Siri even cracked a joke that made everyone laugh. It took me a little bit to notice, but the group had formed a circle, and most obviously, she was the center of the conversation. Her big brown eyes were lit up, her speckled cheeks indented with dimples. I watched her little hands gesture to her speaking. She had an influence on the smiles on our faces, which impressed me.

My insides were churning. At that moment, I began to repress my smile, the realization of my own sad self-beginning to drive that happiness down. The admiration became too strong for my comfort. I glanced at the petite, reddish-haired life of the party pressing her shoulder into mine. As I was about to stand up and escape, feeling like trash as I did, one of the band parents called for everyone to line up for lunch. Relief washed over me and I anxiously jumped in line, my friends all behind. What I didn't notice, however, is that Siri had snuck in line directly behind me. As I fiddled with my shorts in nervousness, she tapped me on the shoulder, but ducked. It was that game. So, I jumped and turned directly around, startling her. She began to laugh playfully, putting her hand on my arm. She kept touching me, and I wasn't sure how I felt about it. I swallowed a lump. Unexpectedly, her expression turned serious, which caught me off guard.

"Roy, there is something serious I want to…tell you."

"Serious, huh?"

She blew out her cheeks like she was about to laugh, but instead, blurted out, "I hear you've never been to a school dance."

I paused, not quite sure where this was going and why she brought it up.

"Is that funny to you?" I said to her smiling face, letting her know I was just kidding.

"Well I think you should go, but it probably wouldn't be fun if you didn't have a date."

"You're right, it probably wouldn't."

There was another short silence. I looked down at my shoes, feeling pressured. Did she want me to ask her to homecoming?

She spoke, "Go with me."

I met her eyes, surprised. A girl had just asked me to a dance. They pleaded for an answer as I stood there, my mouth half open. I began to speak, but closed my mouth. That must've been painful, because she wasn't looking at me anymore. Instead, she twiddled with her thumbs. I squeezed my eyes while she wasn't looking, and forced myself to give her the answer she wanted.

"Sure."

I didn't know how good of a date I would be. The probability of her being disappointed in me for a night full of dancing and fun was very high in my mind. However, to her, it seemed to me it was the most exciting thing ever. I could tell she was trying to hold in excitement. A few moments later, I caught glimpse of Siri even gesturing a thumbs up to Fiona when she thought I wasn't looking.

Well, their plan worked. They convinced me to go to a dance. I can't believe what I had just done.

We placed fourth in our class in consideration of our two performances that day. Moans of mixed disappointment and achievement swept through our band. However, our band director and drum majors attempted motivational speeches back in the lot before we packed up. That wasn't on my mind though when we crammed in to the dark bus. Drumline, of course, always gets back of the bus. Preston and Krysten were in the last seat, hiding under a blanket probably making out. Sean and Nathan were engrossed in their iPods, and I sat with Kyle, aware that Siri was sitting across from me with Fiona. Everyone else in the line and pit seemed to be talking or sleeping.

Me? I was overwhelmed. The idea of trying to appease a girl at a school dance created a discomfort. She's going to want a corsage, pictures with my arm around her waist, the whole slow dancing thing. Why couldn't she ask someone else for the job?

A group of us hung out at Krysten's house for a bit afterwards until it reached a million o'clock and her parents told her we need-ed to leave. Mom wasn't too happy with me when I walked in the door later than she thought I'd be home. She had been sitting on the couch a room away, reading a book, but instantly greeted me and headed to where I was.

"You could've texted me," she had said.

"I'm sorry," was all I could say. She seemed disappointed that I didn't talk about anything else, meaning the competition. But I didn't really want to.

I headed for the stairs at a fast pace, anxious to sleep. I was stopped in my tracks for a second, and suddenly, my stomach start-ed churning to her tone.

"I love you," she almost whispered. I paused my breath, turn-ing around at the foot of the stairs to see her standing, looking up at me across the room in her night gown and slippers.

"And I miss you."

The guilt hit me like a sandstorm. It stung when I realized I had been pretty cold. She had stayed up, waiting for me to come home. Now she was getting sentimental, like she was about to cry. I could hear it in her voice.

"Mom—,"

"It just seems like you are never present."

"I work a lot, Mom. Plus marching band." But I knew what she meant.

She sighed, knowing that to be true. Then came a pause as she rubbed her own arm.

"Can you give me a hug?" She pleaded, walking towards me. I nodded, and openly hugged her. For me, that's kind of big. I'm not a hugger, but I knew she wanted it bad enough. It surprised me when she gripped me as if I was returning home from the military. She kissed me on the cheek, standing on her tip-toes to do so. I finally pulled away gently after what seemed like longest hug, and she looked up at me as if she had more to say, but seemed to hold her tongue. I wanted to question it, but chose not to. Instead, her fingers reached up and brushed the hair almost in my eyes to the side. As I sighed to the amount of affection, she smiled at me.

"You're handsome."

I smiled, wanting to make a sour face.

"Of course you would think so, Mom."

"Well, you should think so too," she said, giving me a playful shove upstairs, "Now go get your sleep. You work too hard."

So I went upstairs, still feeling bad, but somehow, mended and refreshed for the night.

Chapter Four

Homecoming is this coming Saturday, while my birthday is tomorrow. Two events in one week. I've been getting used to the idea that I'm going to the dance. It's been making Siri happy. She and I have been talking even more lately. Anyway, she seems to make extra efforts to relate to me. She and I sat on the curb outside during a break between warm-ups and music. My drums were in front of me, and I quietly tapped on the heads with my sticks while she told me about her weekend.

"So my dad told me he's taking us on a road trip for Thanksgiving break in our tent trailer. I'm excited, but it will just be boring because my sister won't be coming along."

"I understand. Now that John is in college, it's different without him around all the time. My dad misses him a lot," I revealed to her. John is one of those people everyone would miss, and does miss. He's like the light of our household, and always has been. Now Aldin seems to be following his footsteps. He's a pretty charismatic, friendly kid. He's smart. If he let me influence him, Dad wouldn't favor him as much.

"How old is John?" She asked, picking up an odd colored bug and looking at its back closely.

"Twenty," I answered, observing what she was doing. She nodded.

"Most girls wouldn't even touch that thing," I commented. She looked at me and said,

"Well, it doesn't look like it would bite, I don't see any scary fangs, and I am curious at what the heck kind of bug this is," she said, taking a closer look at it. It had half black, half white legs, and red marks on its black backside. It flew out of her hand and onto one of my drum heads.

"No, don't leave me," she said, crossing her arms. I grinned and raised my stick.

She shrieked, "Roy!"

But I only hit the drum head, and the bug bounced and flipped on its back. She began to giggle.

"You think he has a headache?" She said.

"Why he? What if it's a girl, Siri?"

"Well, fine. It can be a girl if you want it to be. What, are your drums a girl, too?" She bumped my shoulder.

"Duh. Those banging jokes are too lame, and I would get sick of hearing that I'm banging a dude or whatever."

"What if you walked in the drum room one day and there was a giant penis spray painted on your drum?" She asked randomly, taking my stick from my hand and bouncing this stick on the drum heads.

"I would trade drums with Preston."

She smiled. Then she said,

"By the way, I just want to say thank you for agreeing to go to homecoming with me. I know you don't like dances, but I think it'll be really fun."

I nodded my head, appreciating her gratitude.

"What color is your dress? I mean, don't you want the flower thingy I need to get to match?"

She snorted, "Wow, you don't have to play dumb. There's no way you wouldn't know what the 'flower thingy' is really called," she said, bumping my shoulder, "And my dress is pale green, kinda like the color of mint ice cream with sparkles."

Liking her description, I nodded, and watched Sean get kicked in the butt by Nathan because he bent over to pick up his drum stick.

That evening, along with an hour's worth of calculus home-work, I actually spent time writing a paper for English. I was having a hard time with the subject, but felt determined to try. I was in my room for hours diving deep into concentration before I finally finished the assignment. Reading over the work carefully, I polished every error and mishap I could find, and decided to print. In fact, I even smiled to myself over the good work I had done. If

John were here, I'd have him proof read it. I didn't really feel like having my parents do so.

The solitude from them was pretty enjoyable. I've barely even talked to them lately. In fact, they don't even know that I'm going to homecoming. Mom would be horrified to find out I didn't tell her I was taking as girl. She would want to be there with the whole pictures thing, thrilled and proud with an annoying flashing camera. It would be so easy to say I have work that evening. When I thought about, however, it made me feel incredibly guilty. It was stupid. They were going to know. I had to dress up nice, keep the corsage in the fridge, etc.

So I shoved the paper in my binder and headed downstairs, forcing myself to address my mom. After the way she had acted the night after the competition, I couldn't just be a cold, jerk son who pushes his Mom away. After all, her hurt face over the whole finding out about homecoming thing would suck to see. When I told her that a girl had asked me to homecoming, I almost regretted it.

"Oh Roy, that's so cute!"

Cute?

"What's she like? Tell me!" She tossed her book down, grabbing a pillow to grip as she looked at me intently. Dad happened to walk in, and when he saw Mom's excitement, sat down by her and looked straight at me.

"What's going on?" He asked, putting his arm around Mom. Now I felt kind of flustered telling the both of them about Siri. It was embarrassing. I probably looked like an idiot, opening and closing my mouth over and over, not knowing what to say. Dad looked at me weird, so Mom cut in.

"A girl asked him to homecoming, and he's finally going to a formal dance," she said ecstatically. Dad nodded,

"Great. About time you experience high school," he criticized.

Mom said, "Will we get to meet her?"

"I don't know. It's not like she's my girlfriend."

"Well, why don't you and…," she paused, waiting for me to fill in her name.

"Siri."

"Yeah, take pictures here!"

"I knew you'd ask that!" I exclaimed, "It'll be our group."

"That's fine," she said.

"I don't know, I guess I'll ask them."

I only said that to make her happy. I know we are already doing pictures at Preston's. I began to head back upstairs, when my dad said,

"Roy, by the way, John will be here tomorrow for your birthday. I called him earlier."

"Oh cool," I replied. It felt nice that is was important enough to John.

"What kind of cake do you want, sweetheart? I'm going to the store tomorrow," Mom asked. I smiled to the fact that I get any cake I want, and said, "German chocolate cake."

Dad moaned, "You just have to do coconut, huh?" He hates coconut.

"More for me, duh."

"Just get out of here," he kidded, shooing me away to my room.

As I walked by Al's room, I expected him to be asleep. Instead, I heard heavy rock. I knocked on his door, with a crazy drumming beat of course, hoping to hang out with him for a bit. I didn't hear an answer or reaction, so I slowly opened the door, curious to see what he was up to.

"Al?"

He was bundled up awkwardly in his bead spread, his tormented face reflecting dim light from his night stand lava lamp. From the sight of me, he covered his face with his blanket. His phone was laying randomly on the floor across the room, as if he had tossed it.

"Please just go away," he demanded carefully, his tone surprisingly soft. But I couldn't. He sighed when I sat on his bed instead. He gave up quickly, knowing that I wasn't leaving until he gave me an explanation. When he sat up, sniffling with messy hair, I realized that he had been crying.

"C'mon, shrub. What's wrong? What happened?"

He looked at me with droopy eyes, and I felt a mass of compassion for the little guy. Aldin threw his hands in the air.

"I guess I might as well just spill it out," he said, raising his voice. I now listened intently, showing him I was by leaning in.

"Grace ended up not wanting to go out with me because she thinks it's weird she's taller than me. So now she's going out with Todd."

Todd is Aldin's best friend.

"She led me on. I mean, why would she make me fall for her so hard, then tell me that?" He hid his face in his hands.

I knew exactly how he felt. Kind of. About the being short part at least.

"Hey," I began, putting my arm around his shoulder, "One day, you'll be as tall as hell," I said, gesturing at myself as proof. He mumbled "I know" under his breath. He didn't really care though. Grace is what he cared about now. I don't have much experience with girls, embarrassingly enough, so I couldn't open my mouth much about Grace.

"And what is up with Todd taking her from you?"

He shook his head, anger appearing in his expression.

"I don't want to go to school tomorrow," he said through a low breath, shaking his head. At that point, I was stuck on what to say to him. So I did my best.

Patting him on the back, I said, "Well dude, just think about the cake and ice cream you'll get later."

He blew out a slight laugh, and plopped himself down, giving me a sign he wanted to try and sleep. So I left, feeling terrible for him. It pains me he wasn't blessed with John's build, where he had always been tall and never had a short stage like us.

When I got to my phone waiting for me with a text on my desk, I saw it was from Siri; "Last few hours of being a child." I smiled. It felt good that a cool girl like her has been thinking of me. I practiced quietly on my pads until I was tired enough to sleep.

The next day after school, the day I had been born on eighteen years prior, I went directly to work. It should be a bummer that I work on my birthday. However, it wasn't that big of a deal to me. I didn't have plans besides the whole happy birthday cake thing my family always does. All attention being put on me usually doesn't make me feel that great, anyway.

I hopped into my Bronco in uniform, hat and khakis included. When I arrived, the manager immediately had me starting on some pizza orders, tossing dough and placing them in the oven. I have been working at Dominos for a couple of years now. Sometimes, I even act as assistant manager when they need me too. Working here is like a piece of cake now.

I watched the clock, the three hours in my shift going by slow. The pace slowed down, so I went to the back and began folding some boxes. Josh, my co-worker and buddy, came hustling back to help just after clocking in.

"Hey dude," he greeted, snatching a box.

"What's up?"

Josh had escaped suspension as well. Once the full story was let known, we were given a bit more grace by the fact that we were stopping bullies in action. Josh is shorter than me, but not by much. He's lanky, wears big shoes, and styles his light brown hair with gel. I've heard the girls say he has lady-killer blue eyes, but some are repulsed by his vulgar humor and language. He talks about sex way too much. It even disgusts me sometimes the way he talks, especially when it's sexual towards girls. I held back from shutting him up when he instantly began talking about some girl he hooked up with. I had just nodded my head and pretended to listen as he rambled on. He instantly shut up when Harry, the manager, approached us. He looked at me.

"Roy, delivery, please. They requested you, actually," he

said, patting my shoulder, "Don't forget you get a pizza on me to take home for your birthday," and he ran to his office to answer a phone.

"Lucky you!" Josh congratulated me with a sarcastic tone.

"Okay," I said, leaving Josh to fold boxes. I grabbed the pizzas Harry had boxed and stuck them in the carrier, heading to my car to make the delivery. The air was chilly, the crisp wind of October driving goose bumps up my bare arms. I shivered, but looked forward to blasting the heat in my car. I cranked some hard rock, the aroma of pizza filling my car. Double checking the address, I thought it was strange. The location had specific directions to a river spot under the name of "Dan Miller."

I pulled up to a place on the side of the road where the directions specified. I decided to turn off my truck and take my keys just in case. I thought about grabbing my jacket, but decided to just go and get it over with. When I grabbed the pizzas and shut my door, I stared out at the trail leading to the river, a cold shiver to the dark chilly air running down my spine. Somehow, I felt nervous. What if they were dudes on drugs, drunk, or ready to steal pizzas and scare me away? Maybe I was just thinking too much. It felt stupid and I continued walking.

I didn't hear any loud assortments of voices, telling me there was no party. It was pretty quiet. For a moment, I began to think this was a joke or something. Before hiking down the steep hill, I hoped they would hear me coming and meet me halfway, or just appear and let me know it wasn't a prank.

"Dominos Pizza!" I yelled out.

I stopped to a sudden movement in the trees beside me. My heart begin to race, and that was when an impact to my head like lightening forced me to the ground. The carriers of pizzas flew out of my hands and into the trees and dirt.

I was shocked and incredibly angry, let alone confused. My temple throbbed with intense pain.

"What the hell?!" I yelled, pressing my hand against the spot that got punched.

Two figures, one very tall, with ski-masked faces, appeared above me. I struggled to scramble away, scared because I knew I was being attacked. They both grabbed each of my arms and threw me down the hill. I tumbled, roots and rocks stabbing me as I tried to control the fall. I grimaced to the pain when I rolled to my landing on the rounded riverside rocks. They hurried down after me, another guy joining to make a trio, and I stumbled onto my feet to try and run for it. At that moment, I was feeling incredibly pissed. I wanted to fight back, but knew a three-on-one would be difficult. I'm no ninja, that is. Instead, I yelled at them, my blood boiling.

"What is this?!"

My heart gained speed with fear as the three of them hustled towards me. At that moment, I realized that I didn't have time to run. I tightened my fists and did my best to fight them off. I forced at least one hit in someone's face, but their power forced me down, and my control was lost.

Siri

Roy's mom seemed excited to be pulling this party together with us. I helped her hang out streamers and balloons, making the kitchen in their house looking colorful. She had been glowing when I told her I was the one who asked Roy to homecoming. She thanked me, even gave me a hug, explaining she hoped he would find a reason to go.

Krysten and Melony had teamed up to hang the "Happy 18th Birthday Roy" banner, bold for him to see when he walks in the door.

"He's going to be shocked," Mrs. Sanders expressed, "You guys are such good friends," she expressed with giddiness in her voice. His adorable little brother was hanging out with us too, excited about the surprise party. I felt bad for him because he revealed that this girl he liked led him on, then went with his best friend instead. Somehow, though, he seemed to be masking it pretty well. What I didn't get was how that girl wouldn't want him for a boyfriend!

"He should be here around six-thirtyish, that's my best guess. He has a shorter shift today," Mrs. Sanders added. She had called his manager and gotten his schedule, keeping everything as secret as possible. He's supposed to walk in the door from work to his friends and family all here to wish him happy birthday.

Fiona came up with the idea, and I was excited to help out.

"Where did Kyle go?" Preston said, sitting at the table on his iPod. Sean and Nathan were sitting against the wall with each other, both playing on their phones as well.

"Watching football with John in the living room," Krysten answered him, tacking in the homemade banner.

"Hey, hey, hey! Is that him?" I nearly shouted, seeing headlights pull into the driveway. I suddenly became stressed that everything wasn't ready yet.

"Did he get off early?" Fiona asked, stretching her neck to look out the window. Aldin hopped up quickly to peer out.

"That's Dad," he said, "Calm down." His voice was so cute. Is this how Roy was? A cute, big-eyed kid with an adorable voice?

Mr. Sanders walked in the door, slightly surprised by the excited, colorful energy of the room. He's a broad man, salt and pepper hair at the tips, deep brown eyes exactly like Roy's. It almost took my breath away at that similarity.

"Whoa, hello everybody," he said. After a moment of studying the way he looked at faces around the room, it was as if they were strangers to him. I watched him address his wife, mumbling that he was exhausted and felt like laying down for a while. Before he left, she hung to his arm, begging him almost to be there to surprise Roy. He just nodded, "Of course," and headed to the couch.

"Kyle," I heard him greet. So he at least knows Kyle, maybe because he's Roy's best friend. But Roy has spent high school with these other people, and he didn't even really know them?

Aldin agreed to watch the driveway when the rest of us felt like lounging in the living room. I couldn't help but study John from across couches. It was bizarre. I had never seen two brothers look and seem so different. John had short, lighter chestnut hair and blue eyes. His build was different, even his voice tone. He wore sporty clothes; a Nike shirt and nice quality basketball shorts. He's obviously an athlete, and it's easy to tell by how muscular he is. He could seriously be a male model or something. Not that Roy isn't attractive himself, but I almost feel sorry for him because he lives in the shadows of such a…well, for lack of words, stud. I couldn't help but notice Melony constantly running her hands through her long blonde hair, staring consistently in John's direction. I could tell she was drooling over him.

John had taken the time to get to know everyone's name. He had known Kyle, Preston, Fiona, and Krysten, which was cool. He attempted to try and entertain us, even. Beforehand, he and Kyle had been hanging out and watching football. They must be bros or something, which seems realistic. They're both so into sports, good looking, and talented. When John had looked at me in the eyes with such friendliness, I was in awe.

"So, Siri, I hear you asked my brother to a dance. That's awesome," he had said, shooting me an infectious smile.

"Yeah…either I will have to wear ridiculously high heels or bring along a stool," I said, immediately comfortable to be my relatable self.

He laughed, catching onto what I was saying.

"He's a tall dude. You know, he doesn't share much. He didn't even tell us he was going to homecoming until last night. We just assumed he wasn't."

"That's weird," I had responded.

"He's just a weirdo."

Now we sat in a circle, playing Apples to Apples. Nathan was winning, but it was funny that he was getting the repulsive green cards such as "repugnant," "chunky," and "distasteful." We were teasing him for it.

"Where the heck is Roy? It's after seven," Kyle said. That got everyone's attention.

"Maybe they needed him to stay later," Krysten suggested, putting one of her cards in the pile.

Roy

I opened my sore eyes to a blanketed blur of black sky above me, the sound of frogs and highway cars stifled by the noisy river just several feet away from my body. Where was I?

My whole body felt iced to the bone, the point of painful numbness. I brought my fingers to my face, disoriented and confused about what I was doing here, and my heart rate began to speed. Sticky wetness coated my fingertips, which frightened me. The moment I realized it was blood all over my nose and chin, I began to slightly panic. Tearing agony ripped through my abdomen area as I tried to sit up, and I clutched it. My other hand fell in a slimy puddle, which I debunked as my own puke. My face felt like someone had dropped a brick on it from a hundred feet above.

I had been tricked. Ambushed. Beaten up. I was here alone, and had been unconscious.

I suddenly felt so helpless, like I used to feel in middle school and back when I was six during that time. It was a pathetic feeling. There was no doubt in my mind that it was a message from Derek and Dion. A little bit of the memory of what happened began coming back to me, which was an overload of pain for my mind. It had been awful. They repeatedly punched and kicked me, no matter how hard I tried to break free or hit one of them back, I failed. It was sick and cowardly of them, and now here I was, defeated and triggered.

I felt the urge to cry as I struggled to get up, my head throbbing. Cancelling my tears, I knew they'd be useless. I had to tough this out. As I clambered towards the top of the hill, I saw they had

81

taken the pizzas. What bastards. That just topped it.

Going back to Dominos seemed like a bad idea. In no way did I want Harry to see me like this, or the general public. Now that I began to think about going home, it sickened me to death. My family will see that I got beat up, and that's the last thing in the world that I want to happen. It'll humiliate me. My mom will freak, my dad will be angry, it'll show Aldin and John I'm weak, and I'll attract annoying attention I don't want to deal with. That thought just made me want to curl up somewhere in the trees and never return home again. Happy birthday to me.

They're waiting for me, and I'm late. I held my breath when I approached my truck, fearing they vandalized it or something. But it wasn't touched. Thank God.

My shoes dragged in the gravel, and my hand shook as I reached for the door handle. A feeling of sickness was settling within me. It began to feel so intense I didn't know how I could face going home. My throat tightened and my heart rate increased. I couldn't even listen to music, and refused to see my reflection in the mirror. I was going numb with distress.

Siri

We all were starting to wonder. Either Mrs. Sanders read Roy's work schedule wrong, or he was seriously late. It was nearing eight. His dad went to the other room to call him, but he came back and let us all know he didn't answer. I studied his Mom, who seemed concerned.

"I'll call his work," she offered, heading to the other room. We faintly heard her speaking to somebody, and simultaneously as she spoke out "what?" a little louder than normal, Aldin got our attention from the kitchen.

"He's here, everybody hide!"

The headlights streaking in from the window got my heart rac-

82

ing with excitement, and I jumped behind a wall between the living room and kitchen. I had a crazy grin on my face, and I met Krysten's anticipating grin. Everyone was hiding behind something. John would cue us for the surprise attack. He sat under the kitchen table in view of everyone.

I held my breath, hearing my own heart beat to the silence. Awaiting his entrance was killing me. I just wanted to see his face!

The door knob turned, his footsteps oddly slow and careful as he entered. John counted down with his fingers, and we all jumped out at the same moment, chaos of an intermixing "surprise" filling the room.

Everything went quiet, and my heart dropped. Roy stood there, decked in his black jacket and hood, staring back at us all in the house with complete and utter shock. Not just that, but horror.

We were too.

A shrill "Oh my god!" came from his mom, who raced to him immediately. The sight of his bloody, bruised face made it so I couldn't breathe. I could tell Roy was humiliated, and had gone through something drastic. His mom reached for his face, and he pulled away, masking it with his hands. John tucked Aldin under his arm.

"Roy! What happened?" John cried, addressing his brother. John's expression read anger. I glanced at Krysten and Fiona, who were both covering their mouths. Kyle jumped up, but seemed unsure whether he should go straight to him. I wasn't sure what to do. Going to Roy with everyone else seemed like it would over-whelm him and cause irritation. Mr. Sanders, who had been in his bed room with his laptop, came walking down the hallway to the chaos, unaware of what was happening. Mrs. Sanders looked back at the rest of us, tears in her eyes, unsure of what to say or do about the party situation.

Roy looked like a cowering dog. It broke my heart to see that this was happening.

Roy

ARE YOU KIDDING ME?

The bright lights in the kitchen revealed everything, my entire audience of friends and family completely seeing my tortured self. The banner, balloons, streamers, cake, the thought….it should've been making me incredibly excited. This was a rare occasion, a birthday where everyone came together, in my house. Not only that, but to actually celebrate something for me. I would have never expected it.

It also made me so incredibly angry at the same time.

My mother reached for my face, tears running down her cheeks, trying to baby it. She was attempting to hug me, cry into my shoulder. Aldin and John looked so immensely dumbstruck and confused I felt my heart in my throat. Kyle was standing near John, looking at me with such empathy it made me feel weak to my knees. All my friends were in the back, unsure what to do or say.

The impulse was there. I wanted to run and hide. I didn't give a shit about my birthday anymore, and I wanted everybody to go away, or I would.

Dad came around the corner with a stack of papers in his hand, but it all fell to the floor when he saw my face. His mouth contorted into a wide gape, his eyes widening.

"What the hell?" He almost shouted, his way of showing worry. I backed away, attempting to run out the door from everybody. There was such intense energy in the room it was making me feel nauseous.

"Where were you? Who did this to you?!" Dad began to shout, making some people flinch with startle. Dad's words were pushing me over the edge into an emotional breakdown. He rushed towards me, wrapping his arm around Mom while she buried her face in her hands with sobs. He almost never shows this much care, and it was hitting me hard. I had stayed silent, my mouth tied shut still with shock from this whole situation.

I felt them. The hot fresh tears, and I wasn't going to let them all see me blow up. Dad reached for me, wanting to gently grip my shoulders and demand answers. My eyes met Siri's, then Krysten's, then John's. Why was this happening to me?

I fled, Dad attempting to hold me back, but I was out the door in a flash, running to my truck. I heard voices behind me, "Roy, don't!" "Please stay!" "You need to go to the hospital!" They didn't stop me from my dash, my feeble escape. I felt low in energy, and running took it out of me.

"Roy!" Came Dad's thundering voice. Mom ran out with him.

"STOP! Please, we don't know if you're okay!" She cried, chasing me to the truck. It was a terrible scene. Everyone came outside. Dad had caught up to me with John, and both of them grabbed one of my arms to hold me back.

I had no words. I wanted to scream till my ears bled, but there was nothing to say. I was now standing up against my truck, Dad's fury implanted eyes searing mine with a locked stare. He was going to see me cry, and it made my chest tighten. I couldn't hold them, and the tears spilled. I bent over against my truck, hiding from his gaze, and wrapped my arms around myself. Crying in front of Dad was one of my nightmares. I couldn't be weak. I couldn't cry if I were a real man. I felt a hand on my head, which was John's. I shook his hand off. After a silent pause, Dad's feet shifted in the gravel after his long release of breath, turning to face my confused audience of friends.

"I think it would be best for everybody to go," he said with a certain sadness in his tone. I squeezed my eyes, so incredibly disappointed and humiliated. I felt terrible for my friends. Everything was ruined.

I didn't even lift my head to say bye. I only heard shifting gravel to footsteps and soft murmurs. I felt hands slip under my arms, helping me stand. Still refusing to look up, I only stared down at my feet. They crunched on the little rocks, next to John's, Mom's, and Dad's footsteps. A hand was stroking my back, another around my neck. I broke from their arms and hands and sped ahead them to the wide open front door.

They sat me down at the table, and I continued to stare down, refusing to look up. The four of them stood there in front of the table facing me, the kitchen light above irritatingly bright.

"Roy," Dad said softly. I could hear his loud swallow, Mom sniffing. I still didn't want to talk. My hands were around my head against my hood. He cleared his throat to my silence.

"Look at me," he ordered softly, but firmly. I reluctantly did what I was told, wiping my reddened eyes with my jacket sleeve. Now all of their eyes were staring straight at my face, gasping at what they saw. I looked into my dad's eyes like he said, which looked painfully disrupted. They also held compassion, which I don't see very often. He seemed to understand the tragedy of this situation. Instantly, I began to feel dizzy, like I was going to pass out.

"Do you—,"

"I'm fine."

They all paused and stared as I fought the lightheadedness.

"You could have a concussion. How hard were you hit?" He demanded.

"They knocked me out."

Now that I had spoken, it was becoming easier to do so. The fact that I was talking about it seemed to put more pain into Mom's expression. Dad had winced.

"Who are they?" Mom asked, swiping her forehead. Dad went on as if he didn't hear her. She grabbed Aldin's hand and squeezed it.

"Do you remember much? Is that blood on your mouth and chin from being hit in the nose or mouth, or what?"

I didn't answer at first. The fact is, I didn't actually know. I remembered some of the punching and fighting, but not all of it. Most of it was a blur. Overall, I was unable to play the whole scene through my heads. Parts were missing.

"Probably both. I hardly remember anything, except being

thrown down the hill at the river and being ambushed."

It was as if none of them could believe that could happen. Their wide eyes said it all.

"Jesus Christ," John said, shaking his head.

"There were three, all in masks."

"Is that all?" Dad asked, sitting down next to me and placing his hand on my shoulder. He could tell I was uncomfortable, so he took his hand off. I nodded my head, but added,

"I think I threw up too."

"God," I heard Aldin say.

"Okay, well no more said. We're taking you to the hospital right now," he said, looking at me in the eyes with sincere concern and forcing me up from my chair. As the attention on me was overwhelming, we all headed out the door, facing the unfortunate aftermath of a ruined birthday. A twinge of pain swept through my veins when I caught one last glimpse of the homemade banner, squeezing every bit of happiness and hope out of my being.

I hate life.

Chapter Five

The hospital felt like the longest process ever. I was there all night it seemed. I only figured they would check for a concussion or something. It turns out I do have a mild concussion, but in danger of internal rupture. That scared me a bit, because I know that could kill me. It turns out, there were no obvious or severe signs of it, and all the blood had come from a blood vessel from my nose. That was a relief.

"Take it easy with that concussion," the doc had said.

So we left around midnight, tired as heck. The ride home was quiet. There was nothing much to say. I had refused to talk about the incident. It made me feel uncomfortable and rigid even thinking about talking about it. I think they could sense that. This wasn't the end of it though. I knew I'd be hearing it constantly about the sick bastards who did this to me.

His hands had grips on my wrists. I was being bound down, unable to wiggle.

"We are going to have a good time today, buddy."

His smile only repulsed me, but he broke eye contact. He became a monster, and I had no control.

Another aftermath of a night. I got hardly any sleep.

Siri

Roy didn't show up to school the next day. A few of us had texted him to find out if he was okay.

No response.

The line looked entirely different without him. The tower in between Nathan and Preston was missing, and it forced sadness into my mood. Preston had tried to make everyone laugh by joking around. His attempt to lift our spirits went dead, and now everyone seemed extra quiet today, unsure what to say. Last night was just awful.

I had my own concerns. Homecoming is four days away. The cuts and bruises on his face will be there. What if he didn't want to go now? I have been so excited about the dance and sharing it with Roy.

When would his spirit be given back? How long will it take?

Roy

Mom let me stay home from school. In fact, she even insisted. Dad had tried to convince me to just tough it out and go anyway. Of course he would. He doesn't want his son being a wimp. I almost didn't care about the looks I would get from people. They already seem to think of me as the rebel type. I just don't feel at it to face the drumline. It's so awkward and embarrassing.

Siri. What about her? I don't really have the desire to go to homecoming, especially after this mother load. It's nothing personal against her, I just don't want to.

"Please Roy, you have to go to homecoming. I can help you conceal the bruises, okay? She's excited to go with you, and she's so cute!"

Mom had tried to talk about something other than the fight. I knew she was tense about it and all, wanting to know so badly who beat me up. She wants the police on their asses. I do too. But how is that going to go down? They used a restricted cell number, a fake name, and a non-resident location for their pizza order. Plus, they were completely disguised. There were no witnesses, just me. I had to tell Harry, who was in fact furious and couldn't believe his ears. He wants to get the cops in on it, too.

I know it was Derek and Dion. It's obvious. They couldn't stand the idea that I had defeated them in a fight. There wasn't anything the school could really do. It wasn't on school property and I don't have proof. They're sick scum and have always messed with me, and are still getting away with it. It fills me with hatred

Every time Mom looked at my face, I could see her distress. She's a good mother, tending to me as much as she can, trying to be affectionate and loving. There's only so much I can take though before it begins to drive me away. Finally, I had told Mom to quit talking about it when she brought it up another time. She was trying to pull more information out of me, asking if I had remembered anything more. It almost brought her to tears again, which made me feel horrible. She cries over me too much.

"I can't help it, you're my child."

I went upstairs to drum for a while. On my music stand was the audition material for The Blue Devils drum corps, my dream. I knew it was a stretch because I would have to travel a little ways in order to audition and meet the staff, but it was well worth it. If it meant getting away from here, it sounded awesome. I thought about how my dad would be resistant, saying it was a long shot and it was very unlikely I'd even make it. "You're wasting your time and money" I can picture him saying. Before I began sight reading, I checked my phone.

Just what I expected. My inbox was blown up with messages from the line. Kyle had said, I'll give you the homework after school. So he was coming over I guess. Siri had said, "I'm so sorry about what happened to you. I suppose it was those D dicks." I smiled. She's good. However, I had no desire to text them back. Fiona had texted me, even Krysten. I ignored them all.

I threw it on my bed and went to my drums. Somehow, drumming gave me an escape and it relieved me. I took the pads off, the notes sounding delicious and flawless. I had become so good at sight reading I was amazed at myself. "You have promising talent," Elliot had told me many times. "There is a solo competition at the first winter show. Write something and show those other staff what you can do." It's not a question, but an expectation.

Elliot is like the proud father I never had.

That afternoon, Kyle did drop by. I had been in my room all day practicing. When he walked in my room, he gave a low whistle to a part I had been playing.

"That was tight, man. What is that?"

"Blue Devils audition piece," I said, continuing to play to show him what I had been working on. I watched him while I played, and he looked down at the drums. It was obvious he was trying to avoid any awkwardness about my face. He nodded his head, grinning at my beats. When I ended, he stood impressed. Taking another pair of my sticks out of my stick bag, he attempted to some of the rhythms.

He stopped and began doing some sticks flips while asking me, "When are auditions?"

"November."

"You doing it for sure?"

"That's the plan. I've got money saved up."

"Good. Elliot would kill you if you don't. I would too. You're too damn good."

There was a pause, and I wasn't sure what to say. I don't think he did either, so he reached for his backpack and threw out a few pieces of paper.

"That's for you. Have fun."

"Ugh," I groaned, seeing that he had written out the English assignment in detail. Plus the homework for math, "You didn't have to do this for me."

"Whatever, just accept it," he said without looking at me. He continued doing stick flip tricks, but I could feel myself tense up. Even though it made me feel kind of bad, I still felt like being alone. He sat on my bed, almost as if he was hoping he could hang around for a while.

Then he said, "Look, nobody really had a chance to give you your birthday presents last night."

I lowered my head, leaning against the wall.

"So, I brought you some. This is from me," he said, handing

me a small package. I lifted my eye brows, curious.

"You got me a present?" I asked. I usually don't care much for when people spend their money and time on me. But I had to accept it. I ripped the little box open to find that it was a Blue Devils Drum Corps lanyard.

"Sweet, where did you get this?" I grinned. I loved it.

"Internet," he replied, relieved that I liked it as much as I did. Why is he so good to me?

"Here's one from Krys and Pres."

I opened it up to find that it was a cigar.

"Wow, how thoughtful," I said. Kyle even laughed.

"Well, you can't expect Preston to get you a teddy bear. By the way, Fiona and Siri wanted to give you theirs themselves."

I rubbed my eyes, "Sounds good," even though I didn't really want them to get me gifts.

"You coming to school tomorrow? I mean, you've gotta come to rehearsal."

"I don't know, man."

"C'mon, just do it. It'll be normal. If you don't show up tomorrow, it'll make you seem like a coward. Especially to Derek and Dion."

"D Dicks," I said under my breath. I raked a hand through my hair, "You're right, I don't want to be a wuss."

He slapped a hand on my back.

"So you gonna continue hiding in here all day, or do you want to go do something?"

I sighed.

"I don't really want to do anything. I just want to practice...and be alone. Please," I said in monotone. He looked kind of surprised. It made me feel guilty. I might have even hurt his feelings a bit.

"Fine," he said calmly, but I could tell that I agitated him. "Sorry," I said, trying to give him eye contact. He didn't really respond to that, just a quick "Okay, seeya" before he walked out.

I skipped dinner. Mom looked concerned when I said I wasn't hungry, but it didn't change my mind. I wasn't really up to eating, especially with everyone at the table. Dad had stared me down, contemplating on whether or not he should force me. He must've decided otherwise. As I laid in my bed, sheets over my face, the event s of last night wouldn't go away. The image of them throwing me down the hill wouldn't stop. I could almost feel the impacts, my body beginning to ache from the memories.

Memories. They were right there. I could feel them coming. The taste of blood was right there on my tongue, the fear and anger dramatic and overbearing. I saw their masked faces above mine, picking me up to lock me in a vulnerable position. Their hands gripped my arms tights as I struggled to get loose, shouting in anger as I did so. The force, the pain; it was so identifiable. I could see it now, trapped and vulnerable. His arms had pinned me down on the comforter, forcing impact into me I couldn't get away from.

I grasped my face, squeezing it in my fingers to the terrible memories invading my mind. I heard myself cry with anger into my palms, my body restless and slippery with sweat. So I ripped my sheet off of myself and sat upright, hoping to wash them away. I checked the clock. It was near eleven. My body felt hot, so I ripped my shirt off, exposing a big bruise on my ribs and one in between. My mirror, five feet away from me, urged me to take a look. I did.

I stared at my sad self, seeing the torturous person looking back at me. My eyes were dark, heavier than I'm used to seeing. Cheekbone bruises on both sides of my face were heavy, my one black eye bold. My sweaty long hair stuck to my forehead, my body appearing untoned and pale. It was now decorated with blue and yellow.

I looked disgusting and unattractive. How could Siri want to go a school dance with me? There are so many other people she could go with.

But I know it's too late. We've already made plans and I don't want to upset her. Laying my head back on my pillow, I played through the music I had learned earlier in my head, my own version of counting sheep. It eventually worked.

I had gone through the rest of the week somehow. Of course, I got a lot of stares from people at school, including teachers. They especially were more apparent when I was walking around with Kyle. It's as if people think it's weird we are friends because we are so different. After all, no one would ever want to beat up a guy like Kyle.

I saw Derek in the hallway, his hair in a gross ponytail. I remember that moment when I stabbed his eyes with my own. I poured every ounce of hate I could into my expression. He seemed to receive my vibe, but didn't respond with submission. He only sneered, "Nice face." It took everything I had not to punch right then and there. In fact, I would have, but there was a teacher ten feet away. I would've been done with this school for a bit for sure. The line, on the other hand, tried their best to act normal, knowing that's the way I would want it. Siri and the other girls had a hard time looking at my face. At rehearsal, Elliot had taken me aside and asked what happened. I told him pretty much everything, and he was really apologetic.

"You can still drum right?" He had smiled, trying to lighten the mood.

"Of course."

He lightly patted my face, "Good, now get back in there tough guy."

I had pretty much avoided the subject every time my family brought up the fight. Eventually, they gave it up, making me promise not to let that happen again. There was nothing anybody could do about it, anyway. Nobody except maybe me.

So here we were, standing in front of Preston's cookie cutter house, taking homecoming pictures in our group. Mom had done her best to conceal my bruises with her own makeup. My man card felt threatened at first, but when I saw the difference, I knew it was worth it. Kyle had McKenzie, Fiona had her date, Melony was with Nathan, Preston was with Krysten of course, Sean was going stag, and I had Siri. The first time seeing Siri admittedly took my breath away for a moment. It made me feel super lucky that she had asked me. Her golden-red hair was down and curled to her shoulders, which was a completely new look. I was so used to her pony tail. I saw that she had super high heels to make up for the height difference, which made me grin. She looked so cute and petite in her little green dress. Not only was she looking beautiful, but her smile was so bright that it changed things for me. I was actually looking forward to spending the evening with her. It seemed too good to be true. We were asked to smile big for the moms snapping pictures on smart phones, including my mom.

"C'mon Roy, smile!" Kyle's mom ordered. I resisted the urge to roll my eyes, and raised the corners of my mouth ever so slightly. I look weird when I smile in pictures. I was mostly focused on the warmth of Siri's little waist against my hand as we stood in our rows.

We finally headed out to the restaurant for dinner. As a group, we decided not to go somewhere fancy or spendy. It was some semi-nice place in a nearby town I had never been to, but the good was decent, and so was the time. We sat at a big round table so we all could see each other, Siri sitting close to me.

"So, what do you think so far? Not so bad, huh?" She asked me, taking a bite of her big burger. I looked around the table at the other girl's plates. They had light pasta, salads, or sandwich halves. I nodded, smiling at her cute quirkiness.

"I guess not. It's the dance I'm not so fit for," I replied. She then brought her attention to my plate, noticing that I had barely touched my spaghetti.

"What's wrong? You'll need your dancing protein," she said, looking at me in the eyes for an answer. That was her way of telling me she was going to make me dance. The truth was I didn't really feel like eating.

So I just said, "I ate a big late lunch."

She shrugged and took another bite. When we got the checks, she pulled out her wallet as if she was going to pay. I put my hand on her arm to stop her.

"C'mon girl, I'm the guy here."

She smiled and nodded. Preston gave a remark in response,

"You sure about that?"

"Shut up, dude."

The commons was creatively decorated to the theme of "Galactic Dream." It seemed kind of lame, but at the same time, the committee had taken the time to hang glow in the dark stars all over the ceiling. Glowing planet props were all around, so were twinkling lights as the stars.

"This is so cool!" Siri had said with excitement as we walked into the loud madness, "My old school was so lame with themes and decorations."

She was eyeing the professional photography area where half of our group was heading. It made me want to groan, but I asked her if she wanted to.

"Only if you want," she said seriously. That was a typical response despite the fact that her eyes were begging to do it.

"Okay, let's do it."

We stood in line for a while, the process long. It gave us a chance to talk though, which was cool. She's fun to talk with. When you talk, she looks at you in the eyes and takes in everything you say. I think it's pretty remarkable.

Once we reached the dancing crowd, my heart began to increase in speed. Preston and Krysten were heading right to home plate in the giant grinding pit. Kyle and McKenzie headed there too, leaving me hanging. So much for keeping together. To my surprise, I felt a little warm hand slip in mine.

"What do you think? Wanna follow?" She asked. I peered at the crowd around us, people who prefer to dance. I figured that if that's where my friends were, I might as well do it too.

"Sure."

96

Siri

My heart felt like it was in my throat as my hand warmed in the palm of his. I could feel my cheeks getting pink, which I tried to hide from him seeing. I didn't know how this was going over with our bodies connecting intimately like everyone else's; ass to crotch. It seems a bit dirty, but it is what everyone is doing now. I would have to lead him. We pressed our way into the tight crowd. My fingers tingled in anxiousness as I reached for both of his hands, placing them around my waist. We began to move to the music, pressed tight against each other and the sweatiness of classmates. I had no idea what he thinking. I had no doubt he probably liked it, but I could tell he was also pretty stiff. Not like that.

Roy

I couldn't complain about being so close to Siri. The feeling was almost too great. However, I was beginning to feel seriously uncomfortable. Being around this many people was giving me anxiety at the same time. I wanted to escape, tell her that I was thirsty. This was exactly what I feared; disappointing her.

"Ease up and relax," she turned her head to say. That's when I noticed how tight my fingers were gripping her waist. Oh shit.

"Sorry," I said into her ear.

The time seemed to pass by slow, fast upbeat songs one after the other. Finally, I leaned down into her ear,

"Water break?"

She nodded, and she grabbed my hand boldly again to lead us out of the crowd. She seemed to be in control. I honestly kind of felt like a lost little boy.

Lost little boy.

I ruffled my hand through my hair, trying to keep certain things away from my thoughts. I even sighed, trying to release whatever was trying to be created. I've been through this before.

"You okay?" She asked, looking up me at me with a puzzled expression. I put on a fake smile and said,

"Yeah, totally. Just needed air."

"Yeah, it gets hot in there."

Once we were given water bottles, Siri asked if I wanted to go sit down at a table. I nodded, relieved. What she brought up was the absolute opposite of what I wanted to talk about.

"So I was told about your one girlfriend, Sophie." I gulped.

"Yeah, what about her?" I said, trying to keep agitation out of my voice.

She shrugged her shoulders, "Just curious I guess. You're a really attractive guy. I just can't believe you haven't gone out with many girls.

I could tell she was on edge, wondering if she was out of line. She fidgeted in her chair, her fingers rubbing the cap of the water bottle. I looked down, flattered, and not sure what to say.

"I just...I don't know."

There was nothing I wanted to tell her. I didn't want to be reminded of Sophie.

"Sorry," she said, smiling to mask her regret. We were both were silent for a moment, thinking of something to talk about. She beat me.

"I like your family. You're brothers are cool, and your mom is so nice."

"You think so?"

"Yeah don't you?"

"They're all right."

She shrugged, hoping for me to talk about them more, I suppose. I didn't really want to, though.

"What are your parents like?" I asked. She seemed happy that I had asked with interest. As she thought for a moment, blowing her freckled cheeks out and releasing air, I stared at her and waited. I

98

was curious to know more about her.

"I have a step dad and my mom. They get along fairly well. Pretty boring, huh?" She said, giving me an expression.

"Nah. Sounds pretty nice," I replied. She gave me a confused expression,

"Well yours seem the same way."

I debated on whether or not I should tell her for a moment, not wanting any pity or weirdness.

"My dad and I don't really get along. I don't think he likes me that much, at least compared to John and Aldin." I spat it out anyways. I watched her expression. It looked like she was trying to come with something to make me feel better or think otherwise.

"Maybe you make it out worse than it really is," she started, "Your dad wouldn't be upset about you getting beat up if he didn't care about you."

I could feel that what she said was true, but my mind went the other way.

"You just don't know!" I nearly shouted, making her jump, "He's always on my case. He never asks me to go anywhere or do anything with him, he doesn't really support me in drumline or even gives a shit about it. There's nothing there. What kind of relationship is that?"

I looked at her face and instantly felt guilty. I had slightly blown up on her and felt like a jerk. She didn't deserve that. Now her expression read confusion and hurt. Immediately, I reached for her arm. Luckily, she didn't pull away.

"I'm sorry, that was stupid. I don't know why I got so worked up. You didn't deserve that."

My heart was sinking. I hoped with all my might she would put that smile back on her face and brighten everything up again.

"You know, your smile seems to make everything better," I complimented, trying to get her unsure look to transform. I pleaded to her with my eyes, and she returned the gaze. Then came that adorable smile.

"Okay. How about we go dance some more," she said, getting up from her chair. At the same time, the DJ announced a slow song. She looked excited about that.

"I love this song!" She said, her face turning red.

Siri

I had Roy trailing behind me, my heart pounding with anticipation. When I turned around to face him, his dark brown eyes showing a nervous side, we kind of went into each other at the same time, his arms falling around my waist. My feet were beginning to kill me in my high heels, but I barely reach his shoulders without them.

"You're still short with those shoes, but not bad," he said, smiling, feeling his breath on my forehead. I was relieved to see a happy expression on his face, especially since that little mishap back at the table. That had made me nervous, frightened me even. But he seemed sorry, and now I was completely forgetting about that feeling his body heat mesh with mine.

I stroked his back with my fingers. The urges to give him affection felt strong and natural. I'm an affectionate person, but with him, I can't seem to stop. When he shifted his arms, I lost my breath, fearing that I was making him uncomfortable.

Shoot, will I be able to do it?

For reassurance, I looked up into his eyes. What I saw made me feel dark inside. I saw withdrawal, his deep eyes peering off over my head without expression. It was like he was trying to avoid me, and it felt like a stabbing pain. His arms wrapped around me were still and stiff. I just didn't understand. However, it was my goal to try and change that. I held my breath for a second, nervous as hell.

"Roy," I said, my voice almost cracking. He floated his gaze back to me. For a second, I was about to discard my idea and just ask if he was okay, but I went on with what I had been wanting to do all week. Now that his eyes were locked into mine, waiting, I couldn't breathe for a second.

Get on with it girl!

"I haven't given you a birthday present yet," I began. I stopped when he opened his mouth, but I think he realized I wanted to continue. Okay, here goes!

"It's not something I can necessarily put in a package."

He raised a brow, but I didn't wait any more. I leaned him towards myself and pressed my lips against his. For a single moment, while my heart was beating crazily fast, he seemed surprised, but gave in and returned the gift. It was pure desire, tingles showering down my veins. He brought one of his hands up to caress the side of my face, driving goose bumps up my arms and to my cheeks.

I was cleansed with relief. His lips felt incredible against mine. It didn't seem to last long enough once we pulled apart.

"Whoa," he said under his breath, looking at me in the eyes in slight disbelief. I began to smile, so happy he liked it. I carefully observed him as the ending of the song was nearing. He seemed looser, the warmness in his eyes there again. To my surprise, he carefully pulled me into his chest. I almost gasped, but instead grinned really wide without him seeing. I was finally getting this hot, talented, complicated boy closer to me, and I felt accomplished.

Roy

We exited the dance in our group. Homecoming was over. The girl who had so well hosted our evening together was arm locked with me, looking very happy. She definitely made me happy...and surprised.

"So, am I mistaken, or did I see you two kiss?" Krysten said with enthusiasm, bumping Siri on the arm. I watched Siri's pale face turn bright red.

"Aha!" Krysten gleamed, "See?" She said, speaking to Preston. I gave them a look, unsure of what was going on.

"Oh leave them alone," Fiona said, winking at me. I gave Fiona a thankful look, especially since I was kind of overwhelmed about this whole evening. Excited, yes, but it's a lot to take in. This girl really seems to like me. The group parted ways in the parking lot. Siri was blowing kisses to the other girls, which made me feel glad for her that she was getting closer to them. It must be easy for her, though. She has such an attractive personality.

"What year is this Bronco?" She asked as we approached it.

"Eighty five," I said.

"Do you ever go four wheeling or anything in this?" Siri asked, hopping up to get into the passenger seat.

"Well, being a guy from the suburbs, it's not really something I do often, no."

"Okay, so if I spotted a giant mound of dirt in a field some-where, would you try and climb it with this thing? I mean, these tires are kinda jacked."

"Just a little. It was like that when I bought it from the guy. And that's a probable case. I feel like I should take advantage of this thing more."

She laughed,

"It's kinda hot," she grinned. I was taken back, and turned to her.

"What?" Does she think my Bronco is sexy? Her cheeks turned red again. Reading her expression, it appeared that she wished she hadn't blurted that out. I just smiled and shook my head, trying to look cocky.

"You are probably the biggest flirt I have ever met in my life," I said. She seriously is. I have never met a girl so touchy feely, con-fident, and brave. I'm not used to it, but it's cool. I started up my truck while she stared down at her legs looking deep in thought. As I backed up, she turned to me.

"Is that a bad thing?"

I paused, frowning.

"No. You're cool."

At the corner of my eye in the dark, the dim radio dash and passing streetlights providing a glow on her face, I saw her smile.

"What are you listening to?" She asked curiously, pressing the button for the radio. Modern rock began to blast, and I heard her mumble "whoa."

"You're a rocker," she commented as I lowered the volume.

"If you want to call it that."

"Me too."

"Yeah," I nodded with a smile on my face, "That's awesome."

As we listened to music during the drive, I noticed her constantly glancing at me. I could feel myself getting nervous. She looked so attractive. I could tell, streaming from the heat of her body language, she wanted me to touch her. Her vibe was infectious.

"This house is mine," she pointed. I pulled over to the curb and shut off the engine to pure silence. I sat still, holding my breath. I swallowed a large lump. I knew she was waiting for me to make the move. After all, it was probably my turn. I finally said something as she began grabbing her bag.

"Hey, do you want me to walk you to your door?"

That killer smile appeared.

"Okay!"

We walked slowly to the steps of her house with no words, arm pressed against each other's. I wanted to kiss her again. Of course, that was the obvious move.

I did it. Under the light of the porch light, I bent down and stopped her in place by grabbing each arm. I heard her lightly gasp with excitement before I kissed her the best I could. My heart was beating fast in my ear as she kissed back with such delicacy. Her face felt so soft against my fingers as hers felt cool against my jaw. We let our lips loose, still in each other's arms and out of our breaths. She gripped my shirt on both sides, a bewildered, satisfied smile appearing on her face as she looked at the ground. My hands slid down to her waist, and she lifted herself up on her tip toes as if to get closer to my ear.

"I really like you," she whispered intimately, her breath hot against my ear. It sent chills down my entire body. I let out a breath,

"I like you too. Thanks for giving me a good time tonight."

"Better than staying home and drumming?" She asked, wrapping an arm around my waist.

We pressed our foreheads together in that moment.

"Way better."

Before letting go of me, her lips gave mine one last brush before turning away. It was perfect.

"Night, Roy," she said softly, giving me a little wave before opening her front door. At a glance inside, I saw her family greeting her.

"Night."

I caught myself smiling the entire ride home. Geez, what have I gotten myself into?

Chapter Six

Homecoming night with Siri was the best I had felt in quite a while. I had so many doubts that it would have been that nice. Here is this girl who, for some insane reason, wants to be with me. She's shown that she wants to care about me more than I even do myself. The feeling is over reaching, like it's too good to be true. How do I even deserve her? How do I react to all of this?

I laid in my bed while my family watched a movie downstairs. It was Sunday night, the day after. My legs were stiff from laying around all day, and I had no motivation. Normally, someone would think a night like last night would only proceed with an excitement for life. Siri should have been making me feel incredibly happy. Deep in my retched soul, however, leaked the dreadful truth. She can't be happy with me. It simply won't last.

"Roy! Come downstairs!" My dad yelled at the foot of the stair way. His tone irritated me, like I was in trouble or something. I ignored him and put on head phones. That way, I'd have an excuse for not hearing him. Quite a bit of time must've gone by. It seemed only ten minutes ago he had put in that movie. Now he was at my doorway.

"Hey," he said, "You've done absolutely nothing all day. Take off those head phones," he ordered. His tone was firm. I threw them off with too much aggression for his liking.

"Don't be like that," he warned. He even gave me the pointer finger. It made me want to laugh. I stood up to face him.

"I just want to be alone," I responded, trying to be careful. He studied me in the eyes as if trying to see if I was lying.

"Well you can go clean the kitchen alone," he barked in irritation. I had it.

"Why are you being like this, Dad? What did I do, huh?"

He began to look angry that I was challenging him.

"Your attitude about wanting nothing to do with us is kind of insulting. You shouldn't be up here all day. Go...do something

105

useful with yourself."

"What, like, go golfing?" I began. I had sarcasm in my tone, "I suppose you were planning on taking me for some 'father-son bonding time.' That's total bullshit."

"Hey, you watch it—,"

"It's not like you want to be around me. So why should I bother being around you?" I said angrily. He was fuming as I walked out past him. A yanking strain rippled up my arm when he gripped it to hold me back. The memory of him splitting a door in half from throwing me into it a few years back invaded my head.

"You are so disrespectful! What is wrong with you, huh? Sometimes you just act like an asshole out of nowhere!" He said with gritting teeth. Of course, he was trying to ignore the truth about what I said. He didn't care. He gave my arm a tough squeeze, then threw me back with the release.

"Congratulations, your kid is an asshole," I spat back, grabbing the first thing I could reach on my dresser and chucking it across my room. His eyes widened.

"My God, I'm gonna kill you, you worthless—," He began hollering, his face turning beat red. Veins began popping out of neck. He was going to start hitting me.

"What's going on?!" Mom showed up, barging in and stepping in between Dad and me. She looked genuinely concerned with the uprising tension. Ignoring Mom, I blurted out my comeback with built up anger straight to Dad,

"Just get off my back and let me do the damn dishes alone!" And I turned my back to the both of them, Mom flinching to my loud voice.

"Excuse me, Roy!" Mom called to me, upset. Dad continued to holler at me with fury. I raced down the stairs, going with the moment, and began scrubbing dishes already in the sink. Of course, the both of them had followed me downstairs. I have to admit, my heart was beating fast as Dad approached me. He shoved me in the back and growled. Aldin became a new audience member.

"Get off my back, huh? You think you have the right to talk to me like that?"

I grit my teeth, holding back from screaming. I stayed silent instead, knowing I had caused enough trouble with my mouth. He continued, almost speaking in my ear with his breath,

"I'm not taking any more of this. You better watch yourself, Roy. I swear to God, you'll be miserable."

Geez. It's as if those words were copy and pasted from Derek's mouth right to his. And how many times does he have to say "watch yourself?" It's getting old. I just stayed silent, refusing to look at him. I watched him shake his head as he walked away, and Mom walked up right behind me, her shoulder annoyingly pressing against mine.

"I don't know what your problem is, but you better cool it," she spoke quietly but seriously. I just swallowed and gave a quick nod. It seemed that she wasn't completely satisfied with my reaction, but she walked away anyways.

The next day, Siri kept trying to make eye contact with me during second period. As we finally exited the building to the field carrying our instruments, she attempted to roll her marimba aside to me. I was walking alone in the back, the group ahead of me and laughing at something Preston was doing. Kyle had tried to talk to me about homecoming before first period. I told him a basic outline, but tried not to make it sound as great as it was.

"She was pretty cool. She even kissed me. I mean, it was all right," I had said.

Kyle seemed genuinely disappointed that I hadn't elaborated.

"C'mon, admit you like her. Everyone assumes you're dating now," he had said.

"Well we're not."

Kyle's face looked as though I had just told Siri the same thing. He knew I wasn't being genuine about how I really feel about her. So he gave up, knowing I was acting withdrawn.

"You look tired today. You trying to hide circles under your eyes with that hair?" Siri asked me with a glow in her eyes. It was infuriatingly beautiful. I thought for a second about what she was saying. My hair was getting pretty long. Thick strands hung over my eyes, so I flipped back my hood and smoothed it away from my face.

"Better?" I asked, trying to be a pleasant person. At first, I have to admit that I was trying to avoid her. The feeling of being around her is too great, and I don't feel ready to deal with it. I don't want her to be around me when I'm in a no good mood. It's like there is this fist trying to break out of my chest to try and punch everything in sight. That's how I felt. She doesn't need that.

"I didn't say it looked bad," she said, controlling the wheels on the marimba down a slant in the asphalt. Her hair was up again today in her high little pony, her bangs in her face. It seemed that she was wearing a little more eye makeup than usual. I really liked it though. In fact, she seemed especially nicely dressed. This was the first time I've seen her in a short skirt. Her bright blue blouse brought out her figure pretty well, even some nice cleavage. She wore shiny dangling earrings and a long leaf charm necklace. She wasn't just the cute, tomboy percussionist she usually is. Hot little lady is what I was thinking. I'd say it even made her look older.

She obviously did it for me.

"So what did you do yesterday?" I asked to just bring up something other than the fact that I was completely staring at her. I thought about how we had kissed, watching her lips as she talked. I'm sure she was thinking about it too.

"Well, I went to church yesterday with the fam, and then pretty much just took it easy. I took pictures of my cat, bought some candy at the store with Kade, and Snapchatted some friends from my old school. That's really it. You?"

Kade must be her brother.

"You go to church?"

"Yeeeah, I don't know. I guess I kinda go for the social aspect of it all these days. It's not that I don't believe in God or anything, I just like to be open about things."

I shrugged my shoulders, "That's cool." She shrugged too.

"How about you?"

"Nah, not really. Not sure there is even a God," I said bluntly. I expected her to frown or even look taken back. She didn't. At all.

Instead, she said, "Isn't it cool that we get to choose? We don't get our heads hacked off, our babies killed. We get to believe whatever we want."

I smiled and nodded.

I had work after school before rehearsal. Harry and my co-workers have finally stopped talking about the ambush. It was the talk of the week. Whenever someone tried to bring it up, I shut down and didn't respond. Eventually, it got old. Harry still wasn't at ease, but he had done his best to track my attackers. There was nothing.

I had a shift with Josh who was flipping dough as I placed on the toppings.

"Who's that girl you went to homecoming with, dude?" He asked curiously.

"She's a new girl from band. Junior."

I knew he wouldn't care much if I described how wonderful she is. I watched him shake his head, and began to predict what he was thinking.

"Going after those band girls, huh? You ever consider going after the hot ones in our grade? You can do it, probably easily. Girls like a good drummer."

I understood what he was saying, but at the same time, it was as if he didn't approve.

"What, band chicks can't be hot?"

He shrugged and gave me a look.

"I've never seen one."

I felt slightly insulted, but pretended not to be. I just didn't say anything.

"Cameron Kroff is having a get together at his house this Friday. You should come, man. Experience a good time."

Huh. I felt intrigued about being invited to a new environment. Knowing that crowd, I figure there will be drinking and weed.

Loads of it. Then I realized that there is a game this Friday.

"There's a football game, dude. I can't."

He blew out his cheeks and let out a short breath. I noticed he was narrowing his eyes at me.

"So? You can't skip just one? Sounds like that band has you whipped," he said with slight animosity.

"That's a weird way to put it," I responded. He begged,

"C'mon, just go. Cameron's got the best stuff. The hottest girls will be there. I'll make it so that they'll be all over you by the end of the party."

I had a voice in my head urging me to just commit to it, telling me I was a prude little wussy for not taking up such an offer. He would think so. To him, I'm a virgin band geek with potential who needs to get laid.

"I don't know, maybe…I mean, I'll let you know," I said, an easy answer.

He paused, and then blurted,

"You're coming. Both you and your dick."

God.

He began talking about sex again, something about how this one girl's tits in his Astronomy class were so luscious he wrote jugs as one of his answers on a test. I bet he was lying.

When I got home after rehearsal, I didn't really feel like eating or doing anything. I just went up to my room and nobody said anything. I was glad. In fact, I just went straight to bed, waiting to be able to escape and just get the day over with. It gave me a chance to just think about things before actually sleeping. I could hear the TV on downstairs, Aldin rustling around in his room next door, and Dad's muffled voice ranting about his frustrations with work. Somehow, I was able to block everything out .

The whole Siri thing is overwhelming. I feel like an idiot. A normal person would just allow himself to be happy about it and make her his girlfriend. I guess I'm not normal. I can't be in a relationship with her. I swear it'll end badly. I'll hurt her, I won't be there for her, or I'll not be able to give her what she wants. She needs better.

Just like Sophie. That's a humiliating memory. She was a pretty bad idea, but an attractive girl. I changed the track in my mind, not wanting to even think about her. Hearing Aldin open a drawer, I thought about how he has been increasingly vocal about how he misses John. John is his idol pretty much. Figures. I guess that's there some kind of hope deep within me that Aldin thinks enough of me to influence him. Sometimes, I feel he really takes in what Dad always says about me: he's strange; he has serious behavior issues. Or to me; why don't you set a good example for your brother? Why can't you be like John? I know the truth though. Why be like me when you can be like John?

Aldin shouldn't be like me. I wouldn't wish him to be. I sure as hell am glad it was me who went through what I did and not John or Aldin. I am thankful every day of that fact. If anyone has to live life with a painful, guilty secret,

It might as well be me.

"You went to bed early last night," Dad muttered as he poured himself a cup of coffee. I sipped a glass of water, but just sat at the kitchen table and read through texts I had never responded to. One was even from John, "Little brotha! Saw pics on fb. Was the dance as horrible as you thought?" I didn't reply, but just tapped my finger nails on the hardwood table. Texting doesn't feel appealing to me, especially lately. I realized that I hadn't even responded to Dad. I just made a groaning noise as my reply.

"You need a haircut, kid," he said making a slurping noise with his sip. When he said that, I just pulled up my hood. He cleared his throat when I didn't say anything. Surprisingly, he continued trying to talk.

"Did you eat anything?" He was now around the counter in front of me. I just stared down at my phone, pretending to be reading something.

"Not hungry," I said barely. He sighed, agitated by my distance. I would be irritated at myself too.

"I hope you're not this grumpy at school, Roy."

I bit my tongue just pretended not to hear him. A couple moments later, he walked away. I let out a sigh, pretty unpleased with myself. There isn't really much desire in me to talk with him, or anyone really. I just want to get through this day and be alone again.

Siri

It was Thursday now. I had been making sufficient effort in talking to Roy all week. It's not like I completely expect him to make me his girlfriend or anything. However, isn't that mutual understanding apparent enough? We would be great together. Something about the way our foreheads had naturally linked, how he had kissed me back with a spark in his body language. I know he likes me—he even said it.

So why is it that he is so standoffish? Did I freak him out? Go to fast? Is it weird that I'm too straight forward?

It's beginning to scare me a little. I can't tell if he's avoiding me, or just waiting for me to approach him. He's really confusing.

"Sis, can we use your flashlight? I need to look in the attic for things to use for our project," Kade said, peeking his head through my door. I was confused at what he meant by "we." I got up from my bed and math homework to grab it from my desk drawer.

"What project?" I asked him. Noticing that he had opened the door wide open, I saw a young boy I recognized. It took me by surprise, actually. I paused from retrieving the flashlight and stared at him with delight.

"Hey, Aldin!"

He hadn't really been paying attention until he turned to look at me. He brightened up and smiled. I love that kid.

"It's you! Uh, Siri, right?"

"Yeah, that's right."

"You know my sister?" Kade asked him, not understanding.

112

Aldin opened his mouth, but I said, "I'm friends with his brother."

"Right, 'friends,'" he said, using quote motioning. Oh gosh.

"What?" Kade asked, raising a brow, "Don't tell me you have a new boyfriend." He gave me a teasingly disgusted face.

"Kade!"

"No seriously, she's like the flirtiest person ever," he directed to Aldin. Aldin grinned, shaking his head. I gave Kade an annoyed look. He just stuck out his tongue.

"Real mature," I said to my little brother.

"Well good luck with Roy. He's like the un-flirtiest person ever," Aldin said, crossing his arms.

"So I've noticed," I replied, my heart sinking a little bit.

"C'mon dude, let's go. I'm hungry," Kade said, steering him away.

"Wait, flashlight!" I called. I heard Kade say out loud "Oh yeah!" I tossed it to him, a perfect toss, and they left.

Roy

I couldn't tell her. Every part of me ached, dread closing in on me like I was suffocating in a plastic bag. She's incredible. We probably should be together, and now that I know what life is like with her, it's almost unbearable to make things right. Or is it right? Is it not right if I don't give myself a chance with her? What if she could help me? What if she gives me balance? But what if she realizes she is too good for me, as she is? I'm not worth it, and it makes me uncomfortable to accept the amount of care and affection she delivers. That's for someone else, someone who would accept it more, that is.

My mind is at a constant battle.

So here we were, sitting in a circle with Preston, Krysten,

Kyle, Fiona, Melony, Michael, Nathan, and Sean. It was right after school. We had all gone to the store together to grab candy and drinks, deciding to come back and hang out in the percussion section. Siri and I had the red couch, hand in hand. Somehow, with our fingers laced together like they were, it was giving me comfort of some kind. It's like she has a magic touch, one that engulfs my entire being with a feeling I've never completely felt; acceptance. She shifted herself and comfortingly placed her legs over mine. Before I realized it, my own hands were placed comfortably on her knee and thigh. I let it be. As for the game, which was in a few hours, I had decided to ditch. It was a first, but maybe what Josh was offering is a good escape. I didn't feel like even going to the game. Even if the line does get peeved at me, they'll get over it. It's a one-time thing. I think. Maybe?

"I can't wait to freeze in the stands, playing repetitive, boring bass parts yet again," Krysten complained with a whiny tone, leaning up against Preston, "Can I play your quads?" She begged, giving him doe eyes. Preston is very particular with who plays his drums, so he contemplated.

"Come on, don't be such a stiff," she said, squeezing his knee. He flinched and rolled his eyes.

"There's no way I'd get stiff with that whiny voice,"

She slapped his leg as everyone else groaned and chuckled. Now Siri was speaking to me.

"How about you? Would you let me play your quads?" She asked, looking hopeful.

"Yeah, let her!" Fiona insisted, "It's not like we have anything to play."

"Yeah, let Fiona be the cow," Sean said. He means the cowbell player. It's an inside joke.

"Booo!" Fiona said, "One of the freshman can do it."

"Wow, where's your spirit?" Preston said to her.

The truth is, I began drowning out the rest of the group conversation. In fact, I had forced myself to be there hanging out with them in the first place. Not that I don't like them or anything, I love them. I just don't feel like being social. I began feeling anxious to leave and head to Cameron's. I want to get drunk and get it over with. The party doesn't start for a bit, but going home and being alone for a bit sounded pretty good.

When I broke hands with Siri to get up, I attempted to walk out without saying anything. They all probably figured I was heading to the bathroom. I just went straight to my truck and drove out, feeling terrible about myself. It's not like they'll miss me much anyways. Maybe Siri, but she'll get over it. She'll have to get over me sometime, anyway. Just like I have to get over her.

I didn't expect Dad to be home when I got to the house. His Sedan was parked in the driveway, him in the driver's seat on his phone. When I walked up to the front door, I pretended not to see him in there. I think he pretended not to see me either. Walking past the kitchen gave me reminders about all the food waiting there for me to snack on. I had no interest really. Lately, I haven't had much interest in anything. There's probably something wrong with me. I guess there always has been, on the other hand. Whatever. Like it matters. Just another addition to the oh-so-strange me.

"Roy," Dad addressed me without expression as he shut the front door. I honestly didn't know what he was going to say.

"What?"

He sighed, sticking his hands in his pockets. A moment occurred where we stared at each other without saying anything. I caught his expression, like he was looking down on me about something I've done. I've come to know that look. I shoved my hands in my pockets to mirror him, beginning to feel annoyed.

"Mom checked your updated grades this morning. We were both pretty disappointed at the results."

I should've known. Angrily, I puffed out an abrupt sigh.

"You and Mom seriously still feel like you have to monitor my grades?"

He shook his head and braced to argue, "Well, it's quite obvious that you aren't capable of monitoring it yourself," he began with a hostile tone, pointing his finger at me. I hate that finger.

"I hate school! And I'm eighteen, so why do you care?" I fired back.

"Well you better change that attitude! Starting now! I don't know what your problem is, moping around and acting like the world is against you! But I'm tired of it. You're an adult for heaven's sake, and you better start acting like it soon!"

I just looked at him. My tightened lips and reddened face probably told him enough.

"A D on an English paper is not acceptable! One more of those and say goodbye to your band."

I completely felt myself break down for an instant. My heart must have skipped a beat, a squeezing force in my throat pressing frustrated moisture to my eyes. How could I have gotten a D on that paper? I actually worked really hard on it. And how does he think taking me out of band would solve anything?

"That doesn't even make sense! I worked really hard on that paper, Dad! It makes no sense why Grebb would give me a D!" I was yelling now.

"Well that sure doesn't make sense, does it? A teacher giving you a bad grade on a paper you did well on! I don't believe it! The point is, you didn't work hard enough!" He yelled back, looking pretty frustrated by me. I felt so enraged I thought I was going to hit him.

"Right! Of course you wouldn't believe me! You wouldn't notice that because he loved John so much, he hates me. You never see anything!" I threw my hands up and walked away.

"You're such a pain in the ass!" He shouted at my back. I tightened my fists, wound my arm back, and I punched the wall with quite a lot of force. I didn't feel much pain because of my adrenaline, and I was disappointed to not even make a mark in the wall. I just saw him lunging for me in my peripherals, tackling me against the wall and gritting his teeth fiercely with wide eyes. My heart was racing, and I was tempted to push him off of me.

"Don't you dare!" He blasted in my face. The grip he had against my t-shirt loosened, and he almost threw me off the wall.

116

I had a swarm of comebacks towards him coming to my mind, but I knew full well it would be a dead end. Watching his angry strut head towards the couch, I ran upstairs to get away from him. Slamming my door as aggressively I could behind me, I somehow fell onto my bed and crinkled my bed spread in my fists.

Self-infliction seemed like the answer at that moment. It was all in the impulse. So I pulled out my pocket knife, took a deep breath, and dug. As a shred of sting engulfed my nerves, I thought about how angry I was at Dad, and how disappointed he is in me. Down leaked the warm crimson to my elbow, the drip falling onto my carpet floor. This one kept bleeding and bleeding, and I let it. The blood kept gushing, on drop at a time from the tip of my elbow. Then came the lightheadedness, which I usually don't let myself get to. I knew it was time to bandage up the mess. Just about three inches down from my wrist on the soft padded side was where I sliced, and it was deep. Normally, it would halfway frighten me to get that deep. But not this time. In a far twisted way, it felt quite good to injure myself furthermore. It fed my fire of hate.

With my dad focused in on the TV downstairs, I knew this was my opportunity to sneak to the bathroom. Inconspicuously, I slid out my door, expecting the hallway to be empty. It wasn't.

"Roy, what the hell did you do? Oh my God!"

I had jumped back, so startled my body froze to ice. I was a deer in the headlights, the kid with his hand in the cookie jar. I was caught. Worst of all, caught by Dad. I had covered my elbow with my other hand to prevent the dripping onto the hallway carpet. That had made the blood smear on my arm, looking gorier than before. I couldn't speak. Nothing even came out when I tried. His face was priceless. Looking into his eyes for answers, they held a significant amount of infuriating concern. I wanted to dart out of there, but I knew I had to get this cut taken care of, or I could be in trouble.

"Are you insane? You're cutting yourself now?" He said wide eyes, disbelief in his stare. I could feel he wanted me to answer him with something, but I didn't have any words. None. He was now shaking his head. Now he felt obligated to help me bandage and clean it, which he wasn't too happy about. I wasn't either. That's the exact opposite of what I wanted. I finally spoke.

"Just let me take care of it," I said firmly, taking my arm out of his reach. He only sighed, knowing that it was a tough situation. Then came the head shaking again.

"How could you be so stupid? So careless? Do you want to be that kid in therapy again? Huh?"

"Stop it!"

He was furious again. I was more. He got right up in my face.

"I will pull you out of everything you do and devote your life to becoming normal if that's what it takes! You are destructive, and dangerous! I just can't believe you. I will put you in a mental hospital if I have to, dammit."

My hate fire was being built bigger.

"Now you clean that thing up good. I better not have to take you to the hospital. Again."

"Why? Why would I go and get stitches? Why not just let myself die of an infected wound?"

Before he went to his room, he stopped to what I had said and turned to look at me.

"Fine. Whatever you please. I'll just 'get off your back.'"

I fell back against the wall, my head filling with starry blindness. I could feel myself falling over, but I managed to stay up straight and make it through the dizzy spell. Dad was now speaking to me, his tone different. It took a few seconds to be able to see him clearly again.

"Roy, are you okay?" He said, his voice lighter, "You're scaring me. You're losing a lot of blood. C'mon." He walked me to the bathroom.

He gave me a cloth to add pressure, which I did while he pulled out the bandages from the cabinet. I just wanted to push him away.

"I can do this myself. Please just leave me alone."

I don't know why he was doing this for me. That didn't change that I was upset with him for not understanding anything.

He resisted, in his body language at least. But he knew I was serious. The tension was still there between us over the argument. I wanted to get away from it.

"Fine," he said shortly with annoyance, "Keep the pressure on." I had managed to make it stop bleeding after a while. I even cleaned it thoroughly, which I usually never do.

I remember one day early eighth grade clear as day. I was walking around the building outside to my next class purposefully trying to avoid running into Derek and Dion in the hall. Unpredictably, one of them had seen me going that way. So they joined me halfway and pinned me against the wall. Derek towered over me by nearly a head's height and began slamming me with hits everywhere he could reach. That had been the day in which inside my mind, something switched and urged me to get him back. Bravely, I kneed him in his junk and put him on the ground. In a flash, my gloating moment was gone when Dion wrapped his hands around my neck and said chillingly, "We're probably going to kill you some day." Now that I look back, what thirteen year old in their right mind would say that? He just wanted to scare me. It ate at me with powerlessness and fear though. I remember feeling that if these two classmates had such desire to hurt me and even toss me a death wish, I must have been such garbage, worse than the garbage I knew I already was from my past. Not just that. The fermented, gooey scum stuck to the very bottom of the dumpster in the dark back alley. I could have hid in a dumpster and never came out, feeling nobody would miss me.

Going home that night, I had no desire to be around my family. It's like I didn't feel a part of them because I was stuck in a whole other world of hidden pain. Dad was making conversation with John at the dinner table and Aldin was lighting up the room. I just sat with my hood over my head, pretending to be nibbling the food I had no desire to nourish my body with. It came to the point where Mom was calling over to me to speak, because I had blocked out nearly everything everyone was saying. Apparently my name was said three times. Dad piped up and ordered me to answer my mom. With a face of stone and no life in my eyes, the only thing running through my mind was that there was nothing for me to say. Nobody knew about Derek and Dion yet. They didn't need to hear anything from my dark mind. They hated it. Especially Dad.

So I said, "I have nothing to say, can't you just let me be?" But Dad, with his need for control, wasn't about to let that happen.

"Roy, you take your hood off right now, stop playing with your food, and treat your family with respect!" His voice was raised just a hair, enough to really shut me down. I didn't give eye contact to anybody now that it was dead silent.

John said, "I don't get why you act so dead all the time. You're acting so abnormal you're drawing this negative attention to yourself." That had annoyed me.

"He's right. And you know what? Nobody wants to be around you when you're being grumpy." Dad added.

I blew it with my anger, "It would be a lot easier for me if all of you would just leave me alone!" Dad didn't like that. I saw John shake his head.

"Then get up RIGHT NOW and get out of here. Don't even bother eating," Dad had said.

I got up out of my chair, "Not like I was anyway, I hate eating at this damn table!"

I heard my mom gasp, knowing I had gone too far. Sometimes the bottled up anger flooded out like lava.

"How dare you say something like that! You should be grateful you have a good family like this!"

"I don't have a good reason to! It's impossible for me to feel grateful about anything!"

I was feeling that at the moment. With so much emotional turmoil from my past and present, I couldn't imagine being happy. That's what I meant. But he didn't take it that way.

I heard Mom shriek, "Richard don't!"

But his hand was too fast and I saw a quick bolt of lightning.

120

My ears were ringing.

"You're mom and I work hard to give you a good life. You better learn to be grateful, because I won't allow that kind of disrespect. Now get upstairs!"

Mom's voice replayed in my head from the middle of eighth grade, "Roy, your behavior is concerning. It's not normal, and I think we need to try something new." Derek and Dion had been so undeniably wicked, controlling my life to nothing but pure dread and anger. I knew I had been acting like a terrible kid. Not only had I attempted to drink an entire bottle of wine in one sitting that I stole from the top cabinet, but I had been skipping out on my homework. I was withdrawn, letting nobody penetrate the endless circle of pain engulfing my life. A trip to the hospital for alcohol poisoning and a report on bad grades had done it. "You have been too much of a burden, and it's got to stop," Dad had told me straight out. That means therapy. My worry came from what I was. I didn't know. The feeling of not knowing was confusing, frightening even. I didn't have any real friends. I hardly spoke to anyone. My brothers were all I had, but even they were distant at the time. Nobody at school wanted to hang out with the weird bullied kid in therapy. "Try drumming. Join your school music program, get a drum set. Drumming could be an excellent, healthy, constructive way to channel any anger you feel often," the therapist had suggested. My parents followed her advice and convinced me to do so. They even helped me buy, instead of a kit, my own tenors. After that, they counted that as good and just prayed I would be normal again. Then I grew.

Now I was threatened by Dad to relive the scene. As I walked downstairs to find him on his laptop, a deep feeling of embarrassment came over me. I resented that he had caught me. Settled in this house between the two of us was an awkward, unsettling entity of mistrust and broken boundaries. What if I had chosen in the moment to cut my throat instead of my arm? He would've been right there. How would he have handled it? Would I have regretted doing so, immense amount of blood squirting everywhere from my windpipe right in front of him?

I must be messed up if I don't think I would have.

My phone vibrated as I stood at the foot of the stairs. I reached in my pocket for it as I caught Dad turning his gaze to me. Kyle; "wtf?" I shoved it back in my pocket.

"Please don't tell Mom," I pleaded calmly, getting no immediate reaction from him but pursing lips and an unsure look in his stare. I knew he probably would tell Mom. He's loyal to her, not me. I sighed when he began to shake his head. So I turned my back to him and headed for the front door.

He spoke, "Why did you do it?"

His tone was firm, like he was demanding an answer in all seriousness, and it carried a sense of disappointment. I stopped, refusing to look him in the eyes. If I told him the reason, it would only escalate into another argument I was not in the mood for.

"Why would I tell you?"

And I bolted out of there, sensing that he was stunned at what I said. I admit that was a pretty big blow below the belt, but no part of me regretted it. It was true.

Siri

That was quite weird. His actions were punching a hole right through me. The absence of his presence was disappointing, but most of all, he left without a care as if he wanted to get away from me.

The vibe I was receiving from the group was "forget about him," "give up," "he's not fit for a relationship." I can see how it's true. It's completely self-destructive. I'm like a rejection junkie. What am I doing?

Some feelings just can't be explained.

Roy

Josh and Cameron were happy to see me once I got there. I pulled up to a three car garage, three stories of a house and two story pillars in entrance to the double wide oak front door. I had no idea this guy was this loaded.

"Hello my friend," Josh greeted, throwing an arm around my shoulder with a bottle of beer in his hand.

"Dude, I thought you'd never come. Anyone who can stick it like that to Grebb is always welcome to my place," Cameron said, handing me a bottle as well. I took it with a smile on my face. He led me to the hangout place, where some people I recognized were spread out on the sofas. One of the girls I recognized, Rachel, gave me a once over. It was slightly offensive the way she did it, like I needed fixing. If I'm honest, she was dressed pretty slutty herself. As I quietly sat down on an open spot, I did feel a little awkward. Eyes shifted towards me as other commotion went on, and I began to feel for a moment that I was out of place. I began to wonder why I had even come.

"Roy, that's your name."

I turned to a girl from my left, who had her black hair tied up in a messy bun. Her make-up was a little dark, but her bright blue eyes were stunning. I knew I had seen her around.

"Yeah that's right."

She flashed me a cute smile, which made me think of Siri.

"I'm Kendal," she said.

"Kendal?"

"Yeah. A lot of people tell me it's cute."

I paused for a second, but decided to say it.

"It is."

I probably shouldn't have. I'm not sure why I even did. Her cheeks turned pink while my stomach churned.

"Well Roy is quite a manly name."

She's pretty bold. Like Siri.

I began to warm up to the group of people. I watched one person after another sip their drinks. I had been taking large gulps of mine. Cameron put on some loud, bass-booming music on a surround sound stereo that I noticed people began to move to. There were over a dozen of us in that large, hollow house. The music made it feel like more.

"Let's get out the shots!" One guy named Grant shouted, his hand on the girl's knee beside him. A minute later, Cameron brought out a tray of paper shot cups full of Jell-O.

"Those were for later," Cameron's girlfriend told him. Apparently she was the one who made them.

"Who cares, we've got other stuff for later," he said, passing the tray around. He ordered everyone to hold off and wait, that we would do it together. I grabbed one, the flavor smelling of strawberry. It sounded great, and I realized I hadn't even eaten anything all day. I was going to get drunk pretty fast.

"To...fake I.Ds!" Cameron shouted, holding his cup in the air. A few people grinned and nodded.

"And to beautiful girls!" Josh added enthusiastically. People whistled and agreed. Then we all gulped the Jell-O chunks down. I began to feel the buzz after about thirty seconds it seemed. Maybe it was just my imagination. I couldn't wait to get wasted.

My phone began to ring, and I saw that it was Fiona. I silenced it. They were going to be mad at me, but I would deal with that tomorrow.

"Who wants to play a game?" Cameron's girlfriend piped up.

Kyle

"I'll kill him, I swear," Preston said. Krysten chuckled at him, clutching his arm.

124

"Babe, you wouldn't hurt a fly."

I knew why Preston was so upset. He can't play Roy's solo, yet our band director will expect Preston to play it tonight at half-time. That's a lot of pressure.

"No, I'll kill him. I think I know where he is anyway," I said. He's probably with that guy Josh. Josh thinks he's way cooler than he really is. The only reason Cameron really hangs out with him is because he deals the best weed, and hooks him up with it. McKenzie squeezed my hand.

"Awe, but what if he had an emergency and had to run off?" She questioned, peering at me with gorgeous eyes telling me to ease up. She looked so pretty in her pink sweater and head band, and we looked like dorks in our marching uniforms. She tells me I'm too hot to be a band guy.

"He's been weird lately," I brought up. There was a significant amount of agreement. Siri made eye contact with me, a sense in her gaze that reflected painful confusion. I shot her a sympathetic half-smile.

"He's probably still shaken up," Krysten said without much emotion. She might be right. He's been acting withdrawn since that incident. It probably shattered him to pieces even though he won't admit it. I still don't even know what to do for him. A big guy like him won't admit it.

"Guys," Fiona suddenly spoke with urgency. She had been trying to call him, and was engrossed in her phone away from the conversation.

"I think Roy accidently answered, like his phone is on in his pocket."

"No way!" Preston grinned, pushing over to listen to the phone. It was tough to hear with the roaring crowd, but we crowded around curiously to listen in.

Roy

"Roy, draw a name," Rachel ordered, handing me a basket full of folded paper. Kendal, sitting shoulder to shoulder to me, said, "Good luck." Whichever girl's name I drew I would have to be locked in a room with her for seven minutes. It's that whole seven minutes in heaven junior high crap, and I was reluctant. Things were slightly spinning, and my stomach was aching. But I reached my hand in when Josh grabbed my hand and forced it into the basket. Then he pulled it right back out.

"Wait, wait a second. Just go with Kendal. You two, in that room, now," Josh said adamantly, giving me a slight, annoying shove towards her. Voices around the room began shouting "yes!" in agreement. I looked at Josh, slightly furious. He threw me a wink.

"Have fun."

Before I knew it, Kendal was lifting me up on my feet and practically dragging me to the closest room. My heart began to pound, and I began to wish I was drunker. She shut the door with a giddy shout of enthusiasm, which almost took away her coolness. Immediately, she began taking off her shirt. It was awesome, but I was beginning to turn red. How uncool am I?

"I've always thought you were hot. I love tall men…and bad boys," she grinned, a fierce look of "I want you" staring back at me.

"Okay."

I was stupid.

"Where shall we start?" She said, sticking herself to me with her shirtless self. I gulped. If my friends found out about this, they would be so upset at me for hurting Siri. I knew this was all wrong. I wanted to suck it up. Here was a girl I didn't really care about. Trying to make out with her and opting out seemed better than waiting until Siri is all over me. That is, if I can even handle a relationship with her. Kendal sensed that I was uncomfortable with being touched.

"Why are you so tense? Just relax and sit down," she said, flashing me a tormenting, sexy smile. She gave me a slight push to the couch. I let myself fall backwards. I was open to kissing her. That's not what she had in mind.

"I know how to make you relax." She was in control. I leaned back, my legs spread out. I attempted to squeeze my legs together as a defense mechanism, but she spread them apart again. My face heated up, and I began to feel sick.

"Kendal," I begged, taking a deep breath.

"Shhhh," she said. I held my breath, her hand gliding up my jeans slowly. Her touch was delicate and felt so great.

"Be a good boy and hold still."

"Just stop." I said abruptly. She did, but with a hurt look on her face. After that moment, I felt terrible. I covered my face with my hands and she backed off, confused.

"What the hell is wrong with you? Are you gay or something? Aren't you human?"

A lot of things are wrong with me. Through my fingers, I saw she had her hands on her hips, waiting for me to say something.

Bumbling idiot, "I'm sorry....I just...I don't know...I¬—"

"Whatever, your loss."

And she stormed out. Bitch. Or maybe I was. What normal person wigs out on being touched buy cute girls?

Now I felt humiliated. A party downer. A loser. How could I go back out there? Eventually, after a few minutes of me and my tormenting self alone in that suffocating room, Josh walked in and asked me what happened? I told him it was nothing and to forget about it. He looked extremely disappointed in me.

"C'mon, Roy. You are not going to do this. You can't repeat that whole Sophie thing. Do you know how lame that is? I'm trying to give you a chance of redemption. That girl wants you!"

That struck something within me.

"So the fuck what?!" I nearly hollered, standing up to face him with tightened fists, "Who the hell are you to tell me what to do with my sex life?"

He was the one who had set me up with Sophie.

"You set me up with slutty girls with rude attitudes, anyway."

Josh looked shocked with wide eyes. He had backed away from me with his hands up, looking betrayed.

He said, "I'm just trying to look after you and help out! Calm the fuck down you crazy bastard!"

I dropped my head. He really didn't have any bad intentions towards me. He was only trying to give me a good time. He just doesn't understand. I met his eyes, and he turned away from my contact, muttering "Jesus." Before I could say anything, he walked out on me, giving me the hand. I think he took my momentary silence as "screw you."

Whatever.

I walked past the group, who were all curious about the fallouts that had occurred. I didn't even look at them. Instead, I walked straight to the kitchen and found the stash of liquor. One bottle was already open, which looked perfect. I didn't even care what it was. I just grabbed the bottle out of impulse and began to suck some down. Whiskey. I popped it out of my mouth, struggling to swallow through intense alcohol intake.

"What are you doing?" Cameron asked, appearing through the doorway. I was caught off guard and almost choked.

"Shit," I gasped, wiping my mouth with my sleeve. The cabinets were spinning. So was he.

"No, go for it if you really want. Just stay out of my Vodka."

Wow, he's a concerned friend. I took another swig and slammed the bottle down onto the marble counter.

"Easy," he said. I was getting there.

Kyle

I was angry. Livid. Why, in any possible state of mind, would Roy even think of skipping out on us for those people? Plus Siri. Poor girl. I mean, they're not official or anything. He's not tied to her. But still, he's led her on and given her hope. That's enough to make it unfair. Once she had heard the girl's voice say "Just relax and sit down," she took off. Roy must have sat down like she said, because his phone cut off.

Krys and Fiona went after her, and I could only sit up here and think about how this guy I thought I knew so well is destroying his relationships with people who care about him. He's an idiot.

Siri eventually returned, the other two girls trailing her with sad expressions. Siri looked disappointed. I looked at Fiona once she sat down and caught her eye.

She leaned towards me and admitted, "I feel terrible. Maybe we shouldn't have eavesdropped."

I shook my head.

"No way, don't feel terrible. Roy should feel terrible."

We performed the half-time show. It went okay. Preston screwed up pretty bad on the solo. I predicted he was going to be grumpy from it. I led the march off of the field, steaming inside that Roy had missed a football game performance the night before a competition while the rest of us were actually here. He was drinking and partying, which isn't bad to do once in a while. I get it, I do it. I can understand that he needs an escape. But not when he ditches his team. I wasn't going to stick up for him this time. There's no excuse.

Roy

Kendal was sitting in the corner of the couch with her arms crossed. She was the only one. Everyone else was up, chaotic laughter filling the empty room. Maybe they were laughing at me. I fell over, feeling dreadful, stomach acid greeting the entrance of my throat. The noise became over-stimulating, drowning me through a vortex of irritation. I wanted to leave.

Kyle

I stacked my drum on the shelf and hung up my harness. Friends were leaving,

"See you bright and early."

I figured I might as well call Roy, see if I can ensure he'll be there tomorrow. What I found instead was a missed call. Cameron. I gave him a ring in return, super curious. It was probably about Roy, considering he was there. There was a pretty quick answer with plenty of noise going on in the back ground.

"Man, what's up!" He greeted, his tone chill. He was buzzed.

"Hey dude, you called me first."

There was a momentary pause.

"Yeah, I did. I did, that's right…...pass that over here!"

"Cam?" Another pause.

"Oh sorry, Kyle. So we've got a problem here…"

Probably Roy.

"So, Roy got way too drunk way too fast. Like, he is friggen out of it. It's depressing. He's like, laying on the floor like he's dying, saying random stuff. It's weird."

"Okay?"

He sighed.

"Look, you're like his best bud, you know? I was hoping maybe you could come and take care of him. Take him home."

"Nobody else there can do it?"

"Well, all the guys are staying over. So they're all going all in. One of the girls is a designated driver, but she refuses to do it."

"Didn't he think this through? He thinks he could go to a party, get drunk, and not figure out how to get home?"

"He was going to stay the night I thought."

"No, no way. He has to be at be school tomorrow at seven a.m."

"For what?"

"Band competition."

"Oh. I had no idea."

"Yeah well, I'll be over there. I'll take care of it dude."

"Thanks bro."

I hopped in my car. This was a best friend's duty, and I accepted it. However, it didn't change the fact that I was furious with him. Once I arrived at Cameron's, I decided not to knock. I just walked in and followed the noise to the main room.

"Kyle!" Rachel greeted, grinning with a pipe in her hand. She jumped up to hug me.

"Hey it's Kyle! Dude, join us!" Dylan shouted, offering me a beer. I politely shook my head, overwhelmed from the commotion of my arrival. Cameron noticed me searching the room, and he knew what for.

"He's behind the couch. We dragged him there," he grinned. Dylan and Josh laughed. I smiled, but knew overall that it really wasn't funny.

"You're hot!" One of the drunker girls shouted at me as I turned my back to them. The other girls giggled. I turned around to face them. I couldn't help it.

"I appreciate that." I said, grinning. They laughed.

"Can you t-t-teach me drumming?" Another one asked, giving

me begging eyes. That made me smile, but I shook my head.

"Guys with girlfriends don't do that!" I heard them moan "aw-wwe."

There was Roy, head buried in his knees, his hair in his eyes. It looked super depressing.

"Roy, c'mon."

He had a slow reaction. I stuck my hand under his arm and attempted to help pull him up. That's when I saw that were was a penis drawn on his forehead. Really? Luckily, it had already smeared. It wasn't a permanent marker. Completely original.

"Let's get out of here, now."

I got him standing up, but he still was bent over. I wrapped my arm around his back to keep him stable. I wanted to blow up on him, call him a senseless idiot. But I held my tongue at the moment. There were many eyes on me.

"Kyle, why do you hang out with him?" Rachel blurted with carelessness. Cameron turned to her to hush up. That was an over the top thing to say.

"He's a freak!" Kendal added. Some people laughed in agreement. Roy attempted to turn around, stumbling, and shot them a dirty look. I forced him to turn back around.

"Ease up," I said back to Kendal. She just shrugged.

A chaos of "byes" echoed throughout the house once we got to the front door. Roy was mumbling something in a low voice, but I couldn't tell what he was saying. I would be on him tomorrow. So would Elliot. He was gonna get it. I let go of his arm to get my car keys from my pocket. He began walking a different direction.

"Roy, what are you doing?" I asked, following him.

"Fuck everything," he said softly. That I did hear out of all his mumbling. I grabbed his arm, but his phone began to ring. It looked as if he didn't even notice. So I reached into his pocket for him and looked at the caller I.D. It was John. I immediately answered. He went at it before I could speak.

"Roy, are you crazy? Mom and Dad have been trying to call

you all night. You're going to be in huge trouble because you're grounded. I'm trying to save your ass, but there's only so much—,"

"John, its Kyle!" I overruled his rant. He stopped.

"Kyle, man. What's up?" He said, shifting his tone.

"Well, your dumbass brother got so drunk he got kicked out of a party. So I had to rescue him. We're here at the house of the party, outside."

"You're kidding."

"Actually, no, I'm not. He's bad, and they were making fun of him."

I heard a short sigh.

"Wow."

Roy had stumbled to the lamp pole across the front lawn. He was looking up at it oddly.

"You said he's grounded?"

"Yeah, something about his grades. My parents are so pissed at him. Dad will kill him if he finds out he got drunk at a party. That won't be pretty. Like, Dad was saying he might make him stay home tomorrow from the competition."

"So I can't just have him stay over at my house?"

He paused, contemplating.

"Well, if he doesn't come home tonight, that may make things worse, you know? They're pretty much waiting for him."

"Okay, well there has gotta be a way to get him there without your parents catching him drunk. We need him tomorrow."

He was thinking again.

"I'll try and take care of that. If he gets caught, he gets caught. But we can try. Just drive him here in his truck, and I'll drive you back to your car wherever it is."

"Sounds good man. God, he's lucky you happen to be home tonight."

"Hell yeah, he is. I was going to a party here in town, but Reya came over here for dinner instead."

"Okay, seeya man."

"Take care of my little brother."

Roy began coughing quite a bit. I went over to him and patted his back.

"You okay?" I asked.

"He's gonna kill, gonna k-kill my, k-k-ill me," he stuttered through breaths.

"He might not catch you, c'mon." I tried, leading him to his truck. I asked him for his keys. He didn't seem to listen, so I pulled them out of his pocket. He kinda wigged out about that.

"Sssstop touching me," and he yanked my hand off of him. It annoyed me a bit, but I let it go. I opened the car passenger door, forcing myself not to help him in. He stumbled, so I ended up helping him anyway. He made some mixed up comment about how he wasn't my grandma. I don't know. Once I hopped in the driver's seat, I searched his glove box and ash tray for gum or mints. He actually did have some gum. I pulled out a strip and ordered him to chew it. He did, but in slow-motion.

"Roy, why?" I began, hoping to get something out of him. He lifelessly stared ahead, very slowly moving his jaw to chew. I stared him down, but he ignored me. So I started the engine and gave up.

I attempted to turn on music, but he switched it off. He was so drunk that he wasn't in a relaxed, partying mood. He was uncomfortable, disturbed, and depressing. It began to scare me a bit. He mumbled something, slurring his words, but I couldn't tell what.

"What the heck are you saying?"

He began to moan a bit. Even in the dark truck, I could tell he looked terribly pale. He unstrapped his seat belt.

"I'm gonna puke. Pull over," he muttered, beginning to open the car door as I was traveling at forty. He was going to literally plunge into the road.

"Roy! Stop!" I nearly screamed, gripping his jacket to pull him back. I skidded to a stop, my heart racing, and he immediately flew out the door once I had it slowed and tumbled to the ground. Then he puked, supported by his knees and elbows. It was ridiculous. I came out of the car, slamming the door behind me. I took a quick look at the road in either direction, but nobody was around. It was late.

"God, what the hell, man?" I said. He was in agony, vomiting up a storm. It was disgusting, and I turned away, shoving my hands in my pockets with frustration. He slowly stumbled to stand up. When he did, he just stood and stared off into the distance, his face purely reflecting something I didn't even recognize. I didn't know what to do or say, standing there tensely holding my breath. I was about to suggest leaving, like I really wanted to. But he spoke finally, and I was confused.

"Perfect, Kyle."

Brief silence.

"What?"

He was staring right past me, and began walking forward, practically running into me as he did.

"Where are you going?" I demanded.

No answer. I realized where he was walking though. We had parked just short of a small, high bridge over the river. I followed him.

"C'mon, man. It's cold and late. We gotta get."

Still no reply. He walked to the ledge of the bridge, placing his hands over the concrete to peer below. He was so slow and tipsy. I took a deep breath of cold air, the exhale through my nose a visible cloud. Roy just stared at the water blankly. I got chills.

"I'm a piece of shit," he mumbled loud enough for me. I gulped a lump, sucking an icy breath into my lungs.

"Roy, c'mon. You're not a piece of shit. Please don't—,"

"Don't....," he paused, wincing, "bullshit me, Kyle," giving me a glare so dark it was chilling. I sighed and stared at the ground. I knew I couldn't say anything to convince him otherwise.

"Enough of this, we're leaving know," I urged. I snatched his arm, but he shook me off and immediately began tearing off his jacket. His gaze was focused out off in the distance.

"Roy!" I pleaded, "Let's—,"

"Do you think I would break if I…I jump-p-ed? Head crash, instant death," he struggled to say in a relaxed voice. It was frightening to hear him say that.

"The freak dies, everyone is happy,"

"Roy—,"

"All the shame, the pain. What he did to me. What I did. It'll be gone, so will the no good, s-s-sick kid."

"Roy, stop it!" I was so confused, especially by who did what to him.

He began to climb on the concrete barrier. I leaped at him and snatched his arm, yanking him off. He lost his balance and fell to the ground. I let go of his arm, shocked. When my palm felt wet, I looked to see. It was blood. So I looked at his arm to see a big, bleeding gash. I didn't know what to do. He was on the ground, looking like he was crying. I don't think he was, but it looked like it. I crouched down, feeling uncomfortable. With concern, I grabbed his arm to see the cut, but not just that. Along his arm were sporadic markings and scabs that appeared to be scarring.

"What is this?" I demanded.

He buried his face in an arm, yanking the other away from me.

"Why are you so hostile?" I asked.

A wind picked up, filling the silence with whispering leaves to the roar of the river. I helped him up, accepting that he didn't want to answer. He put his jacket back on, and we walked together back to the truck. As we did, he hid his face from me, as if embarrassed.

I tried to process what had just happened as I drove. Roy had passed out, and I was left feeling incredibly disturbed in the silence of the drive. I gave John a ring once I parked the truck against the curb in front of their house. He answered right away and I was relieved.

"Okay, man. I got a way to sneak him in. Aldin's got the cover.

Is he all right?"

"He passed out."

John has no idea.

"Okay, I'll be out there in a sec," he said. He came out the front door in a few seconds, running to the truck. John opened Roy's door.

"Wow, he reeks. And is that a dick?" John commented, pulling off his seat belt, "So Al will distract my parents in the garage while we can run him upstairs. It's a great act, he's a freakin' kid genius."

He lightly slapped Roy's face to try and wake him, but he barely reacted.

"Okay, well, we need to hurry. Help me carry him," John ordered. I fled and joined him on the other side, wrapping one of Roy's arms around my shoulders. The two of us rushed to the front door, and John listened carefully inside. He even opened the door slowly to peek.

"Awe yeah, that's my bro. Coast is clear," John whispered, leading us inside. My heart was beating fast, hearing commotion going on in the garage. But I trusted John's judgment. We made it to the stairway, and I felt relief.

"Make your footsteps quiet," John said with fear that the staircase was nearly over the garage. We stumbled to his room and lied him on the bed. John gave me a fist bump.

"Good work man," I said. He nodded, but then looked like something was wrong.

"My parents will smell the alcohol."

That's right. We both looked around his room for something.

"Where's Lysol when you need it?" John said.

"Lysol? You want his room to smell like flower boos? Plus that might make it worse. Just cover him with a blanket."

"Right," he said, throwing one on top of him, "now you take off his shoes," he grinned. I shook my head, and slipped them off onto the floor.

"K, c'mon! I'll wipe the penis off later," He urged, turning the light off. I took one last look back at Roy, hoping this was a one-time thing. What I had seen earlier had caught me off guard, and I feared he could do worse.

Suddenly, a commotion went on downstairs. Everyone was coming in from the garage. John and I were still upstairs. John hit me in the shoulder.

"Dude, Dad's coming upstairs! Hide in my room!" He hissed. I dashed out of there like he said, and the footsteps up the stairs got to the top.

"Dad, Roy got back," John said. I stood by the door to hear the conversation.

"Oh really? Well where is he?" I heard Mr. Sanders say.

"He went to bed, he was tired. He said something about having to stay late to load the truck for tomorrow."

Nice, John. There was a pause, and I held my breath.

"All right then."

I heard a door open, which probably meant he was checking to make sure Roy was sleeping.

"By the way Dad, one of my friends texted me and she's stuck without a ride, so I'm gonna take off and help her."

All I heard was a mumble of "all right, whatever."

Now I was stuck. I didn't have a way of knowing how to get out or where the family was around the house. I texted John, "what do I do?" A few seconds later, he replied, "out the window." Really? Was he serious? I ran to the window and began to see how it was possible. There he was in an instant around the corner in the back yard. He motioned for me to open the window, so I did.

"Kyle!" he shouted in a hushed voice, "Climb out, and go to the tree over to your right!" I did, and began to feel confident. I'm a great tree climber.

"I'll be down in a sec!" I said, rushing to the tree. I descended like a freakin' monkey.

"Nice," John said. He followed me.

"I begged my parents to take my window screen off so I could

138

hang out on the roof. They actually let me," he grinned, opening the fence door. Suddenly, Aldin comes through the back sliding glass door. John addressed him, giving him a high-five, and I gave him one too.

"Don't give our position away, little man," John said, continuing to walk.

"Nah, told Dad I was taking a piss."

"Atta boy," John smiled, leading me out.

"Seeya Kyle!" Aldin whispered.

Love that kid.

We hopped in Roy's truck, and John made a comment.

"I'm using his gas."

Normally, hanging out with John is a lively time. We always talk it up, joke around, and ramble about sports teams. But tonight, what I saw disrupted me. I think John began to notice.

"Is something wrong, man?" John spoke up, turning down the music. He switched from the radio to the CD player. Some hard core metal song was first on the playlist.

"God, never mind. He listens to music you would cut your wrists to."

Ironic.

Releasing a tense sigh, I said, "I saw a lot of shit tonight from Roy. It scared the hell out of me."

John's expression contorted into a frown. He abruptly turned his head at me as if he had no idea.

"What? What did he do?"

I wasn't exactly sure how to put it or where to start. There was a lot on my mind.

"Has…," I began, trying to gather my train of thought, "has he ever talked about hurting himself?"

I think I put John into a deep thought. He stared straight ahead at the road, like he didn't want to answer.

"Okayyy, what did he do? It's obviously serious."

"He said some weird things, like he called himself a piece of shit, and talked about how dying would make everything better and make everyone happy."

"Wow." He rolled his eyes.

"John, have you seen his arms lately?"

"No, why?"

"Exactly. He hides them by always wearing long sleeves. And why do you think?"

He looked puzzled, but it came to his mind. He began shaking his head, gripping the wheel tighter.

"No, it can't be. It's too stupid. I thought only fourteen year old girls cut."

"It's stupid that he drank too much, probably on purpose, and that he tried to jump off a bridge to kill himself. His arms are covered in cuts, man."

John ruffled a hand through his hair.

"He really tried to kill himself?"

I sighed, "Yeah. And he tried to jump out of the moving car."

"Dammit, I know my brother is weird, but I didn't think he is actually emo."

"Well something is up with him, and if he's suicidal, then something needs to be done."

"You mean, like, he needs help or something again?"

"Again?"

"Yeah, you don't…," he paused, not sure if to continue. Now I was curious.

"Don't know what?"

"Well, I thought he might have told you at some point. But maybe not. Just don't say anything."

I shifted in my seat, and he continued.

"During the time that he was getting bullied really badly in middle school, he started getting out of hand. My parents were convinced he was on drugs or something. He just stopped being

140

him and turned into a scary, depressed person. He became violent when he got angry, and Dad hitting him a lot definitely made things worse I thought. But of course, we didn't know about the bullies. He never took his shirt off and hid his bruises well. He tried to kill himself and it really caused a scare. There was a period of time when we were little kids, maybe when he was like six or seven, when he was doing some weird shit. Like, he would pee his pants randomly, he was doing some really strange play with his toys, and he had uncontrollable temper tantrums. Plus, he hated Aldin. He would do things to Aldin behind our backs, and he was like two. Even later on, he still bullied Aldin, but I think I understand why. It made him feel like he had some power because he had none against them at school."

That was some strange information to hear, definitely a side of Roy I didn't know about. I can understand why he never told me.

"Wow," I replied. He continued.

"So at the time in middle school, they took him to therapy for a short time. He had tried downing a bottle of wine and had to be taken to the hospital for alcohol poisoning. That was what had done it. So in his therapy, they gave him drums, meds, and called it good for a while. Of course, that was when he entered high school and he started growing. Then the assholes started leaving him alone. Those guys, whatever they were doing to him at school, were really messing him up. He really hasn't been someone completely stable since before seventh grade. I wish I could go back. I wish I had known what they were doing to my brother. I would have tried to save him. But I was self-absorbed and clueless. I don't think he's recovered from it even now. I mean, he has a self-esteem issue, and sometimes I feel like he's depressed. Obviously depressed enough to do something drastic. He's a pretty cool guy, but he's not right in the head right now."

"Well he did something drastic tonight."

John nodded, then pursed his lips and sighed.

"Whatever he's going through, my dad makes it harder on him. Puts pressure on him. I think he's just cracking, you know?"

141

"Well that's for sure. He vents about it enough."

"Seriously, dude. It sucks living with them when they're always at each other's throats."

"Yeah, that's what I hear."

"I know my dad has this thing about Roy reflecting him, and he has to try to fix him so that he doesn't embarrass him. You know, especially when dad and I have always clicked so well, what's he supposed to do with a son who's completely different? And in his eyes, different in a negative way? Like, I kind of understand, but at the same time, he doesn't take the time to try and understand him, you know?"

"You sound like a father yourself."

He smiled, "Well, when you live with it long enough, you begin to understand things. Roy takes Dad's hard-headedness too hard though, I think. He interprets it as "he hates me," you know?"

"Yeah, but…it doesn't mean he doesn't like, care."

"Yep. And if I tell him that Roy tried to kill himself, he would take it seriously. Dad would do anything for him, really. Roy just doesn't believe it. I wish he could see the side of Dad that I see. I don't know if he can if he continues to act the way he does."

"Well, seeing the way he reacted to that whole birthday thing…"

"Yeah, exactly. If Dad knew who did that to him, he'd hunt them down and kick their asses. He's that type of guy. I've seen it. Roy just pushes him away when he tries to help him."

"He seems to be pushing everyone away lately."

"Oh, I haven't been home a lot lately, but that seems probable."

We arrived at Cameron's.

"You gonna join the party?" John asked, grinning.

"Nah, I'm too responsible. Too lame." I said, lightly hitting his shoulder. He nodded.

"Course. Thanks for helping Roy. We should have just let him rot in his misery and made everything easier."

"No kidding," I grinned, climbing out.

Before I shut the door, he said, "You should come to a college party sometime. I'll let you know. It's gonna happen."

Sweet.

"Sounds great, man. Seeya."

I went to my car, unsettled about everything I heard and saw. What a night.

Chapter Seven

Roy

"Roy, this is a very special thing that we do together, okay? You're very special, and that's why I choose you to do it. You're doing a good thing for me. You are a good person for doing this."

It was getting stuffy in the corner of the closet. I moved the large coat on the hanger out of my face so that I could see him through blurry eyes.

"C'mon out, it'll be okay," he smiled, grabbing my hand. A resistance in my mind tugged on me to get away, but I was so little, and he was so big. Besides, he said it would be okay. He picked me up and held me in his arms, placing my hands around his neck.

"Don't be afraid, little buddy. You do this for me, and I'll give you a giant bowl of ice cream later, okay?"

My eyes got huge, and I began to nod my head.

"And remember, I accept you. You're perfect. But if you tell Daddy about anything, he won't love you anymore."

The smile on my face faded, but was replaced with guilt.

"Do you understand?" He demanded, his eyes hard and firm. I became nervous, so I just nodded.

"Say that you understand, Roy. Say it," he urged, a cold look in his eyes staring hard back at me. I became frightened.

"I understand," I said softly, hoping that he would accept my response. He continued to stare at me as if to make me afraid, my heart pounding. He finally eased up.

"Okay. Now go in the bed room and get ready for me."

He let me down, and I did what I was told. I raced to the momentary seclusion. Small room, wood panels, musty smell. I peeled my clothes off and waited on the bed, the hollowness of a space with a lack of love suffocating my existence.

"Get up moron," an irritating voice called at me. I felt a hand shake my body from the shoulder. I'm pretty sure I groaned.

144

"I have orders. Now get your ass up," John said, ripping the covers off of me.

"Leave me alone, what the hell?" I grumbled. Why was he being so persistent?

"Hello, your competition?"

I sprang up in an instant, my chest freezing up into a ball of ice. As I did, a rush of pain swelled behind my eyes. How could I have forgotten?

"Oh my God, what!?" I nearly shouted, startling John. It was kind of funny the way he backed off, but I was completely lost. He crossed his arms.

"John, what happened to me?" I demanded, pressing my hand to my aching head.

"Uh, well, you got really drunk, Kyle went and brought you home, told me about your little adventures, and then here you are, forgetting your big day."

Little adventures?

"Wait, what?"

"Oh, not to mention that we had to both carry you and sneak you up here from Mom and Dad. They don't know. Yeah, you're welcome."

Wow.

I rubbed my face, so disoriented. I felt completely stupid for what I had done last night, whatever it was. Now I had to race to the school and face my angry friends.

"Oh God."

"It's obvious something is going on."

I didn't want to hear it.

"Just...stop. I don't care."

He looked like he was ready to argue.

"Okay, well, I'm sorry that I care," he said, his tone sarcastic, "and you better thank Kyle for saving you last night. He wasn't too happy about it."

I didn't say anything. Kyle is a saint for doing that. He really shouldn't have. Now I felt embarrassed to face him. When I got up and went to my dresser, John sat on my bed as if he wanted to talk. I stopped and turned around.

"What, John?"

He gave me a dirty look.

"What is your problem?" He said defensively. He crossed his arms. I hesitated with him looking at me.

"I'm not taking my shirt off in front of you," I said, crossing my arms too.

"What? You embarrassed? You don't want me to see your ripped ribs?"

"God, just shut up," I piped up, turning around. It angers me when he judges my appearance, especially when his is so dang perfect.

"Why are you starving yourself, huh? Are you back to that? And don't think I don't know about your arms. Yeah, why don't you roll your sleeves up?"

I lashed around. How does he know?

"Who told you?!" I said, thinking it might have been Dad. That surprised him, especially since I didn't deny it.

"Don't you know? Things come out when you are drunk," he said, giving me a look. I was beginning to panic on how much he knew. What did I expose to Kyle?

Tightening my fist, I said, "John, what did Kyle tell you?"

He sat and thought for a moment, staring at me in the eyes as if weary about telling me.

"You talked about killing yourself, and that everyone would be better off without you. Apparently, Kyle stopped you from jumping off a bridge."

Dammit.

John stood up and walked to my tenors. He picked up the sticks and began tapping the drums.

"Just don't do anything stupid. If you need help, get help. Don't go and do stupid things. You're beginning to scare people.

Even me."

And he walked out, tossing my sticks on the floor.

So even though I felt incredibly stupid for how reckless I was last night, I did know one thing I think: that my secret was still safe.

I felt sick to my stomach driving to the school. The whole thing with Kyle is awkward. Same with Siri. For the first time, I just wished the whole day would speed through so that I could get it over with.

When I walked to the percussion section after grabbing my uniform, the drumline seemed to ignore me, as if they didn't want to make a big deal of anything. Siri didn't even look at me. That made me feel worse. I would miss her talking to me. I caught Kyle's eyes from across the section. His expression didn't say much, but I knew I had to talk to him. When I approached him, he waited for me to say something.

"Look, man, I don't really remember much about what happened last night."

He nodded his head as he uncrossed his arms.

"K, well, whatever. I'm just glad that we have our quad player," he said, surprisingly calm. I thought he would have been angrier at me. He got Fiona's attention.

"Hey, why don't you tell Roy what happened last night," he said to her. Fiona widened her eyes, like she wasn't sure if she should. Now I had to know.

"What are you talking about?" I demanded, searching both of their faces. Fiona looked at Kyle. He nodded. I was becoming incredibly nervous.

"Well," she began, "I was trying to call you last night to see what happened to you, and I think you accidently answered," she said, looking at the ground. Preston happened to hear our conversation, and he grinned.

"Something like 'just sit down and relax,'" Preston said in a high, girly voice. It took me a second to figure out what the heck

147

they were talking about.

"Who was the girl?" Kyle asked, "Was it Kendal? Is that why she was so pissed at you?"

That struck something in me. I felt anger towards them for listening in on an incredibly horrible personal circumstance. That must be why Siri isn't acknowledging my existence. I think Kyle saw that I was fuming.

"Whoa, man, calm down. That's all we heard," he said. Preston was going to make a comment, but Kyle shot him a look to cool it. I walked away from them towards Siri. I felt terrible. She looked like she was struggling to zip up the back of her uniform. I had the urge to go and help her, but I had no idea if she would even let me. Suddenly, I felt a hand on my shoulder from behind.

"She'll forgive you, she's too cool to stay mad at you. Just be patient," Fiona said calmly. I nodded, thankful that she is so forgiving and helpful.

"What do you think I should do?" I said, hoping she would give me some kind of girl advice. She took a surprising turn.

"Come here," she ordered, pulling my arm. I was curious, so I followed her. She led me to the empty drum room where we would have privacy.

"This is weird," I said under my breath. She gave me an odd look.

"Okay Roy, spill it. How do you feel about her? Because everyone is confused about it, especially her. The best advice I can offer to you is to be straight forward and tell her. So tell me, okay?"

"What?"

She rolled her eyes.

"Come on, don't be dumb. You asked me what you should do. So talk to me. Maybe telling someone about it will help you understand it even better."

"But what about last night?"

"Well, I mean, you can apologize about that, but it may not matter if she hears from you what she wants. And that is that you care about her, which you obviously do. So what is holding you back? I mean, why did you hold hands with her yesterday, then just leave without saying anything?"

I rubbed my eyes, unsure of what to say.

"I don't know, Fiona."

"C'mon, you must know."

I just stared at her. I didn't feel like sharing. How did she think I would?

"Roy, please. Don't just bottle things up like you do. It doesn't get you anywhere, and it just frustrates people. I'm trying to help you, okay? How do you feel about her? Why are you holding back?"

I sighed. The truth is, I really do like Siri. I've been definitely crushin' on her, especially after homecoming. She's different, and special, and adorable. Somehow, I am drawn to her in a way I've never been drawn to anyone else. I just don't think being in a relationship is a good idea. Fiona was waiting, hoping I would say something.

"I like her, okay?" I said, letting my arms fall to my sides. She crossed her arms, forming a smile.

"Okay, well there's a start."

There was a silence, like she was waiting for more. I just shrugged.

"Well, then why isn't she your girlfriend?"

I raked a hand through my hair. There was no point to this. If I told Fiona that I don't think I'm good enough for her, she was only going to try and butter me up, tell me that's not true and all of that stuff.

"C'mon, Fiona, you're not my therapist," I said, opening the door to walk out. I think that shocked her, taking it as rude.

"Wow, really Roy?"

"Sorry," I mumbled on my way out. I should have been nicer about it.

The day went by. I didn't socialize much. Just when I had to.

149

So I admit, I stared at Siri a lot. I know that Fiona is right. I need to man up and tell Siri what I'm thinking. She's waiting for me to.

Elliot was mad at me. I was sluggish, and he could tell I wasn't completely there. I thought he was going to yell at me in front of the whole line. I was afraid he would. Instead, he just gave me the most scorning glare he's ever presented me when we finished out first rep in warm-ups. It just made me feel just great. I didn't even feel good when I performed on the field.

I know I deserved it all though.

We sat in the stands, watching other bands perform before final scores were announced. It was already dark. I had my pad and sticks out just drumming quietly to myself. I wasn't in solitude, though. Kyle was sitting by me, Nathan to my other side. That is, until I received a text from Siri. I was completely surprised. "Come and meet me at the truck?"

I stood up and got out of there, leaving before Kyle could ask anything. Through the chilly air, I walked back to the lot where our band truck was, my heart beating to nervousness. I had absolutely no idea what she had in mind. What the heck did she want to talk to me for? Then I saw her, secluded, sitting on the gate of the truck. She swung her dangling legs wrapped up in her coat. Dang, I was shaky.

"Hey," I said, approaching her. I shoved my hands in my jacket pockets, hoping that I wouldn't be an idiot and say something wrong. She didn't quite smile, but acknowledged me.

"Hey," she said back, blowing out a short breath.

"I'm surprised you want to talk to me."

She looked at me in the eyes.

"No, I just feel a little bad. I mean, I feel like I might have pushed you or pressured you into being with me. And I'm sorry. Sometimes, if I want something, I'm a little assertive."

Interesting how she thinks that. I would have thought that it was all my fault.

"That hardly crossed my mind."

She looked a little relieved, studying my face in return. She has been a little pushy about it, I admit. I'm not comfortable with everything she does towards me, mainly because I don't feel ready for it. However, it doesn't necessarily mean I don't like it.

"Are you sure?" She asked with an innocent look, standing up and walking right up to me. I lost my breath for a second.

"Don't think for a second that it's your fault. I'm just afraid."

"Did anything happen with that girl?" She asked calmly. It was a jump of a subject change.

"No. I'm not really good for you, Siri."

That really confused her. A loud roar erupted from the stadium. "Huh?"

"I have certain issues. I'm not normal...at least as a boyfriend would go. Trust me, you don't want to be with me."

Her expression looked tormented. So was mine. My heart ached to every vessel.

"Roy, I don't understand," she said, looking like she was holding back fresh tears.

"I...I know, I'm not sure I even do, either."

That caused her more confusion. She began to shake her head. I felt it in my throat, right there, being thrown to the tip of my tongue. I had to let it out.

"You're amazing."

She looked as though she lost her breath. She didn't know whether to smile or feel rejected.

"Why don't you let me speak for myself? What if I don't care whatever issues you have?"

It was hard to hear. I had no idea why she even liked me so much.

"Why? What's in it for you?"

Her smile faded, "God, why are you so hard on yourself, Roy? Give yourself a chance. Give us a chance. I mean, geez. You make yourself sound like you're worthless."

I looked at the ground. I knew she was right. I am hard on my-

151

self. But I also can't help it if I don't even like me. Not knowing what to say, I just continued looking down. She took my hand, and I got warm chills.

"Can I tell you what I know?" She said rhetorically. I could feel her warm breath. Her eyes were big and sweet. She had something to really say.

"I know that you're not like a lot of other guys. But I know what I feel, and it's strong, okay? I'm not even sure what it is, but it's like there's this force. When I'm not around you, I feel like I should be. I want to be. Something about you draws me in. Now please, please tell me if you feel it too, like I think you do."

Here it was. That moment. She bared her soul, and now was standing there, a foot below me with those adorable, begging eyes. I had to do it. She felt it, I felt it. It felt right, and I was an idiot for not giving it a chance. Somehow, she was an inspiration for me to take the leap. So I opened my mouth and grabbed her other hand. It was so in the moment.

"I'm sorry I've been weird and confusing. But it's true, I want to be around you, too. I've never felt like this before, and home-coming was one of the best nights of my life. I want this, I'm just scared. I admit it. I'm scared I'll disappoint you."

She looked extremely happy at that moment. It lifted me, and I then felt a very good feeling float inside. She squeezed my hands.

"I'm willing to take that risk with you. I'd rather risk feeling hurt than wondering what it ever was," she smiled. Then came a moment of silence. I think that was our cue to kiss. She was staring at my mouth the next second, and I acted upon it. It felt like such a quick apology and conversation. Now here we were again in an instant. I bent down, and our lips met in perfect harmony. They were soft and warm, so was her hair in my fingers. God, it was great. We didn't stop, actually. We kept going. There was nobody around. The truck was open, and we both climbed up somehow with our hands still on each other. We sprawled on the floor of the truck, hands gripping, our tongues swirling. Her hands were gliding along my front side, her cool fingers on my chest. My hands were reaching everywhere, and she was actually letting me. I wanted every part of her. It was crazy good, and I was grateful, so incredibly happy at that moment having her so close to me, so intimately. I hadn't felt this close to someone since…since…

My hands began to freeze, as did my chest. His face came into my mind. His hands were Siri's stroking my body. Oh God. That disgusting, sickening guilt. There it is again. It's what I was afraid of. I wanted to scream with frustration for the disruption.

We slowed down to the loud breathing, the crowd in the stadium coming back again. Just in time.

"We better go," she said grinning, grabbing my hand. I nodded, standing up with my arm around her waist. I was so disappointed. Every damn time a girl touches me, I go back to that.

BACK TO THAT! I hate it, and I hate him!

Siri

Finally! I mean, seriously! Finally! We're getting somewhere. I pretty much got weak in the knees when he told me I'm amazing, especially with those killer dark eyes. Gosh. I feel alive.

Roy

She texted me the next morning. It put a smile on my face to see her name on my phone. "You were quiet for the rest of the night, everything okay?" Hmm. She was concerned. I just said, "No worries, I'm fine. Just a lot on my mind." I hoped that would be a good enough answer for her. It was true. She was on my mind, but so was that bastard I hate.

As I walked into the kitchen, I noticed that I actually had some kind of motivation to eat this morning. I pulled a bowl of cereal out

153

of the cabinet, but heard footsteps behind me.

"So, you're actually eating something, huh?" Dad said to me. I was slightly startled.

"Yeah."

He didn't say anything. Instead, he walked up behind me and blocked me from getting into the box.

"I'm making breakfast, so you can save that for the week."

"Okay."

I went and sat down at the table while he pulled out some pans and placed them on the stove. I began to pretend that I was engaged in my phone. It began a second later.

"You're behavior is concerning. And yes, I did tell your mom about your arms. Not only that, but John made us aware that you aren't eating much and that you've been doing potentially dangerous things to yourself." Potentially dangerous?

"I figured," I sighed.

"I almost felt oblivious for not noticing, but at the same time, you isolate yourself a lot."

I raked my hands through my hair, feeling uncomfortable to be discussing this. That was when my mom walked in. She seemed to instantly know what we were talking about.

"I need to see this, Roy, okay? Will you please roll up your sleeves?"

I did not want to. I was very uncomfortable and irritated. She sat down by me when I didn't even budge.

"Show her, Roy. She has the right to see," Dad ordered. He even pointed his spatula at me. God!

"Why? I'm eighteen," I said, hiding my face with my hands.

"Oh come on, don't be ridiculous," she said, hitting my shoulder.

Okay. Whatever.

"Fine!" I said, whipping my head up. I ripped my sleeves up, acting irrationally.

"See? See?" I said, putting my arms out in plain view for her.

Etched in my skin were numerous scars, deep and dark. They shouted out pain. The pain was exposed, and it felt like I was naked. She gasped.

"I present to you my personalized Etch A Sketch." And I stood up humiliated, ready to walk away. A hand stopped me, gripping tight with angry fingers.

"How can you be like this, you inconsiderate scumbag!" Dad fiercely griped at me, "Look at her!"

"Don't call him that!" She yelled at him.

She was crying. I was a terrible person obviously. A terrible son. Dad knew me well. I was so angry that he put me in this situation. What did he expect? Of course she's going to be upset. Of course I'm going to be resistant and uncomfortable.

"Mom, I'm sorry, I didn't mean to upset you. Let go of me!" I yanked my arm away from Dad. He had a furious look in his eyes. Mom was whimpering.

"What did we do? Are we horrible parents to you or something? Why, Roy, why?" She cried, making me feel worse.

"Because I'm an 'inconsiderate scumbag,' that's why. Aren't I right, Dad?"

He didn't say anything. He just glared at me, fuming. Mom shot Dad a dirty look.

"I don't really care if I get hurt, Mom. But I care if you do. That's why I didn't want you to see. Now it's a bigger deal than it really is."

"Hey, it is a big deal! That's messed up behavior! It means that something isn't going right in your head, and you need help! Help that we don't know how to give you!" Dad said.

"That's right," Mom said, wiping her tears, "that's why we enrolled you in therapy. We did yesterday."

"What? You did?" They really did?

"Yep. It's non-negotiable," Dad added, going back to the pan, "And we mean soon."

"Because you are eighteen, we can't completely do all the paper work. So you are going to fill them out today."

"I'm not really hungry anymore," I said, starting to walk away.

"No, you're eating. I don't care if I have to force you. I want you to be healthy," Mom said, ordering me to sit down.

"Yeah, no more of that walking away like you constantly do. It's insulting and cowardly," Dad said, pulling out strips of bacon. I just swallowed.

"Right. Because the conversations with you Dad are always about what's wrong with me. How can you blame me?"

He just released a breath and shook his head.

"Well, because, you tend to make things difficult," he said. Geez. There it is again.

"Point proven," I said in return. I slapped my hands on my lap.

"Well look at you, proving my point too," he smiled smugly. That made me angrier.

"Why can't you two just get along? Don't you know how tiring it is?" Mom chimed in, rubbing her forehead. Neither Dad nor I said anything. It's just how it is. All that was heard was the frying of the bacon and the sizzling of the sausage after that point until Aldin came downstairs. We assumed John was sleeping in. When he did come down for breakfast though, Dad hit it off with him, talking away like they were best buddies. It fired me up so much inside I stayed silent the entire course of that torturous breakfast. Then Dad had me clean up while he and John and Aldin began to watch a game.

Mom tried to talk to me while I was cleaning. I was trying not to be cranky with her through my frustration with Dad. If I'm completely honest myself, it did sting. Its sucks being constantly ridiculed and then left out of his bonding time. I just acted like I didn't care. I really wish I didn't.

"You don't talk to us, so maybe whatever it is that's bugging you, you will be comfortable telling the therapist."

"Yeah," I answered, scrubbing crud off of a plate vigorously.

Then the all famous quote, "We do it because we love you."

156

Gag me.

I had work that night. Of course, Josh was scheduled too. It was pretty awkward. We completely ignored each other. I'm even a little blurry about what we had argued about, but I could sense by his body language he didn't want to talk to me. So I returned the favor. The ignoring was working pretty well until he told me that I should go mop up the corn meal on the floor with my useless, baby dick when he slipped. That set me off, especially since he wasn't trying to kid around. If Harry wasn't ten feet away a few seconds later, I would have decked him. At least, I fantasized it. It's not worth getting fired over. Maybe he will eventually get kicked out once other people finally get sick of his sex-crazed mouth. Nobody likes hearing about the chicks he hooks up with or goes down on every dang weekend. What's his problem, anyway? Why is he so obsessed with sex? Maybe it's hard for me to understand. After all, I can't even handle sex. What a prude I am.

The week went by. I actually spent quite a bit of time with Siri at school. We held hands in the hallway, and some classmates gave me curious looks and stares. Cameron even asked me about her. At the same time, he tried to sell me dope. I accepted.

I can still feel myself holding back when it comes to her. She can sense it too. Maybe she believes I'll come around eventually. I don't know. I'm just trying to stay on my toes. I also couldn't stop thinking about therapy all week. I don't want to go. I mean, I really don't feel fit to bring up all my crap. I don't want my parents to be into my personal thoughts and life. It's awkward and embarrassing. Besides, they didn't even talk to me about it. Initially, it was Dad's threat. Now it feels like a punishment. I guess, in all fairness, I would have resisted anyway.

Siri

I wanted to go to Roy's house Friday night so bad. Unfortunately, he wasn't too thrilled about the idea. The group couldn't hang out, they each had something going on. It put me in an exciting position to spend time with Roy. He was going to meet my family. Dinner was my Dad's idea. He was curious about Roy.

I admit, my heart was pounding. I stared out my bed room window facing the street until his truck pulled up under the street light. I grinned like an idiot, especially when I heard Kade from downstairs shout, "Siri's boyfriend is here!" I was dressed a little nicer for him tonight. My family would notice, which is a little embarrassing. But he's worth it. So I ran downstairs all excited, my stomach twisting in a knot with nervousness for the awkward introduction.

"Someone's excited," my mom exclaimed. I smiled, waiting at the door for him. When I heard the knock, the door rushed open by my shaky arm. When I saw him, tall, his hair brushed out of his eyes, I said "hey" with a smile. He returned it. This time, he wasn't wearing his black jacket. It was replaced with a black button up shirt. Of course it's black.

"You're looking colorful this evening," I said, grinning. That got him to smile.

"Ha, ha," he said, stepping inside.

"Hi, Roy, I've heard a lot about you!" Mom greeted. She rushed over to us with her crazy big, overly friendly smile. I looked at Roy to read his body language. My mom is a very loud, friendly, over-joyful-in-a-good-way person. I figured it might overwhelm him. He seemed fine. Her hand was already on his shoulder, gesturing him to come in and make himself at home.

"You are tall, wow."

"Six four," he said, nodding.

"How cute is that height difference?" She said,

"Oh, Mom," I responded, placing a hand on my cheek.

"Well, he's cute, Siri. Just like you."

Oh gosh. She's a bit much.

I led him downstairs to the basement for a foosball challenge.

"She thinks everything is cute," I said to him.

He smiled, "I can easily tell she's your Mom."

"Ha, yeah. That's what people say. You wouldn't believe how different my sister is. She's really quiet, reserved, and timid."

"No kidding?"

"Nope. Then there's me. I'm the weird middle child."

"You're not that weird," he said, placing a hand on one of the foosball table handles.

"I eat peanut butter and pickle sandwiches, I hang car fresheners above my bed, and I play with silly putty when I watch long movies."

Roy

"Yeah, maybe you're right," I responded. She shot me a competitive grin. But I spoke before she did,

"I bet I'm a weirder middle child than you."

She stared at me for a second.

"Well how so?"

"Oh come on, it's almost like I was adopted in my family." It's true.

"Yeah, but you have the exact same eyes as your Dad. That's hard to miss. Your brothers don't."

"What, do you study my family's eyes?" I joked. She laughed. Then came a silence. She asked me a serious question, but acted nonchalant about it.

"Do you ever wish that you were the oldest or the youngest?"

I've been over that many times inside my head over the course of my life.

"Well…yeah. I guess so."

"Really?" She asked. That was just a placeholder for "tell me more."

I sighed, "I don't know, I mean, I was taught young to sacrifice for Aldin because he was the baby. At the same time, John was Dad's boy. So in certain ways, yeah, it kinda sucked. But I would never wish upon either of them to have been in my position."

"Really?" She replied. She smiled because she said "really" twice.

"Yeah, just certain reasons."

"Really?"

I rolled my eyes and tried to poke her by pushing the handle towards her. She backed away and dodged it, grinning.

"Way to ruin my serious moment," I said.

"I'm sorry," she said through a laugh.

"Tell me something else I don't know about you," I asked. There's so much I want to learn about her. She was silent for a second, looking a little serious. But she just looked up at me and smiled.

"I was a major ass tomboy in middle school. Never wore pink, never wore makeup. I wore t-shirts and jeans every day."

"Really? Me too."

She beat me at foosball. I expected it, of course. She actually has one she plays often. She's cool because she didn't brag about it. Kade went on about how Aldin probably has a new girlfriend. It kind of pained me that I didn't know this. I haven't spent time with the kid at all this week. At the dinner table, I was a little nervous. I was quiet, but Siri's parents made a good effort in keeping me engaged.

"So, we hear you are interested in auditioning for the Blue Devils this year?" Her dad asked me. He had friendly eyes, and when he addressed me, it seemed he was legitimately interested in hearing me talk. It took me by surprise how he brought up DCI.

"Yeah, that's right. How do you know DCI?"

"My older brother played for the Madison Scouts for four years."

"Sweet, what did he play?"

"He actually played the Sousaphone. But uh, Blue Devils, they're up there among the best. Good for you."

"Thanks," I replied, feeling pretty cool. Siri shot me a smile. I smiled back.

"Your brother has been over a couple times, he's a nice kid," Siri's mom said. I nodded.

"Yep, everyone likes Aldin."

The rest of dinner it went fine. I didn't say anything awkward or stupid, and I think they like me. Siri took me up to her room to watch Netflix on her laptop. As typical as can be, her dad made us leave the door open. Somehow, Siri and I got talking. She told me about her sister and her cousins, her biggest fears, what her favorite things in the world are…and by each moment, it seemed that we were getting further and further away from actually watching a movie. She unfolded her big, fluffy quilt. Automatically, she threw it on my face. Now my hair was all crazy. She giggled, so I took the quilt and threw it over her and wrapped her up. Her laughter was muffled, and I began kissing her face through the blanket. I could hear her shouting "I can breathe, maniac!" So I said "Too bad!" and picked her up and hugged her tight. Then she was lightly punching me so I'd let her go.

"What are you doing to her?" Kade interrupted from the doorway, looking confused. Siri shouted from under the blanket, "What does it look like? He's raping me!"

"Hey, Jesus!" I shouted back, tossing her back. She bounced and unrevealed her grinning face.

"I'm just kidding," she said, giggling. Kade gave her a dumb look and walked away.

"You…are ridiculous," I said. She was breathing hard.

"Proud of it. But your messed up hair is a little more ridiculous," she said, shoving me. I shoved her back, but she just leaped on top of me and began kissing my lips like crazy."

It was awesome.

"I like it when you're ridiculous," I said. She smiled and rested herself on me. It was a pretty cool time. When I left, it pained me. I wanted to stay in her presence forever. It was fantastic to feel that way. It gave me something more to look forward to. Her.

I worked long shifts the rest of the weekend. Josh still ignored me. I returned the gesture once again. I didn't need that. I picked up my sticks a lot as well, perfecting the audition material. It helped me get the frustrations about Cameron's party and Josh off my mind. That whole event is still bugging me. Kyle hasn't really spoken to me much lately. It's been kind of odd. I feel like he's not trying to make it noticeable, but it definitely is. He's been distancing himself. I can't blame him. I'm a crappy friend, and he's got many others.

"Hey, weirdo," John greeted at my bedroom door. He only came home for Sunday evening.

"Hi," I said, finishing a reply to Siri's text.

"Is that her?" He asked, walking to me on my bed.

"Yep."

"You should invite her over here. Seriously," he suggested.

"I really don't want to. I like it at her place better."

"What's that supposed to mean?" He asked, crossing his arms.

I looked up at him, not knowing that I had said something wrong.

"I don't know, just do."

"Well get over it, Mom would be thrilled."

I sighed. John doesn't get it. He may love being here with this family, but I'm different.

"Come downstairs, quit being a loner, and come hang out with me and Reya."

I rubbed my eyes, not feeling very social. He waited for me to

162

reply or get up or something. So I got up to make him happy.

"That's the spirit," he said, putting his arm around my shoulder. When we went downstairs, Reya was on her phone checking Instagram. She perked up.

"Hey Roy, how are you?"

"I'm fine, thanks" I replied.

"Good," she responded, turning her attention to John, "Becky tagged us in this photo from the party. She turned the phone around for him to see, but it was in my plain sight as well. John stiffened up, I could tell. He let out a tense, brief sigh, and then I saw what he was worried about. There in the picture, arms around each other looking all happy with their grinning faces were he and Reya, and Kyle and McKenzie. That really agitated me, the sting setting in pretty quick. I looked at John's face, showing him how angry that made me.

"Roy, it's not a big deal--"

"When was this party, John?"

He sighed and looked at the ground.

"Last night."

He had the nerve to invite my best friend and not me. He's never taken me to one of those college parties. Reya looked confused, looking back and forth at John and me.

"So what? You and Kyle are all buddy-buddy now?" I said. I knew I was being irrational, but I couldn't stop. My fears were being validated right in front of my face. John and Kyle are good looking, popular, and fortunate. They deserve each other. Apparently, I don't. I mean, what am I? He prefers John over me. It's so typical.

"I guess so, yeah. Besides, you were working."

"Whatever. I guess you know my work schedule, huh? Because I'm sure that if you knew that I worked last night, then that would have been the reason why you didn't invite me long before."

"C'mon, Roy. You're overreacting. Kyle's cool, and I thought it would—,"

"Right, cooler than me. I know that," he threw his hands up and rolled his eyes as a reaction.

"But you would invite your brother's best friend to a party behind your brother's back? How do you think that's supposed to make me feel, John? Especially since he's been not even talking to me."

"I'm sorry, Roy, okay?" he said harshly. He was frustrated by my reaction.

I ran upstairs to have alone time with my pocketknife, hearing John say behind me, "There he goes again."

I heard Reya say, "I don't get it, why is he so mad?"

"Because he's Roy. Nobody gets him."

I didn't tell any of my friends about my first therapy session on Monday. The only people who know are the people in my house, and it better stay that way. I hate to say it, but if I can keep it a secret from Siri as well, I'll feel better. I just don't want to be even weirder than I already am to everyone.

Dad went with me to my first session. I wanted to tell him that I can handle it myself, but I chose not to when he was actually acting calm and cool about it. He really wanted me to go through with this whole therapy thing, so he tried to make it as easy as possible for me, acting like it wasn't a big deal and it may not be so bad. Behind all that though, I knew he just wanted to make sure I wasn't skipping out like I wanted to.

She was the same therapist I had in eighth grade. There had never been a real diagnoses except for depression, and they forced me to shove pills down my throat. I had talked about the bullying problems and the unofficial middle child syndrome or something of that nature. At least I got the drums out of it. She figured before that drumming would become my new stress reliever. I was thankful for that idea. She's an attractive women; slim, shiny, full brown hair, flawless skin, and a soft voice. I at least like being around her, which is a plus.

She started off, "Roy, I want to know how your drumming has been going. It's been a while since we've seen each other. I thought that may be a good place to start."

I told her about my high school drumline and DCI, but eventually transitioned into what she really wanted to hear; the emotional part. The whys. I'm not exactly sure what I really got out of that first therapy session. It was only about my anger and destruction issues, and that won't change overnight. She's not going to stop me from cutting myself. I don't want anyone to be all worried about me and my problems. My dad was trying to get out of me what we had talked about it in the session. But the thing is, I'm eighteen. He doesn't have to know anything anymore. Lydia (the therapist) can't enclose any information. So I made it clear to Dad that I didn't want to talk about it.

"Well, at least you were able to talk to someone," he said.

"Yeah."

Dad attempted to make conversation on the drive home. I didn't know what to say to him when it went beyond the small talk. He hardly knows who I am. Can I say that that makes me a little sad? Sure. A father is supposed to know his son, as so the normal assumes. But then again, maybe I really am not his. The stork dropped me off at the wrong doorstep. The misfit standing in the middle of the professional portrait usually gets the extra-long stares, the double takes. Who's this kid? He's got long dark hair and wears too much black. His lighter haired, blue eyed, athletic brothers resemble him hardly. You wouldn't know he's Richard's if it wasn't for those eyes.

At least, that's what it seems like.

Siri

At rehearsal Monday night, Roy seemed a little quiet. Krys, Fiona and I tried to involve him in conversation. The awkward atmosphere that appeared between Roy and Kyle was noticeable. Kyle avoided Roy when possible. It bugged me. I mean yeah, Roy was kind of a douche that one night, but we've all forgotten about it and forgave him. By everyone, I mean all but Kyle it seems. I don't know what happened, but I was curious to know.

I felt warm hands on my shoulder as I reached in my locker for my mallets. I grinned, and he pulled me around to look into his neutral, brown eyes. I wish I could tell what he's really feeling.

"Roy?" I asked, curious about what he was doing. His hands were hooked on my upper arms, the hair on his forehead barely exposing his eyes.

"I just wanted to do this," and he planted a quick kiss onto my lips. It surprised me, but it was a pleasant surprise.

"Oooooh!" Preston teased pathetically from across the section.

"Cool," I smiled, taking hold of his hand once he let go of my arms. He's usually not this affectionate.

Later, after rehearsal ended, Roy left before me. I walked him to his car, which he appreciated.

"Text you later," he had said, giving my cold hand a squeeze before hopping in his truck. I watched his tail lights disappear around the corner of the street.

I searched for Kyle. He was talking with Preston outside the drum room.

"Here comes lover-girl," Preston whispered loudly. I shot him a look, but I knew my face was burning red. Kyle reached into his pocket to check his phone, but he knew I was coming to him.

"Kyle, I want to ask you something, is that okay?"

He looked up, nodding.

"Yeah, sure."

I gave Preston a look to go away, so he did. Kyle crossed his arms, a sign that he was closing himself off.

"Can you tell me what's up with you and Roy? It's weird, and I can't help but to want to know."

"He hasn't told you anything?" He responded. I shook my head, confused. Maybe it really was a big deal, especially if Roy hasn't said anything to me.

166

"Why don't you ask him?"

"C'mon."

Does he really think that's a good idea?

"Fine. Let's go outside, okay?" He said, leading me behind him. We went out to the lonely, chilly air. I didn't realize it was going to be a confidential, intimate conversation. He looked in every direction suspiciously before speaking.

"Look, I don't want to freak you out or anything, okay? But he's just a really unstable person. I don't know what's up with him, especially lately. He's mentally off."

"I get that. But what makes you so concerned?"

He stared at me in the eyes in silence, a contemplating look that began to worry me. He was seriously concerned about telling me.

"Okay, here's the thing. This isn't something that should ever go around, but I know you are trustworthy. You can't tell anyone, you swear?"

"Yeah of course. What is it?" I asked urgently. He took a deep breath and looked at his feet before he brought his eyes back up to mine.

"He's suicidal, and he's a cutter."

"What?"

"Siri, the only reason I'm actually telling you this is because I know you and him are getting close. Since you wanted to hear it, I think you have the right to know what you have in store."

I took a deep swallow. I didn't want to believe it.

"Are you sure?"

He sighed sadly, "When I drove him home that one night last week, he was drunk out of his mind. He was embarrassing himself at Cameron's party. Then, he was talking about wishing he was dead. That's when he threw off his jacket and was going to jump off of a bridge into shallow, rocky water. I saw all of the cuts on his arms."

I didn't know what to say. When I buried my face in my sleeve with stinging, hot tears, he put his arm around me.

167

"C'mon, let's go sit in my car."

It was nice of him, and I nodded. He led me to the passenger seat, and even opened the door for me. He shut his door, and then came the mere silence with my sniffles.

"I know it's hard for you to hear, I just want you to know that it's the truth."

I nodded and choked out, "I believe you, but it's just really hard." I was struggling to speak.

"He's been my friend for a while now. But I don't think I really know him that well anymore. I don't understand his behavior."

"You mean how…how he is all anti-social and impulsive and moody?"

"Exactly. You notice it too?"

I nodded.

"He scared the crap out of me, Siri. I am just trying to disconnect myself from it, because it's just draining. Not only that, but he's not really a good friend. He didn't even show gratitude."

That made me incredibly sad.

"This is something you have to tell somebody, Kyle. You have to tell his parents that he's suicidal! They have to know, because he needs help!" I said, worried about Roy.

"I told John. I know he told his parents. His parents are making him do therapy. He went today, his first time since middle school apparently."

"What? Are you serious? But why wouldn't he tell—,"

"Roy doesn't even know that I know. I didn't know he went in middle school, either. John told me. He keeps to himself about a lot of things, so don't take it personally."

"Oh, that makes sense. He doesn't even want me to have dinner at his house."

"Yeah, he tries to avoid his family as well."

All I could do was sit there and wonder why. I could tell Kyle felt really bad for me. This was all overwhelming.

"Siri, you're a sweet girl. It'll suck to see him hurt you."

I felt gracious that Kyle cared.

"It's too late to turn away, Kyle. I...."

I stopped myself, wondering if I should say it. But I did.

"I'm really falling for him."

He looked down, fiddling with his thumbs. Then he spoke through the tense silence.

"Just be careful, okay?"

I looked at Kyle in the eyes, nodding.

"You know, he warned me to stay away. He's so afraid he's going to hurt me. He feels like he's not fit for a relationship. He just thinks so low of himself it makes me sad. But...why?"

"There could be dozens of reasons. He's a complicated person. Don't know much about his past. I really don't know, unless he went through some trauma long ago that he hasn't told anyone about. I mean, who knows."

"Trauma?"

"Well possibly. He's a secretive person and he acts like he has some crap hidden underneath. It's possible. My mom is a social worker. She has been through so many abuse cases and stuff with kids, and a lot of them just don't say anything about what happened to them because they are afraid for different reasons."

"But, his dad doesn't seem to be abusive."

"Unlikely, but possible. If something like that did happen, it could have been anybody at any time. He's shown similar behaviors to the abused kids my mom has dealt with, so it's been at the back of my mind as a possibility for a while, I've just never, ever addressed it. I mean, personally, if I was molested or something, I wouldn't want anyone to know. It would be threatening to my man card, you know what I mean? It's complicated."

"Molested? You jumped right to that?"

"Sounds extreme, I know. You never know. I'm just saying it is a possibility. It could be bullies or something that caused trauma even, you know? Or he could just be depressed."

"You would think if he was abused by someone in the family,

his brothers would be off too."

"Yeah, so it seems unlikely."

There was a silence for a bit.

"Siri?"

I snapped my head up.

"You okay? You with me?"

I hadn't realized I checked out, lost in my thoughts. What he had just brought up triggered my own memories.

"Yeah, yeah I'm fine. It's just…intriguing what you just said. It….I have a lot on my mind, it's just a lot to process. I'm afraid for him, you know? What if the help he is getting isn't fast enough?"

"I don't know, I'm afraid too."

I reached myself out for a hug, and he accepted. It was a mutual feeling of worry.

"I better go, thank you Kyle," I said, wiping a tear. Before I shut the door, he got my attention.

"Hey," he said.

"Yeah?"

"I'm sorry."

I nodded.

"Yeah."

Could it really be?

Roy

The next few days of school were nothing exciting, except for being around Siri of course. She's my safe haven. Grebb hasn't been on my back lately, mainly because I've been sitting in the back of class, quiet, not trying to disturb anybody. I'm completely failing that class anyway. Same with calc. I might as well drop them both, make Dad pissed. The drama about John and Kyle leaving me out and ignoring me has also been really getting to me. It sucks. I don't trust either of them, but then again, it seems I hardly ever have. Kyle has always been a best friend to me, but I've always known I'm not necessarily his best friend. He could have given up any time, and he did. Same with Dad. Could never trust him. He's never understood me.

"C'mon, leave me alone!" Shouted a shrill, recognizable freshman voice.

"Shut up, chubby," Derek said.

I caught Dion's eye looking directly at me. He and Derek were giving me a show. Now I had two choices. One, I swore to Derek that if he ever bothered Michael again, I would kill him. I could help Michael and give the D dicks what they want, an opportunity to have me in their grip again if I don't pound their faces in. They wanted to show me. Two, I could walk away and ensure I wouldn't get into any trouble with anybody. Derek pulled Michael by the back pack into the bathroom away from the crowd. Nobody had really gathered to watch yet. I had to help, the fire was burning like crazy in me. They just couldn't get away with it. I threw my back pack on the ground aggressively and stormed into the bathroom.

"Roy!" Michael shouted with relief. He was struggling to get out of Derek's grasp.

"Oh look, the big hero!" Derek sneered, shoving Michael on the ground. I knew I had to be smart and not hit first, but that was going to be hard. I hated them so much.

"What the hell are you doing, huh? What's the point of this?" I said firmly, trying not to yell.

"What are you, a counselor? Shut up," Dion snapped, "You know the drill." I wanted to snap his neck.

"I heard you got clobbered a few weeks ago. How is that face?" Derek said.

Kill.

"Just let him go."

"Uh, no. We need to have our fun first. This marshmallow is ours." He picked up Michael and dragged him into a stall. Dion gave me a "what are you going to do about it?" look.

"Stop, now!" I shouted. Michael was begging him to stop. All of the memories, the pain they had caused me, the trust I had lost in the safety of school; it flooded my mind. Michael was their momentary victim to get to me. No matter how much it would cost me, I couldn't let them do it. I took a few quick steps towards Dion and landed one big punch into his nose. I was too quick for him. He shouted in pain and went to the ground, holding his face. I barged into the stall where Derek was trying to shove Michael into the toilet. He was ripping off his clothes, which freaked me out. That really did it. I grabbed him by the throat, and with great strength, pulled him backwards. He lost his balance and fell on his back and I went down with him. I was able to roll over on top to straddle him and began punching him in the face over and over again. I continued to beat him, blood going everywhere.

"How does this feel, huh? You like it? At least I'm man enough to show my face while I do it! I'm not some little, easy dork to beat anymore, huh?! I can pound your face in now!"

Dion was trying to pull me off by my throat, but I didn't stop.

"Hey! Stop this, now!" Some teacher cried. Dudes were pouring in now, and at least couple more arms were trying to pull me off. They finally succeeded. My fist was bloody and sore, and the adrenaline still wasn't completely depleted from my veins. I was bigger and stronger than I used to be. I have the power to beat him. That felt great. At the same time, it felt terribly sickening to see what I had caused for myself.

"Sanders, you're through. Get to the office right now!" Grebb nearly shouted. Great, it just had to be him. The crowd of guys began to leave. The entertainment was over.

"Roy, I'm sorry. I didn't want to get you in trouble for me!" I heard Michael tell me. Oh well. It wasn't his fault. Grebb was trying to escort me out, and I took a look behind me at Derek. He was still on the ground. I found it hilarious that nobody really cared.

172

Everybody knows he is junk.

I sat and waited in the office. The look Grebb has given me before he left made me feel like worthless scum. That's what Dad will think when he finds out. It made me feel sick to my stomach again to think about facing my family. I know that this school might get rid of me. Mom will cry, Dad will yell at me, John will shake his head, and my little brother will have a terrible influence. What am I going to do?

They called me in, and Derek and Dion walked out. It hated seeing their disgusting, threatening looks, but felt accomplished for seeing the blood on their shirts. Kaye looked at me coldly when I walked in.

Siri

I went in the band room after school to practice some scales. Preston and Krysten were in the loveseat corner, doing whatever. Preston had his sticks and a pad, and Krysten was trying to get his affection.

"Guys! Hey!" Kyle barged in from the entrance. It wasn't a greeting of excitement, but seemed as if something was terribly wrong.

"What!" Krysten jumped up. Preston continued playing on his pad and stared at Kyle.

"I just heard that Roy got in huge trouble, got in a fight."

"Oh God, are you serious?" Krysten sighed, rolling her eyes. Kyle looked at me.

"I heard someone talking about it who saw most of it, said Roy was brutally punching Derek Fawman to the ground."

I couldn't help but gasp. I didn't want to believe it.

"Cools," Preston said nonchalantly, still drumming.

"What the hell, Preston? This is a big deal. It means we're

173

probably going to lose him in the drumline," Krysten said.

"He could be expelled," I said. I didn't want to start crying again. Preston looked slightly offended that we had ridiculed him. He's one of those guys who has the emotional level of a crocodile and doesn't always follow things.

"Okay, sorry. That sucks, poor us and poor Roy, I just hate Derek. I think it's awesome," he corrected, looking at Krysten for her approval.

"It's just really stupid. Sure, I get how he would want to kill Derek and Dion. They deserve it. But he lets it out at school where he can get into trouble, and can't control himself. Now it's affecting all of us," Kyle said. He was venting. I could see in his face that he was really disappointed. As much as I hate that those guys tortured Roy back in the day, this situation sucks too much to feel happy about his fight victory.

Roy

It was a ripping, unimaginably horrible feeling when they told me that I was going to have a hearing about whether or not I should be expelled. My parents were already notified. I know I shouldn't have punched Derek as much as I did on school grounds. It just felt like what I had to do during that adrenaline pumping situation. I had had it. I mean, come on. After all that they've done to me? All of those times they had gotten away with punching me in the bathroom? It's weird how this world works.

The worst was coming to my mind as I walked to my truck before the end of school. Why has my life been such a struggle? Why do I have to make decisions that cause trouble? Why is it that I can't seem to ever be completely happy? I felt so alone. Going home seemed like the worst option. What I wanted was Siri. I've become attached to her, but I don't want to be at the same time. I know she wants me to count on her, however, I don't want to spill all of my troubles on such a beautiful person who doesn't deserve to feel my pain.

I wasn't sure about calling John when I first thought about it. I could stay with him in his apartment to avoid Mom and Dad. It was a bit of a drive from there to school. At the same time, I'm not sure he'd really want me to. He'll probably tell me to go home and face them instead of prolonging it. I know John would be disappointed with me. John is only understanding to a certain extent.

I had no idea what to do. It seemed like hours that I was sitting in my truck, just thinking. What about drumline? What about Elliot? It'll all be over if they kick me out. No senior year winter show. No marching band championship. Kyle is probably mad at me if he's already heard. The word is going around that I'm most likely a goner, I'm sure. We'll see. Even though I hate school, I'd hate alt. ed. even more. I finally drove off to the river and sat on Brittany. I pulled out the pipe Cameron had sold to me, filled the bowl, and began sucking in hits one after the other. I got a little high, but wished I had something stronger, something more destructive.

Staring out at the rippling water, I thought about all the organisms settled in there, just living out their lives with no responsibility, no fear, no ridiculing. No right, no wrong, no guilt, no anger. How nice that must be. I'm sure that bug floating on the water never had to deal with such awful human emotion. Lucky little bastard.

I sat for a long time. My pocket rung, so I pulled my phone out to look at the caller I.D. It was Mom. I ignored it. Thinking about the money in my account, I figured that I could leave and disappear. That would mean that my DCI funds would be lost, but at least I would be able to escape all this wrath. Besides, maybe I've been silly all of this time thinking I'd actually be able to do DCI. Would they really want a weird guy like me? I'm pretty hopeless.

Mom tried calling me again. It made me feel guilty, but I ignored her. My stomach was growling, which reminded me that I had eaten almost nothing all day again. Oh well. I was beginning to

175

have thoughts again, suicidal thoughts that is. It could be so easy. In fact, I was wondering why I hadn't driven me and my truck into a semi already. What I need is something quicker and easier, something a little more for sure.

My phone began ringing once again.

"Leave me alone," I growled out loud. I was surprised to see that it was John. I bet Mom called him to call me. Fine.

"Yeah?" I answered.

"Geez, man. C'mon, just call Mom. She really, really needs to talk to you."

"I bet she does. I'm just not ready to."

"Well we are worried, okay? We're afraid you're going to hurt yourself or something. Please, please, please Roy, c—,"

"I just can't. She's going to start crying and everything."

"Look, she's pissed, but is more worried about you being okay right now than being angry about your school problems. There is a lot going on right now."

"Why don't you just tell her you talked to me and that I'm okay?"

"How do I know you're okay? How do I know you're not cutting yourself right now, or trying to think about killing yourself? Huh?"

He was right. I didn't make a comment, because there was nothing I could say.

"Grandpa Joe is in the hospital. He had a stroke. It happened today, and Grandma Helen found him on the bedroom floor."

"What!?" Are you kidding me? My mom's father is on his death bed? At a time like this? God. It made me feel worse.

"Yeah, I'm not kidding. So it's bad enough that all of this shit happened today, and she needs to know that you are okay because she's freaking out about it all. She's really stressed out, so please, go home, okay?"

"I can't believe it."

"I know, we need to go see him tonight. It could be his last night. You can't just disappear."

"Fine, seeya later."

He paused for a moment, "Okay then, bye. Go home!"

John and I haven't been very warm to each other lately. I know it's my fault. I looked up at the sky, the white clouds getting darker and greyer by the minute. The time must have flown by right before my eyes, because it must have been six or seven already if it was getting dark. John was right. As much as I loathe the thought of facing everyone one with my shame, I couldn't kill myself at a time like this. While I was driving home, that sickening feeling of dread setting into my entire body. I blasted my killer metal. I saw that Dad's car was in the driveway. Siri had called me while I was driving. She probably heard. I just couldn't talk to her at that moment, pulling into the driveway behind Dad's car. I felt like throwing up.

Walking to the door seemed like the most tormenting moment I've experienced in a long time, even worse than when I got beat up. At least then, it was pity. This is shame. When I opened the door, Mom, Dad, and Aldin were sitting at the kitchen table, most likely discussing the stroke. It looked like they were waiting…for you know who. When Dad lashed his head towards my direction, I could see he was going to be pissed. His face was already red.

Mom stood up out of her chair with a tears stained face, "Roy!" I was frozen.

"YOU!" Dad hollered, his chair flying from under him and tumbling on the ground. Jesus. I was stunned and frightened at the same time and couldn't even react. His temper was already blown, and there was nothing I could say or do. Here it was.

"HOW COULD YOU! ARE YOU ABSOLUTELY OUT OF YOUR SENSES?" He was now screaming, pretty much in my face. I began to back away. I had to try and defend myself.

"Dad, I had to!"

"NO YOU DIDN'T!"

I quickly glanced at Mom and Aldin. Mom was whimpering, Aldin was wide eyed and shocked.

177

"Jesus! You got this far into high school, and you act like an animal and throw it all away! I don't care what it is you did! You are absolutely out of control."

I felt so angry, so repressed. I wanted to scream. It really hurt and sucked.

"Richard calm down!" Mom tried.

"NO! I will not! Dammit, we were too late with the help! I didn't raise this! You're not my son!"

"I HATE YOU!"

His hands came so fast. It wasn't just a hard, stinging slap. It was an actual punch. It caused me to fall backwards against the counter, which also hurt. I bent over holding the eye that he had hit.

"Richard!" Mom shrieked. Dad had backed away, the hot-headed son-of-a-bitch. He says I have anger issues? What about him?!

"Jesus," he said under his breath, "Roy, I really didn't mean that—,"

"Yes you did, don't lie to me," I snapped, looking straight at him back in the eyes with my own anger. He frowned at me at the same moment that John walked in the door. John stopped and paused, feeling the heavy tension. Everyone was silent at that awkward moment. I saw John staring at my face in the spot Dad had punched. He didn't say anything.

"Roy, I am unimaginably disappointed in you. God, I just…I don't know. I mean, what the hell? What do we do with you?" Dad grumbled, his hostile tone heavy.

"God, Dad, you don't even know my story! Geez, and I'm not expelled yet! It's not determined!" I yelled, stinging so strongly inside I felt I would break. I had to stay and look strong in order to hold myself together. I couldn't just buckle. I swear that I swallowed so loudly that everyone could hear it.

"Well, if that school expels you, you're on your own to find a way of getting a diploma. I'm not going to help you! You did this! Good luck with your pitiful life," He fired again. Ouch.

"I can just get out of your life and move out. Who says I need you anyway?" I said back. He crossed his arms and gave me a "really" look.

"No, you're staying! At least until you can get a diploma and graduate! Which you will!" Mom battled through her tears, "I don't want you to struggle!"

Dad began to shake his head. He left the room and ran right upstairs. I made eye contact with Mom.

"I just can't believe this," Mom said, shaking her head. It felt so awkward seeing Aldin and John both staring at me. Shock was in the air still that Dad punched me in the face. They had seen him hit me numerous times before, but not in a situation this tense. Suddenly there was a racket coming from the stairway. What now?

"Richard? What's going on?"

Then I saw it. My beautiful, expensive, black tenors being carried to the bottom of the steps in his unforgiving arms.

"WHAT ARE YOU DOING!?" I shouted. I blew up.

"NOW DON'T YOU GET HOT-HEADED! YOU AREN'T SEEING THESE FOR A MONTH!"

"YOU CAN'T DO THAT!"

I was so angry, so red, so consumed with loathe. I hate him, I hate him, I hate him!

"Richard, that's too far! Those are very important to him! There are other ways to handle this. Take his phone privileges away or something, but not this," My mom tried to defend.

"No. Maybe he'll learn to get his priorities straight. Something extreme will teach him. Until I see him fighting to improve his grades and getting a diploma, he's not seeing these!"

"I NEED THEM!" I screamed. Dad shot me a fuming look.

"Dad, please, don't do that to him," John tried.

"Now you be quiet!" he pointed at John, "I'm the authority, I make the decisions." Mom put a hand on John's shoulder.

"Why don't you just kill me, huh?!" I said to Dad, my fists clenched.

"Oh don't even start that crap. You're going to act like a man and deal with it. We're leaving in a few minutes here, so you get yourself together and quit being dramatic, God dammit!"

I had so much to say. I could have kept the argument going for another hour. I wanted to leave and runaway. The consequences would have been too much to live with though. There are people here who would worry about me too much. I don't want to be that selfish right now. Besides, what kind of person would I be if I didn't visit my grandfather on his death bed? All I could do was take in the pain and anger and save it for later. I'm good at that. I've been saving pain almost my whole life.

Everyone was silent now, and I just stared at the ground, watching Dad take my drums into the garage. All I could think about at that moment was hurting him.

"Okay, let's just put this all behind us for the night and focus on Grandpa Joe, okay? I don't want any of this negativity lingering when we are around him. Is that understood?" Mom demanded, looking at both Dad and I when he closed the garage door.

"I agree, now we need to go," Dad said, grabbing his coat from the couch arm rest.

He passed away just like that. He was determined brain-dead when we had been in the waiting room for a while. Grandma Helen and Mom were holding onto each other, crying. It was pretty awful. My grandfather was a pretty cool man, but he and I never got close. He and Grandma got annoyed with me when I was little. I was a pain in their butts when John, Aldin and I would stay with them for a weekend. I peed my bed every night. I would be defiant, and do whatever I could for attention. One time I went into Grandpa's closet and put on one of his really nice suits. I went out to show him, but I knocked a coffee mug off the table and spilled it all over the pants. He was upset, and I remember going into the pantry afterwards and scratching my skin until it bled because I was mad at myself and wasn't sure how to handle my emotions. I remember resenting Grandma for adoring Aldin so much instead of me. We would walk in the door at the beginning of our stay, and

Grandma would come running in saying "Where's Allie?" I turned into dirt.

Everything happening at this time was too overwhelming for me. Being ambushed and beat up, getting nearly expelled, punched by my dad, my drums getting unrightfully taken away, the whole thing about Josh and Kyle, and my family in distraught from that and the death of Grandpa. I wasn't sure how to handle it all besides just shutting myself off emotionally. I stayed in my room the next day. Siri had called me and asked if she could see me. I said it was nothing against her, I just felt like being alone. She seemed a little worried and sent me a text; "Im here if you need me." That was a good feeling for sure.

The next day was the same. I had absolutely nothing to do while being stuck at home. After school, Siri and I took a drive. I brought her to Brittany, my blood stained escape. We talked about little things and listened to the river. She wore a thick, red flannel shirt that was large enough to cover her legs when she brought her knees to her chest. She had red Toms on her feet to match. This was the first time in a while I've been down here with someone else. In the lighting of the bright clouds, her freckles were clearly defined.

"You're staring at me," she said with a little smirk. Her mouth had curved into a crooked smile.

"I didn't...I didn't realize I was."

"You okay?" She asked softly, cocking her head to the side. Siri doesn't know about everything completely. My stress levels are high, but that doesn't mean she should know. I stood up from Brittany after spotting a flat rock on the ground. Picking it up, I gazed at the water for the perfect spot to skip it. Before I knew it, Siri had begun searching the ground for rocks as well.

"I like contests," she said, bending over to pick one up.

"Oh yeah?" I grinned. I wound my hand back and tossed it at the water. It skipped twice.

"Dangit," I sighed, expecting at least three skips. I turned to her, waiting for her to throw. When she threw it, it didn't even fly

181

flat. It plunged into the water. I hacked out a laugh to make fun of her.

"Jerk," she puffed, shaking her head. I began searching the rocky ground again for the perfect candidate.

"Got a good one," I said out loud, bending over to grab it. Out of nowhere, Siri's shoe smacked my back end, sending me into the ground. It didn't hurt, of course.

"HEY!" I jokingly yelled, getting back on my feet. She giggled like crazy, pointing a finger at me while trying to control her laughter.

"You bent over."

I crossed my arms, letting her know she was in "trouble."

"Really?" I said.

"I'm not scared of you!" Siri grinned. We stood about five feet from each other, staring. For that time being, she had been my medicine. The distraction was refreshing. We eventually wound down and headed to my truck. There was something on my mind, and I had to thank her.

"Thanks, by the way, for not…asking about things. Being with you for a while took my mind off of it," I stared ahead at the road.

Seeing her head turn in my direction, I looked at her too. She rested her cheek against the head rest and smiled at me with her milk chocolate stare.

"I know."

I gave her a smile before returning my attention forward.

When I dropped her off at her house, her step dad happened to be in the driveway. He gave me eye contact, but didn't wave or make any expression of greeting. Dang. I delivered him a short wave before taking off. While driving, I thought about Grandpa's memorial service tomorrow. I'm going to be reunited with Mom's whole side of the family. I'll be seeing everybody bombarding me with greetings and questions.

Then… it hit me like a smack to my face. I couldn't even breathe when that realization came over me. Oh God.

He will be there.

Chapter Seven

Roy

I dreaded the service so much. I could feel myself beginning to shut off, emotionless and unsociable. I didn't eat. Mom noticed and asked if I was okay. I just shrugged my shoulders. She tried to hug me. When I refused her hug, I could see she was holding back tears. I just wanted to get everything over with. I knew I was getting anxiety or something, and it felt like it was attacking me. I didn't know how to control it.

"Roy, come on, why are you acting so weird?" John had said, trying to give me eye contact. I refused to look at him. I turned away from him without saying anything. He just sighed, shook his head, and walked away. Typical reaction. On the car ride there, I took out my phone and looked at a picture of Siri I had taken when we were playing foosball. She looked incredibly beautiful and pure, something I wish could have consumed me at the moment. Seeing her cute, smiling freckled face gave me some kind of hope, that with her nearby and there when I need her, it could help my anxiety, sooth my tenseness.

We arrived. The five of us walked to the entrance of the church where the service was being held. Some of my cousins were across the parking lot, waving at us. John and Aldin were waving back. It was a bit of relief being around family other than my immediate. I felt suffocated by them. At the same time, I felt a bit awkward by the way I was feeling to be addressed by relatives asking me "How are you?" What do I say? Hey, thanks, I might be expelled from my school. You see my black eye? Pretty obvious, huh. It was a gift from Dad! My grades dropped, and oh! I am also enrolled in therapy because I'm a messed up individual who cuts himself and has attempted suicide! Life has been fantastic!

I sat alone and in the back. Family members were looking back at me, giving me odd looks. Nobody said anything, though. Thankfully, I was left alone. I don't believe I was very welcoming after all.

Then, an arrow pierced my chest. It was a terrible feeling, one that felt like I was going to fall and break. I saw him. He looked older, more wrinkled, balder on the head, holding Aunt Marie's hand as they found their seat in the pews. I broke a sweat.

"Roy? Don't you want to get on the bus? School is over, I'm sure it'll get lonely here. Go on, the bus driver is waiting for you, sweetheart."

Dread. Reluctance. Fear.

"There's my special boy. C'mon Roy, I have a special request of you today. It's a fantastic surprise, you'll love it! We have to hurry, though. Your mom is picking you up earlier today."

Depletion of innocence.

"Roy, Honey, you wet your pants again? Kindergarteners don't pee their pants. What are these bruises from? Did you play too rough at school?"

Blindness.

"C'mon Roy, it'll feel good."

Disgust.

"We are gathered here to celebrate the life of Joseph Dalton McFray."

"Don't cry, Roy. C'mon, you're a big boy. Big boys don't cry. You're father doesn't like criers. I don't like criers. Crying isn't going to make me stop."

The woman next to me wiped a tear from her cheek.

"If you tell anybody about what we do together, they will not want to be around you anymore. Do you understand? Now c'mon!"

"But I don't want to, it hurts!"

"You do this favor for me, I'll do it for you."

"No!"

"Don't make me hit you! I will!"

Paralyzing fear. He had before.

"If you tell, I will hurt you! I will hurt you and your baby brother too! It'll be your fault! You want that? Huh?"

I couldn't stand the sight of him. The rows of pews and backs of head were all a blur, my body feeling frail and ready to crack. Being in the same room with him was giving me horrible anxieties. The pastor's words in the microphone were like hollow murmurs, and I heard nothing he was saying about my grandpa.

I walked out. I felt chilled, like I was going puke my worries out. Luckily, my exit wasn't noticeable. Sorry Grandpa, I know I should have been paying my respects. I went off to a Sunday school room off in the halls of the church. I closed the door to silence. Being alone with my thoughts almost made me feel worse, and I knew only one person who could soothe me at the moment. I needed a distraction before I could have slipped off into a longer, vivid flashback.

"Roy? Hey," she greeted. I could picture her face.

"Hey," I said, sighing with relief that she had answered. It was a Godsend.

"What's up? Is the memorial service over?"

"Uh yeah, it's over. I just felt like hearing your voice. It always makes me feel better."

"Awe, you're sweet. Did you wanna hang out? We could do something fun to get your mind off of everything."

"I would love to, but…umm…it'll have to be later."

She paused, "Okay."

We talked for a half an hour more until she had to go. I was incredibly thankful for that distraction. My mind was now on her as opposed to the other crap. I thought about how she had been so brave to ask me to homecoming. I must have been intimidating, considering I'm a tough hide to puncture. I hadn't expected to have such a great time that night. She has such a sweet, caring, spunky personality that just makes me excited to be around her. She'll never be boring. She's unique looking. She has this really cool

185

colored hair that is subjective to both red and blonde. It matches the freckles on her face, but also makes her light, sparkling brown eyes stand out. There is no other person I have ever met that is like her. It's impossible to see how I can ever let her go. I never felt that I could be capable of loving someone, let alone someone being capable of loving me. Whatever it is that we have together, I love it, and it's a miracle.

I sat in there for quite a long time, distracted by thoughts about Siri, or anything else in the world besides the man who had put me into a regression. I was missing the reception, all the family talk, the stories of my grandfather, visiting with my cousins. I should be out there, not sitting in this room like a lonely idiot. I was half-expecting John to call me and ask where the hell I was, but he's sick of me, I know it. He doesn't really care at the moment. That's when I got a text from my cousin Jessica, who is just a year older than me. Out of my cousins, she is the one I have been closest to all these years. She's the one who would force me to go on walks with her while we visited to make sure I was doing okay. I told her all about Derek and Dion. She cried when I told her about them beating me up in the bathroom at school. I got a bruise from Dion smashing my cheek bone into the toilet seat before plunging me into a putrid mess. That sucked. I told my mom that I ran into a wall.

Every once in a while, Jessica will send me random messages that are supposed to lift my day. It's definitely cool of her. She lives a few hours away, which is why I could never really went to her when I felt lonely and beaten back in middle school. That was before we had our own cell phones. Right now, though, I'm sure she's looking for me. I called her. Maybe hanging around her away from the pedophile could be better than shutting myself off.

"Roy! Where the heck are you? I was so excited to see you!"

"Hey Jess, I have been in the bathroom throwing up. I think I ate something that made me sick."

"Seriously? You mean you had to miss the service? I'm so sorry!"

"I'm okay, no worries. Can we meet outside? I need air."

"Sure, yeah. See you in a sec."

Thank God for people like Siri and Jessica in this world.

I slipped through the hallway, peeking around every corner just in case. Seeing him could regress me back into another realm I didn't want to be in again. I got to the exit, and she was already standing there waiting. The sun was peeking out of the clouds, and huge sense of relief cleansed through me.

"Hey, thanks," I greeted. When I took a good look at her face, it was obvious she had been crying through the service. She perked up when I arrived.

"Hey there, Roger. You okay?" Sometimes she calls me that, as in Roy Rogers.

"Yeah, totally fine."

She smiled and handed me a cup of liquid.

"Its pink lemonade, I thought maybe you might need it to get rid of puke taste."

I smiled. She's too cool.

"You're good," I said. I sipped some to go along with the act. I didn't realize how thirsty I was. At the same time, I could tell she was observing me. She looked good herself. She's a little over-weight, but is pretty in the face and presents herself well. A few things about Jessica: she's very forward, charming, and she lost her virginity when she was thirteen. I'm one of the few people who know that. I've always admired her confidence in herself. That's something I lack dearly.

"You growing out you hair? It looks good." She looked past my beaten face purposefully. I was thankful of that.

"Ha, thanks. People having been commenting that it's getting to long."

"Well, you don't want to hide those lady killer eyes."

"Don't make me gag."

"Awe come on. So, Aldin says you have a girlfriend?! Roy, that is so exciting. You have to show me a picture of her! I want to

187

know everything!"

I could tell my face was flushing red. Then was when I realized that I had somebody here to confide in about Siri. Jess crossed her arms and tapped her foot teasingly, waiting for me to spill the beans.

"Her name is Siri. She pursued me, actually. She's beautiful, funny, and more than I deserve."

"Awe, don't say that! I'm sure you deserve her. God, you need to learn how to be cockier about yourself."

Yeah, says the promiscuous one.

"You're the queen of cocky."

She gave me a look. Oddly, she peered inside for a moment as if she was going to do something sneaky. I couldn't imagine her being that type.

"What are you doing?" I asked. She connected her speckled green eyes back with mine.

"I want to hear more about Siri, but first, I wanna show you something."

She stuck her hand into her purse and dug for a moment. What she pulled out was tin foil.

"Jess, what the hell is that?" Without warning, she grabbed my arm to have me follow her. We scurried to a small shed that happened to be unlocked.

"Seriously. What are we doing?" She shut the door. I was pumped with excitement, but was nervous at the same time. I had a good guess about what would be in that foil.

"You can't tell anybody, okay? You're my favorite cousin, so I want to share it with you, show you how much better it can make you feel."

She unraveled the foil to this brownish powder. I gulped.

"It's smack, well, heroin technically. But I like calling it smack. It's the most fitting."

I was staring at with her with wide eyes. I would have never thought that out of everyone, Jessica would get into drugs. And here? At a church where our family is inside mourning over our grandfather? It seemed messed up.

"Why now?" I asked her, unsure what to do or say. The substance was screaming at me. It was an intriguing idea. I felt like getting messed up, taken out of this place. It was incredibly stupid and destructive, but that seemed like the best part of it.

"Why not?"

I stared at her in the eyes while she gave me a contemplating look. Something was off. She was hiding something. I almost asked her what this was all about, but she was already inhaling it. I was at a loss of words all of a sudden.

"I'm all about sharing," she grinned, "Don't be afraid, it'll be great."

"I'm not afraid," I reacted.

I took one look down at the powder I was supposed to snort into my brain. I wanted to. What I didn't want was my family being able to tell that I'm intoxicated.

When I began to hesitate, she spoke, "Look, I was unsure my first time, too—,"

"It's the timing. I'm already in a lot of trouble. Being high around my parents are the wrong people to be with, you know? They'll ruin it."

She looked slightly disappointed by the sinking of her head, but seemed to understand.

"Yeah, I know. The timing is bad. I'm sorry—,"

"No, I want to. Can I just save it for later?"

A crooked, devious smile appeared.

"Anything for you," she said, slipping the rest into my back pocket. Her fingers seemed to linger around that back area for an extra moment. Okay, I understand that we have a connection, but she really likes me. Why so much?

"Thanks," I said without much expression.

"So," she began, "Siri."

"Right."

Jess and I sat and talked for a while in that shed. It was a bit claustrophobic and odd, but I went with it. I released how Siri is the only girl I've ever met who is worth it.

"I just don't get why you didn't ever date more. You're a hot shot, talented drummer. And you're cute, even if you could use a touch up."

I'm really not.

"I know you probably don't understand. I'm not sure I do either."

"Well, there is a lot we don't understand about ourselves, I suppose. But, the important thing is, she sounds like a keeper."

Very much so.

"Yeah, I just hope I get to keep her."

"Show me a picture!" Jess said, beginning to make random dancing movements. Fair enough. I pulled out my phone.

"Awe, she's ginger!" She exclaimed.

"I suppose so."

My phone buzzed. I picked up.

"John?"

"Dude, don't know where the hell you are, but we're leaving now. Everyone is saying their goodbyes." He seemed pretty down. It made me feel just a little guilty.

"Okay," I replied, hanging up the phone. I turned to Jess, who was making shaky movements with her legs.

"Oh yeah, it's really kicking in, baby," she said, nodding her head. I ignored her.

"Sounds like the reception came to an end. Ready to get out of this shed?"

She stuck out her lower lip. I gave her a playful shove. When the both of us stood up, she spun me around abruptly. It took me by surprise a bit. She stuck out her finger and began poking me in the chest.

"You. Make Sure. That you try it. Call me when you do, okay?"

And then, yes, right there in that cold shed, my biological first cousin clutched my head…and planted a kiss on my lips. For the first second, I thought it would be nothing. You know, a friendly family peck on the lips. I wouldn't have minded, with her at least. But she kept locked on, wet, slow, and far too intimate. The moment I was going to push her off of me, she let go instead.

She read the shock on my face. I could feel my mouth gaping open. What the hell was that? My cousin just kissed me! With one pat on my chest, she walked out, the words slipping off of her tongue, "Love ya."

What?! I hadn't said anything to her. I was too stunned. The door closed behind her, and I was once again left alone, shuddering in disgust. I raked a hand through my hair, so confused. How could she do that? Was it just because she's not herself on the drug? I know she's a sexual person, but the Jessica I know would never go for the incest.

I walked to the car with my head down trying to get what just happened off of my mind. Mom was hugging her sister Renee, Jessica's mom, and they were both wiping tears. Mom's other sister, Marie, wasn't in sight. Therefore, I didn't have to worry about running into my uncle. John was leaning against the car with his arms crossed. When he saw, he looked a little angry. He even gave me a head shake.

"God, Roy, you missed the entire friggen thing. You really had something more important to do?" He said coldly. Man. That really made me churn inside. All I could give him was a shoulder shrug. Feeling uncomfortable, I shoved my hands in my pockets. I couldn't tell him anything. He rolled his eyes. Aldin appeared by my side in a moment.

"Why are you such a jerk?" He piped up in a breathtakingly serious tone. That stunned me.

"What?" I defended, looking at Aldin. He was genuinely upset as well. I had no idea they would be this upset with me.

"You heard him," John said, uncrossing his arms. I had no words. With the two of them glaring back at me with scorn, it was

191

almost too much to handle. When I didn't respond, John turned his shoulder to me, rolling his eyes again.

"Whatever. Just…whatever."

I lost my breath, feeling terribly guilty. What was I supposed to say? How was I supposed to handle this? They couldn't know about why I really skipped out. They just couldn't. Mom didn't even look at me while she walked to the car. She completely ignored me. So did Dad. In fact, the car ride home was so tense and so silent I was beginning to feel nauseous. I sat in the very back by myself, feeling isolated.

Siri texted me and said, "It'll make me super happy if you invite me over for dinner sometime soon!"

Okay, I can completely understand how she would want me to. But with the tension going on in my house right now, it may be awkward for her to see. When we were close enough to see our driveway, I saw a red SUV I didn't recognize parked beside my Bronco. I didn't want to ask Mom whose car that was because of the odd tension suffocating us all in the car. But she answered my question anyway.

"Looks like Mark and Marie beat us."

What?

"What are they doing here?" I blurted with a little too much hostility. Dad parked the car and shot me an odd look in the rear view mirror.

"They're staying the night with us, Roy. Geez," she responded, sounding annoyed.

"Why?" I said. John looked back and threw me a dumbass look.

"Can't you figure it out?" He said, rolling his eyes. I was seriously becoming pissed at John.

"They're flying back out to Denver tomorrow morning. I offered our couch bed so we can visit," she continued.

I didn't want to panic. I needed to stay strong, act like nothing was wrong. Uncle Mark was here, in my house, too close to the proximity of my personal space. I was going to suffocate.

I was gone. Away. My emotions were solid stone, non-penetrable. I skipped through his mass, standing there outside the red SUV. My eyes strayed away. He didn't exist, and I was a zombie. I knew my family would roll their eyes to my standoffish behavior. Typical me, running off to my room to be alone. They would never believe that that man molested me. He'd get over a dozen character witnesses in court, no doubt. Being accused of pederasty? Yeah right. He's too sleek, and would never "hurt a fly." It's sick. It makes me sick.

When I shut the door to my room, I heaved a big sigh. I wasn't sure how I was going to handle everything. At a time like this, I wish I could call up Kyle and ask to sleep at his house. I know Preston's mom wouldn't allow a school night sleepover. John and I are tense with each other. It's not like he'll gratefully let me stay with him when he leaves tonight. It's a mess. The stress was building up tightly in my chest. I was numb from the cold slab of steel I had become in my existence to this house. I needed to feel.

I pulled out my pocket knife. My arms were too obvious because I had done enough harm. I lifted up my shirt to expose my body. I definitely have lost a little weight. Geez, hadn't really noticed it before. I've been a terrible eater lately. Mostly skimpy butter on bread and handfuls of cereal or crackers. It's just enough to keep me going. I lost desire to eat any more. There, right against my ribs, was where I made a slice. It was going to leave a nice scab. I bandaged it with the stash I began to keep in my night stand.

It was a decent release. I could hear their voices downstairs, chatting away, having their "visit time." Hearing Uncle Mark's voice could send me backwards, and I wasn't up for that. I placed on my head phones and turned on my music loud. I felt myself relax, my limbs sinking into the mattress, facing the wall against my bed. I had a picture there above of our drumline group at finals last winter season. Sometimes I search their faces, think about how fortunate I am to have friends like that. I know that I have been cold to them lately, especially by how I snapped at Fiona. She was only trying to help me. I do appreciate her. One time early junior year, she was beginning to show signs of interest. At Krysten's house one night, she "accidently" fell asleep on my shoulder. Her leg was pressed up against mine, which surprised me. I wasn't sure how I felt about it. We began talking a lot, texting every day. After a while, Fiona began acting like I was a brother other than somebody she wanted to date. It was as if she had given up. I felt it was better that way.

I sent a text to Siri telling her that I'd meet her at her house to pick her up at seven and we could go eat somewhere. My parents would resist, but they can't control me. She texted back with a smiley, agreeing. It was almost six, which means I had a little time to relax my mind. I wanted to get rid of as much anxiety as possible before seeing her. Then I could go sneak out John's bedroom window to avoid seeing anyone in the house.

I lightly dozed.

John

It was cool to see my aunt and uncle. They used to live here right in town, but moved to Denver when Uncle Mark got a better paying job. We haven't seen them for years and years, mostly just phone contact. Mom was in the kitchen preparing dinner. Aunt Marie was helping her out, and us guys (excluding Roy of course) sat around in the living room. Mark is a pretty social guy and it's nice to have him here hanging out.

"Smells good in there!" Dad called to the kitchen. Pot roast.

"Gosh, those ladies sure know how to make good pot roast. I'm telling you, I'm spoiled by Marie's cooking," Mark said.

"Uncle Mark, do you watch football?" Aldin asked.

"You kidding, bud?" I'm a die-hard fan. Been to every Broncos home game . Wouldn't miss one."

"Really? Lucky!" Aldin said.

"Absolutely. You a Denver fan?" He asked him. Aldin nodded, "I'd root for them."

"High five, little man," Mark said. He said, making a loud slapping sound.

"Wow, that was a good one," Mark grinned.

We began our football talk. I turned on the TV to a sports channel. I laughed when Mom groaned from the kitchen. We became engrossed, and then Uncle Mark spoke up,

"Where the heck is that other kid? What's he doing? I hardly saw him at the service," He asked. He looked at Dad, who shrugged and gave a "don't bother" look.

"In his room," I said.

"He's on the brim of being expelled. He keeps getting in fights at school. Cathy and I have to go to a hearing Friday to determine whether or not he'll be kicked out," Dad said.

"That's not good. Dang. He was a good kid though. Didn't he ever play football or basketball? He's got the perfect build for it."

"Yeah, no. Not him," I said.

"Roy's a band geek," Aldin brought up.

There was a small moment of silence.

"Oh," Mark said, folding his hands in his lap. It got quiet. In the next moment, Mark stood up and began to stretch his arms.

"I wanna go talk to him, tell him to get the heck out here," he said. Dad nodded.

"You can try," he said.

"He hasn't been very friendly lately," I added.

Roy

I opened my eyes. My playlist had ended. I looked at the time on my iPod. It was nearing seven. Time to get Siri! I threw my head phones down and went to my closet to grab casual shoes. I still had my black button down shirt on. I decided to change into something else, so I threw it off and searched through my drawer.

Someone knocked at my door. I paused, standing in place. I did not want any visitors right now. Holding my breath, I said "Who is it?"

The door opened without permission, thick fingers curling around the side.

"It's me," he said. There was Uncle Mark's face, wrinkled lines, piercing grey eyes. I was being stabbed by a thousand knives at that moment. Here was the man who took away my innocence. The man who had used me sexually, caused me physical pain, tore me up emotionally, and straight out raped me. Having him stand there, closing the door behind him, brought back the very feeling I had endured during that one year of my life. My throat tightened up like a dried prune.

"What are you doing?" I managed to squeeze out. Naturally, my fists were clenching at my side as my muscles tensed in every point of my body. I don't think he cared how uncomfortable I looked. His once over of my shirtless body shot a creepy chill straight down my spine.

"Hello Roy, it's nice to see you."

I turned away from the gaze of his repulsive eyes. They reminded me of that familiar pain.

"I'm up here for a reason," I said in a low, warning voice. I faced the floor squeezing my eyes shut to the hope that he was going to disappear. It's as if he didn't even hear me.

"You're quite the grown boy. Or shall I say man? Look at you, it's too bad you didn't join sports. Either way, the girls must be all over you."

What? Why is he saying all this? Is he trying to relate? Compliment? Be a creep? I stood there, frozen in place, and I could hear his footsteps on the carpet head towards me.

I got off the bus and stared at the house knowing what I had coming. I approached the front door where he was waiting for me.

196

He greeted me with friendly smiles, picking me up in his arms and swung me around. I giggled, too distracted from the rush to notice where he was carrying me. He threw me on the bed so I'd bounce, which I liked. He did it every time. He told me he'd be right back and to stay. I laid in the bed, thinking about what we were going to do today. I began to feel uneasy, uncomfortable once again. I was hungry for lunch, but knew he wouldn't feed me until I did my duty. The longer I waited in there, the further into a deep, drowning dread I began to dive into. I wanted to get out and escape the nightmare, get home to the safety of my mother. When the thumping of his boots made it way to the bedroom, my heart began pounding. They got closer and closer. I didn't dare hide because I knew he would get mad, so I stayed there…like a good boy.

"I didn't say you could come in here," I said under my breath.

"Awe come on, don't be rude, bud. It's been a long time since we've seen each other."

"How's my special boy?"

"Just…leave me alone. Please." I turned away from him.

"What's your problem?" He said. C'mon. He dared to take another step towards me. At last, he put a hand on my shoulder. I shook it off.

"Where is this cold, resentment coming from, huh? I'm just a friendly guy wanting to make conversation."

"You're little, and I can easily hurt you if you don't do what I tell you. Don't even try to fight me."

"I'm a closed book."

"You can't push me away that easy. You may be big now, but that doesn't change anything." he said softly. I could feel his hot breath on my shoulder.

"It changes everything."

"It doesn't have to."

"No."

"No, what?" he said slowly, slipping his hand around my arm to my bare chest. I stared at the wall in front of me, focusing on my lamp shade. I didn't respond. My pulse was crazy, my face hot.

"C'mon, you know you'll always be my special boy."

That sparked it. I jumped back from him aggressively, almost knocking stuff off of my dresser, and gave him a threatening glare straight into his eyes.

"I am not, and will never be again, you understand me?! Now get out!" I growled, quiet enough to not be heard from down stairs. He held up his hands, slightly smiling as if he wasn't going to take me seriously.

"Whoa now, no need to get mad."

"Didn't I tell you to get out? Huh?" I fired at him. I raised my fist. That make him chuckle, which really pissed me off.

"You're not going to punch me, Roy. Don't be ridiculous. You and your fighting habits? It hasn't gotten you anywhere, has it?"

How can he think he can just come up into my room and touch me? He's disgusting.

"I will if you touch me again, I swear to God."

He tightened his lips and stared at me, thinking.

"I took care of you, remember? This is how you repay me? They've given up on you downstairs, trying to involve you in the family. I'm just trying to care. I don't want to give up on you," he attempted. Oh please.

"Using me as your sex toy wasn't taking care of me. Don't try to guilt trip me, I know what you're doing. You are being your manipulative, piece of shit self. If only people could know how sick you are," I said nastily.

His expression was priceless. Wide eyes, flushed face. He became flustered.

He grit his teeth, "Nobody will believe you. Look at you. You're a loser, probably into drugs and cutting, feeling sorry for your pathetic life," he pointed at my arms and my fresh cut, "Just think. If you try to bring out some story and accuse me, whose going to believe you? You'll just be getting yourself into deeper trouble, especially with your dad. He's going to throw you out and

198

accuse you of being gay."

I swallowed, my throat feeling roughly tight.

"Yeah, exactly," he said, reading my fear, "So don't even. You will lose. You won't see the last of me either. I'll hunt you down, do whatever I can to sabotage your life for even trying. I will. Don't you think I won't," he said with wild eyes.

I was so frozen in the moment, my blood turning to ice. There was no way out. He's always going to win.

"Just get out," I managed to say. I hate him. He gave me a look.

"I thought we had an understanding?" He said, reaching his hands down to his belt. He began to slip it off and I could hardly believe it. I couldn't breathe I was so revolted. I attempted to turn away, but he gripped my arm and yanked hard.

"Let go! You're sick," I yelled through my teeth, pulling hard to get out of his grasp.

"Don't make a big deal out of this!" He fired back, refusing to let go, "Just do it!" At that moment, I was out of control horrified. It was bringing back everything, all the trauma, all the disgust.

"Your hits are useless. You're too small to fight back, don't even try."

I'm big now. Bigger than him. I can beat him, bust up his face. I swung my free arm back, and before he could dodge it, I planted one sick, cracking punch right into his nose. His clammy hand let loose of my arms and he shouted in pain. Both of his hands went up to his face to cover his nose. Blood was rushing out, making rivers down and around his knuckles. I backed away, justified, but completely horrified. Blood was spilling onto my carpet, and he was now shouting at me.

"What did you do?! Marie!"

I was scared out of my wits for what was about to come. That was it. This was that point I've feared most. I hit him, and I can't take it back. Everyone will see what I've done. I felt like throwing up, and hearing the footsteps up the stairs was petrifying. Mark frantically pulled up his pants and refastened his belt.

199

"It's coming, look how scared you are you stupid kid. Your life is over."

The air in me stopped flowing. My bedroom door flew open, and guess who was there to see first? Yes, Dad. He looked absolutely blown out of his mind at the scene. Aunt Marie followed him and shrieked, covering her mouth with her hands.

"Oh my God, Mark, what happened? There's so much blood!" She cried. Mom, John, and Aldin appeared there too, each of them with horrified expressions. Some eyes were darting over to me in disbelief. There was nothing I could say, nothing I could even think of. Seeing Dad's completely and absolutely furious eyes meet mine was climax of my fear.

"WHAT DID YOU DO!" He screamed.

"Oh, it's broken!" Aunt Marie said, shooting me a deathly look. Dad kept eye contact with me, the veins in his neck popping out. He looked scary mad, like he could kill me right there.

"Roy, what did you do?! What happened?" Mom was shouting at me. The commotion was overwhelming.

"You have nothing to say?!" Dad yelled. I didn't move or say anything. I turned into a stone cold rock again.

"I was just trying to talk to him," the crazy man lied .

"Get out! Get out of this house, right now!" Dad hollered, pointing. I looked over at my usually compassionate mom, who gazed at me with complete disappointment. The feeling I gathered felt so bad at that moment that I knew. I knew I was going to end everything. I clenched my fists, and with nothing on my feet, said nothing, snatched up my black button up shirt, and pushed past everybody's angry eyes glaring right at my face.

I did as I was told and raced outside to my truck. I was done.

Chapter Nine

Siri

It was nearing seven thirty, and Roy hadn't been responding to my texts. Maybe I was being a little bit paranoid. I mean, things happen. I doubt it has anything to do with me, and he wouldn't be late on purpose. I decided that he if doesn't show in ten more minutes, I'd call.

My step dad was wary about me hanging out with Roy when he heard about the expulsion.

"He's not expelled yet, he has a chance to tell his story," I had said.

"Just be careful, Siri. You can't always help a person who is troubled. It can end up taking a toll on you."

I understand his point, yet it doesn't change things. I sat in my room, standing up every now and then to touch up my makeup and kill time. I spent quite a bit of time looking out my bed room window at the street, waiting for his truck to lift my spirit. Fifteen minutes had gone by, and I was becoming nervous. I dialed. It went to his voice mail, no surprise.

Disappointed again.

Aldin

I found Mom bawling her eyes out in the bathroom with Dad trying to coax her.

"I don't get it! Why? Why did he do that? Why is our son like that! What did we do?! What if he's going to hurt himself?" She continued to wail. I could hear Dad's voice trying to comfort her, letting her know they'll find a way to get Roy to a mental hospital or something. It was such an awkward atmosphere filling up the house. Talk was going around about how awful my brother is and that he must be mentally ill. It sucks to admit, but maybe he really is. He's so off and on. He'll be cool, funny, and playful. Then suddenly mad and depressed. Now he doesn't pay attention to me. John and I don't get his distance. Now he might be getting expelled from school, he hardly attended the funeral service, and he punched his uncle in the face? For what? Coming in his room and trying to make conversation? All because he wanted to be "left alone?"

I mean wow. Come on.

John already left. Without him here, I feel kind of alone. The adults are all being chaotic, and I'm just sitting in my room, wondering where the heck my brother is going to go tonight and if he'll come back.

This family is so close to being normal. Why does Roy have to rupture that chemistry? Why does Dad have to get so mad at him all the time? It's tiring.

I admit I'm scared. I don't want to suddenly never see him again.

Roy

I wasn't in the mood for music. I wasn't in the mood to see Siri. In fact, I shut off my phone. There was no way I was going to burden her with my problems. She doesn't need it. Uncle Mark is right about me. I'm a loser. My family doesn't need me, and I don't need them. I don't deserve my friends. I don't deserve Siri's concern. Sitting in my truck, the reality began sinking in. I could never face my family again. They must think I'm ill. I mean, I can't tell them why I really punched him. Enough said. I can't do it, and I never will.

It was dark out, hardly any cars in the sight. The road I parked along the side of is in the middle of the country. I had never felt so alone. The silence was slightly eerie, especially from hearing my own heartbeat. It won't be beating for much longer. That sounds terrible, even to me. But it's true. I don't want to be here anymore, especially when I hate myself so much. I'm down in the lowest, the deepest I've ever been. I've reached a dead end. Ahead in the distance, I saw bright headlights making its way towards me. I could tell it was a semi-truck, which was perfect. It would cause enough damage to probably kill me. Following my impulse, I started up my truck. It could be so easy. How fast is he going, like fifty or more? I could park in the road with the driver's side facing the oncoming. Instant death. At least, that would be ideal.

Then I began thinking again, my face getting hot to my increasing pulse. This would cause a major scene. That innocent person in the giant truck will have to live with killing a teenage kid for the rest of his life. I couldn't do that to him. I needed a cleaner, less destructive approach. Therefore, I turned off the engine. Carbon dioxide poisoning would be perfect, yet where? I don't have a hose or garage. What I need to do is go to the house. I could search around while everyone is gone tomorrow. There are so many ways to do it and I'm certain to find something. Yes, my family would later find me dead, which is pretty barbaric and tragic. At the same time, they would find out eventually. No need to prolong it. Besides, I'm so mad at my father that it provides a little twisted sense of pay back.

I leaned my seat back as far as it would go, and poured in a little heat in from the engine. I reached into my back pocket and pulled out the stuff Jessica had given me. I figured it would be a long night.

Siri

He never said anything. At all. I arrived at school the next day, feeling absolutely depressed. I didn't let it show first period. I was looking forward to talking to him during second. When the time came, I sat on the loveseat before class started. If I didn't hear from him, chances are nobody had. What the hell?

When I saw Kyle walking over to the section, we made eye contact. It surprised me when he didn't break it. He was heading towards me as if he could sense I was off from something Roy did.

"Siri? Is everything okay?" He asked me, leaning on the arm rest.

"Well, if you must know, Roy and I were supposed to hang out last night. He blew me off and obviously shut off his phone."

Kyle made a face, as if he was realizing something.

"Wait, do you know something?" I said, begging him to tell me. He lightly nodded, took a look around for listeners, and went back to me.

"John called me last night. He said…..he said Roy got into huge trouble yesterday and he was…..God. Okay, his dad told him to get out."

"What?" I blurted, my mind running like crazy.

"He asked me if I had heard from him or if he was staying with me, but I said no," Kyle continued.

"But…but what could he have done?"

Kyle shook his head.

"I don't exactly know. John wasn't specific. I just know that Roy is gone, and nobody knows where he is."

"Oh my God," I squeaked out, covering my mouth. What if he's out trying to kill himself or something!

"Yeah, I tried calling him. Got nothing. I mean, it sucks because there is nothing nobody can really do," he said, looking down at the floor.

"Kyle, I'm scared."

He looked at me in the eyes briefly and sighed.

"Me too. I feel horrible, like it's partially my fault for pushing him over. I shouldn't have blocked him out."

"No, don't blame yourself. You did what you had to do for yourself," I tried, putting a hand on his shoulder. He nodded.

"Thanks, but…I also should have listened to the signs instead of avoid them. You can't just bail on a friend when they cry for help."

"He doesn't want help, though."

"Yeah, well that's what he wants us to think."

I nodded and he stood up.

"Look, if you hear anything, let me know," he said solemnly, patting my arm before walking away.

I felt sick to my stomach about this whole situation. Roy is pushing everyone out, meaning it's possible the worst may happen. I want to stop him, find him. With any kind of assurance that he's okay, I'd feel better. I didn't want to let tears fall in front of everybody, so I tightened myself up. What was I going to do?

Roy

I opened my eyes to day light, my eyes heavy and groggy. It took me a second to adjust to where I was before I remembered what I had been through last night. Sleeping in my car made me feel like such a loser. Without thinking, I turned on my phone to check the time. It blew up. I wish that it did literally, but no. Nine missed calls? Fourteen new text messages? I couldn't stop my curiosity, so I checked out who had all called me. Mom tried four times, John tried twice, Aldin once, Siri once, and Kyle? Really? Wouldn't expect that. All of those people are supposed to be pissed at me. Texts in order of when received...

John, "why? just why?"

Just stop.

Mom, "Stay safe."

Aldin, "Come back home. Please don't disappear."

Gosh. That one gets to me.

Siri, "I thought you said 7?"

Picturing Siri's disappointed face makes me want to rip myself apart. I'm a horrible person.

John, "don't do anything reckless and stupid, k?"

Mom, "I want you back at the house tomorrow. We are going to talk."

No thank you.

Siri, "Is something going on?"

Josh, "You really embarrassed Kendal. I found out last night what you were missing."

The fuck? Shut up, Josh.

John, "fine, don't respond then."

Jessica, "I'm really sorry for today. I shouldn't have done that and I know it probably made you extremely uncomfortable. That wasn't like me. Some of my shit was brought up and I was a bit out of sorts."

Wow. I'm really glad that she said that. It was cool of her to apologize, because what she did really weirded me out.

Siri, "Okay, just talk to me when you can. I hope you are okay. <3"

Oh man. I feel so bad. She's too great.

At that moment, I was ready to burst up into tears. I probably should have, just to get it over with. But I didn't. I'm not going to let them stop me from ending my life. I've have already made my decision. I turned on my truck after seeing in was almost ten. The longer I wait, the more I risk my parents coming home early from work and catching me in the act. I was twenty minutes from home, yet it seemed like the longest drive I've ever been on. I'm a ticking time bomb. That's when my phone buzzed on the seat to my side. In my peripherals, I could see capital S. What could I possibly say to her? She's important to me, but there are some things I can't face that trump everything else. I pulled over, getting a strong feeling to just check what she had to say.

"Please. Please, please, please just let me know that you are still alive. Yes, I know that you are suicidal. It kills me, and I don't want it to kill you. Just say something to give me peace of mind. Where are you at? I'm sorry if I'm being really nosy, but can you blame me? I'm not just going to back away now when you push away. So please. Respond."

I let out a loose breath. Would it even do any good? Or should I say at least something? So I gave it my best shot.

"I'm going home."

I pressed send. I held my phone in my hand in disbelief about what I had just said. But it was a bold move on my part. Without trying to think anymore, I turned my phone off once and for all and threw it behind my seat. I was done with it.

Ten minutes later, I pulled up to the house. I was antsy to get out and run, my veins filling with rigorous adrenaline. So I burst through the front door like a maniac, scanning the living space for a place to start and ideas to swarm me. It doesn't matter to me if I'm being irrational. At this point, I don't see any reason to be rational. All I know is that I want to cease to be anything. Or, to correct myself, maybe I would choose to be a rock. Then at least I wouldn't feel a damn thing. Ever.

Under the sink cabinet is a fix. I fantasize, bitter slime rushing down my throat, swirling around my tongue, agonizing in cold whispers the last thing I will ever taste.

A shiver ran through my body straight to my bare feet, cold on the linoleum. In a moment's pass, I realized the empty silence of the house. What will be the last thing I hear? In all hopes, I wouldn't want it to be my parents. I need to hurry.

I rush to the medicine cabinet as it beckons. Opening the door reveals an easy solution; a present, just for me. I couldn't ask for anything more. I start picking through the bottles, letting them drop on the counter below. The impacts are like gunshots echoing in the silence, so I stop. Then I find the one. In my hand I hold Dad's sleeping pills.

Good thing for me, I have an idea of where he stores his special liquor. Double whammy. I hurry upstairs to my parent's room, trying to ignore my childhood pictures in frames on the walls. The nausea of the situation begins to set in. But I ignore it. I'm a rock for God's sake!

I saw the bottles in his wardrobe one time, I swear. That time was an accident in the game of hide and seek with Aldin. He hides them there for a reason. Me.

Aldin. I sure hope that he will be okay. Doubt was beginning to grow again. The guilt of letting down a person who looks up to me so much, or at least used to, makes me want to puke.

No. I can't do this to myself. I am determined to finish what I started.

I thrash open the doors, gritting my teeth and growling deep in my throat. I feel like tearing everything he owns apart! I grip a handful of his sweater and jackets, then I notice it.

The hell? The compartment embedded in the side threw me off. I think for a moment, the silence here gain. I have never noticed that little feature. There is no liquor here, but now my curiosity is aroused. I flip the little brass latch and pull the door flap down. My blood freezes for a breathtaking moment.

Yes.

I pull out my new deadly weapon. Goodbye world.

Noticing that it was already loaded, I searched the hand gun until I found the safety, and I switched it off. Thank you, Dad. You made it easy. I hastily stood up, fearing I would change my mind in a quick moment. Making my way across the hall to my room, I held my head up high and forced every thought out of my head. My mind was ready to spin like crazy with memories of my entire life, but I wouldn't let it. So this was it. I brought the cool barrel to my temple, my finger floating on the trigger. I was able to stay strong and completely narrow everything on my mind down to the cold silver against my skin, my sweaty hand clutching the weapon, creating cramps in my muscles. Squeezing my eyes shut, I only hoped my finger could do it. But it couldn't. My arm shook and my eyes watered with tears. Things began flooding my mind again, such as my mother's cries. Time felt like seconds, but it was really minutes going by with that stiff trigger on my finger.

Then it happened. It was a disruption I hadn't anticipated, one that make me swarm inside with intense fury. Out of nowhere, this crazy thudding against wood began rupturing the quiet, empty house. No fricken way. Immediately, I could tell that it was someone desperately pounding on the front door downstairs.

"DAMMIT!" I scream with a sudden burst. I clenched my fists, flipped the safety on quickly, and chucked the gun to the ground. It was incredibly stupid, but I was so close! The door downstairs had already opened, and my body froze to what I heard. A familiar female voice began calling my name.

Jesus.

Siri

"Roy?"

The moment I had seen his truck parked in front of the house like I had hoped, I stopped even thinking. My impulses carried me to his front door that I had ended up barging into. I scanned the kitchen, seeing prescription bottles and medication spewed all over the counter and onto the floor. That was when I had begun shouting his name, fearing the absolute worst. I could be too late.

"Where are you?!"

The house was silent.

I sprinted to the living room, checking the couches, the downstairs bathroom, and I even briefly scanned the garage. My feet carried me to the stairway. If he was laying down dead already, I don't know if I could take it. The anticipation was horrifyingly sickening. My stomach was a knot. I fear I will never see those dark brown eyes look at me again, or be able to feel the warmth of his hand in mine. He's the one I want to spend all my time with. Most of all, I would be angry. Angry that nothing had been done to stop him. Angry at him for even doing it.

Even though I had been frantically running through the downstairs area, my feet were now going in slow motion up each step. The silence of the house gave me chills.

"Roy?" I said again but softer, hearing myself whimper. I

wiped my damp eyes with my finger, trying to control myself somehow. Then I heard a sound. It was muffled and soft, like a voice. A male voice. Then…a sniffle?

"Roy!" I said enthusiastically, and now I was leaping up the steps. His bed room is the first on the right, and I quickly opened the door. I gasped, because there he was, sitting up against his bed. His head was low, his body shaking.

"Siri," he choked out, hardly looking up at me.

"Oh my God!" I shrieked, seeing him there in a breakdown. I caught glimpse of the hand gun sitting in front of him on the floor, which caused me to fall on my knees and wrap my arms around him. I had made it! His arms immediately fell back around me, and they were shaky as well. He felt so tense, sitting there heaving out cries like I would never imagined coming out of him. It was overwhelming, shocking even. Now I was crying harder. Not just leaking out tears, but full on bawling along with him. We held each other in that moment, the both of us pouring everything out.

"I'm so glad I got here, I'm so glad I got here," I said, choking on my words. When I said that, he squeezed his arms tighter around my back, gripping my shirt. My face had fallen into his shoulder where I squeezed my eyes shut, so relieved that he hadn't shot himself.

Minutes had gone by. He never let me out of his arms. The both of us had went through the cycle of crying, still shaking and sniffling. None of us said anything to one another. We just stayed in the moment, making our way to laying on the carpeted floor where he was holding me into him. I was in disbelief about what had just gone down. I actually have him here, alive, holding me like I want. The world and I get to keep him.

We wound down until the two of us were calm. I began stroking his hair, letting him know how much I cared. I finally decided to speak.

"I'm gonna kill you for what you put me through," I said softly. He began shaking again, and I was wondering if he was beginning to cry a little more. But no, he was laughing. I smiled, relieved. He still hadn't said anything.

"I can't believe you were going to do it."

When I heard him sigh, I almost wished that I hadn't brought it up.

"I just can't believe your timing. I was ready to. I was going to. But I couldn't with you here." He talked slowly with a heavy voice.

I gulped.

"It's like a miracle," I said. He was silent, like he was thinking over what I had said.

"You're a miracle," he said. That got me smiling, feeling his breath over the top of my head. His body was warm.

"Can I just ask you why? What went wrong between last night and now?"

Roy took a deep breath, held it in for a moment, and let it out, as if he was reluctant to tell me.

"It's complicated, and I can't talk about it."

That was it. I let loose of his grip and sat up. He seemed a bit surprised as I gazed into his eyes with a serious expression. He raised a brow. Seeing his tear stained face and melting brown eyes was a new look. It even took my breath away for a second. I had something bold on my mind, like always, I suppose.

"Look, you need to understand something, okay? I get that you have something you don't want to share. I've had serious secrets like that before, too. But that something is what pushed you over the edge. It was bad enough to make you want to end your life. You need to get rid of that, okay? That is the only way you can help yourself."

"S—,"

"Either people will continue to bug you about it, including your therapist—yes, I heard—or it's going to continue bugging you. I don't want you to die. Nobody else wants you to die."

He looked at the ground and shook his head.

"Please, Roy," I begged. He refused to look me in the eyes.

"It's not that easy, Siri," he said in a low voice. I could tell he was irritated.

"It can be—,"

"No, you don't understand. You can't just push me and expect to have me tell you everything, okay? It doesn't work like that!"

"Roy—,"

"You just don't get it! And nobody will!" He raised his voice and stood up. My eyes welled up with tears for his reaction. It stung. Roy paced around the room for a moment with a hand on his head, his expression pained.

"I'm sorry," I said, pleading him with eye contact. He returned my look, dropping his hand and sighing.

"Me too," he said, sitting down in front of me on the floor. The two of us were silent for a minute while he seemed to cool off. Meanwhile, I picked at the carpet in deep thought. I knew what I had to do, and I felt ready. If there was a time, this was it.

"Hey...," I began. He immediately looked up at me, curious, ready to hear me.

"I have something that I think I'm ready to tell you."

"Yeah?" He said, shifting his position.

"Umm...," dang, I didn't know how to start, "There is a lot that most people don't know about me. I mean, nobody actually, except for my family."

"What?"

"Yeah. I...," oh God, will I be able to do it?

Roy was silent. The only sounds in the room were the two of us breathing, and I began fiddling with my thumb.

"I was sexually abused years ago...by my real Dad."

My eyes immediately went to him to read his reaction. It's like my heart had stopped beating momentarily, waiting for him to respond. He was sitting cross-legged, and he shifted one of his legs up to rest an arm on. It looked like he was struggling, so I continued.

"It lasted for five years, until I was thirteen at least. Ummm...

212

yeah. He was the coolest dad ever to everyone else, which is what made it so hard. Nobody would never have guessed what was going on."

When I looked at him, he was intently watching me. I had his full attention.

"It didn't happen all the time. He was real sneaky about it, mainly when Mom was gone or when we would be home alone together. I never understood why he had to go there. I thought for a while that he loved me most or something. It was really confusing being the "special one." I hated it. I remember feeling so confused about it all…you know…loving my dad and not wanting to lose him, but wishing he could go away so all that he was doing to me would end. Sometimes he became violent when he got forceful. He tended to verbally put me down too, call me a—well, I won't go into detail."

Roy just stared at me. He looked like he wanted to say something, but didn't know what.

"One day, I decided I had enough. I always thought that nobody would believe me if I told, or would think I went along with the sexual stuff and that it was my fault too. All of that repression and fear had built up, and I became unsure of myself. I had been masking myself every day. My mom had taught me how to be a cheerful person, and not let your problems and sorrows burden others in your life when you could help it."

He nodded, "I can definitely see that," Roy said.

"Yeah, exactly. You would never have known, right? I didn't want to be that girl at school who had been abused by her dad. I wanted to be liked. I wanted friends and to appear happy for everyone so that they wouldn't suspect anything. I decided that I had enough of that. Dad was causing me a lot of pain, and I was sick of living with it."

"Siri, I'm…I'm so sorry," Roy said. His voice sounded odd.

"It's all over with," I said. There was a short silence.

"So…you…you told?" He asked.

"Yeah, I told my mom. She believed me too. All that time I had

213

been so scared to mess up my family and get my parents divorced, but also that people would think I'm lying for attention or something. I mean, yes, she was shocked and it took a bit to sink in. When I did it, I knew I would become safe and it would all be over. It was like someone had taken a freakin' refrigerator off my shoulders. That was when I found out he had been doing it with Ellie, too. Ellie and I both had no idea he was doing to the other. I wasn't as special as I thought."

Roy

I admit, soaking in her story was difficult. I was in complete disbelief, and wasn't sure how to handle myself. I mean, I would have never known!

"Roy…are…are you okay? You just look really uncomfortable or something," she asked me, taking my hand and stroking my knuckles with her thumb. She had told. She was brave enough to do it. I ended up ignoring her question.

"I...um...that was brave of you, you know, to tell."

She nodded.

"It was definitely one of the hardest thing I've ever had to do. But it changed things all for the better. Sexual abuse is…it's just a horrible thing to do to a child. I learned through my therapy how much I had actually suffered from it. Same with Ellie. She's been through loads of therapy. She used to cut actually because she became so depressed."

The similarities between her story and mine are undeniable. The fear of telling, not being believed, and how her sister cuts. It's all real. It's not just me. It was them too. Uncle Mark is a force on me that I cannot reveal easily. I would love for him to be exposed, but the consequences for myself are too risky. I'm a guy who was molested by a guy. It's disgustingly humiliating, demeaning, and definitely not what I want people to know, especially Dad, John, and Aldin.

"Is he is prison?" I asked.

"Well, he was sentenced to jail time. But it wasn't too long until he went through loads of treatment. He moved away, doesn't talk to us a whole lot. What is that, four years ago? So yeah, he's not really a part of our lives anymore. It makes me sad every day. He…he broke my heart I guess."

This was making me sad for her. I wasn't expecting to feel this way, especially when she wiped a tear from her eye.

"Were you scared of him after you told?" I asked. She thought for a moment.

"Yes, a little. He was forced out of our house after I was able to tell my story to the detective. My sister did too. Luckily, Kade was never touched. I was really scared of that. Okay, seriously, you don't look okay. What's wrong?" She asked, squeezing my hand.

This was the moment where I had to make a real decision. She had been through what I had been through. Our stories are different, yet they're the exact same. Hearing it from someone who had been through the revealing process, it got me thinking about how telling somebody might seriously change things. But it may not. I can't expect anything.

"My parents are expecting to talk to me today. One of the reasons why I wanted to escape today was to avoid telling them something. There…"

I stopped. Was I really doing this? I looked straight at her. I had messed up her ponytail, and her bangs were in her face. The sweet brown of her eyes held a reflection of concern, but sadness that I had caused. She was right here, willing to listen to my story and actually believe it. Here is someone who won't look at me like I'm disgusting, for telling such a "useless lie." She would understand. I actually have this right now.

"Whatever you feel you need to say, don't be afraid. I'm here."

She's too great.

"I broke my uncle's nose last night."

She jumped a little and covered her mouth, but was able to tone down.

"What?" She said, "There's probably a good reason, huh?" She took both of my hands. Her affection towards me is endless. I'm just used to it now.

"Yeah. Unfortunately, the fights I've been in lately didn't really help me much."

She agreed, nodding her head.

"So that's why your dad kicked you out?"

I raised a brow, "How did you know that? And that I'm suicidal? And that I'm in therapy? Are you my personal little spy?" I said. Seriously, how?

"Actually, Kyle told me everything."

No kidding?

"Really? Kyle?"

She nodded, "Yeah, John tells him things. They're both really worried about you, you know. Kyle's waiting for word to know if you're okay, actually. He feels terrible for blocking you out."

"He said that?"

"He did. Today. You should talk to him."

I don't want to talk to Kyle. There's nothing to say.

"I don't know."

"Yeah, you're right. You need time."

I sighed. Just minutes ago it seemed, I was ready to die. I would have pulled that trigger. Now, the forces of nature have brought me to this moment where things are changing in just seconds. This girl was abused by her father? How in the world could he have hurt her like that? The bastard. Looking at her and trying to sink all of that in is hard to put in a picture.

"Anyway, why did you punch your uncle's face in?" She said, trying to remind me what we were actually talking about. I knew we had gotten off topic. It was delaying what I know I needed to say.

"Oh, that."

Here I go, second guessing myself again. It was a strong feeling inside me screaming to tell her. Do it! You can't leave her hanging now! That would be too cruel. You owe her an explanation! Look at her, she's an angel. It won't hurt to tell. It may even make your relationship stronger! It won't get better from here if you don't!

My running mind was right. I have to tell her. There's no turning back.

"Okay," I said, heaving a sigh. My eyes still felt irritated from crying. My palms were becoming sweaty.

"I have...secrets. Let's just say that...well...my uncle is the cause of them. Bad secrets. Hurtful, deteriorating secrets....ones.... oh God," I sighed and placed my face in my hands, "...ones similar to...yours." I hung my head low, not sure how far into details I should go. I was only comfortable to a certain extent. When I looked up into her eyes, it nearly killed me. She knew. She could tell, and her look was so compassionate.

"Roy...are you telling me...that you—,"

"Yes, he...did. He did it to me, when I was six. Many, many times. My uncle."

Her hand went up to her mouth again, then the other one. Her eyes were wide, but I could tell she didn't want to act shocked. Our hands disconnected, and now my heart was beating fast. Someone finally knew my secret. It's been twelve years, and I could feel it wanting to spill out all at once like word vomit. I looked at her face with uncertainty, but it was replenished with security. It was as if we were both feeling the same emotion.

"I've never told anyone. Ever. I don't want to tell my parents or anyone but you."

She scooted towards me, hoping to lean herself on my lap. I let her, feeling her warmth. It was a soothing feeling.

"It's the hardest part," she said calmly, rubbing my arms with her fingers, "You're not alone."

I was ready to continue.

"I just have a messed up situation. He tried to touch me again last night, after all of these years. Just being alone with him in a room again got to me. My natural reaction was to defend myself now that I actually can. But he's very good at threatening me. Who knows what could happen. First off, I can't imagine my parents believing that such a friendly, normal guy would do something like that. Especially when they're mad at me already, you know?"

Siri nodded, "It may seem like the scariest thing, telling your parents, especially if your uncle has scared you against telling for so long. My real dad had always told me that if I told, he wouldn't love me anymore and neither would Mom."

"Wait, he said that?" I asked without hesitation. "If you ever, ever tell them about our little secret, you will be in big trouble. They will be very, very mad at you. So will I." Siri looked up at me. She looked adorable.

"Yes."

"My uncle told me similar things. I've never forgotten."

She seemed to hear me exactly. Without saying anything, she heavily sighed and gave me a squeeze.

"Whenever something comes up and reminds me of the abuse, I get a little bit depressed. Sometimes it's hard to get through it. I used to see a shrink, but I stopped going a year ago. I figured out a lot about why I was acting the way I was from what I had gone through. Back to what I said about how I masked myself every day, sometimes I would get home from school and lock myself up in my room and not come out until morning."

Sounds exactly like me.

"I've gotten to the point where I'm able to let go a lot of it when it comes up. My parents have been incredible with supporting me. I began piano lessons as an outlet, and music became an amazing healing tool. The experts say that trauma never fully leaves you, but I try really hard to see that it does. I mean, I want to live my life not having to feel what I felt during that terrible time, you know? I just wish it would never haunt me again."

I know exactly what she means. She lets it out with music too. That's cool.

"You seem to handle it amazingly. I mean, look at me? Look at my life and my relationships? I just can't seem to get it right. I...I don't even really know myself. I mean, who am I? Really? I don't seem to make any sense to myself most of the time."

She sat up from laying in my lap.

"Roy, I know exactly what you mean. I felt that. I felt that exactly!" She became enthusiastic,

"I used to feel like he owned me. I felt like he defined who I was because of what we did together. That was my life, and I didn't know any better. It took me a long time to realize that that wasn't me," Her eyes were welling up again, "But you haven't been given the guidance to let go and heal. You can't compare yourself to me, because everyone copes differently." I pulled her into me.

"God, I just...I still can't believe it. How did we get here? How did we find each other like this? I mean, I don't know what I would do without you."

She kissed my neck.

"I know, I know. I told you I felt something."

We sat in a moment of silence together, taking in this whole situation. It was unusually crazy, and I held my girl in my arms, taking note of how impossibly out of this world my morning has gone. It was so much at once I wasn't sure how to sum things up. It was jumbled up like a thousand puzzles in my brain. I shoved the gun under my bed temporarily, and we moved to my bed where we ended up holding each other face to face. In soft voices, we continued to talk.

"I want to thank you for not asking me for too much," I said. This was quite intimate for me.

"I'm not necessarily sure how to talk about everything without losing myself, so thank you for not pushing me. I'm still kind of in disbelief that I had even said anything. But with you, it was easier telling you now that I know you had been through it too."

She took hold of my hand and our fingers laced together.

"Well you need that. I want you to know that I want you to be happy and to heal. Healing is incredible, and I want you to feel incredible, because I think you really are," her voice was soft, her breath sweet.

"I don't know what to do now," I said. That part was killing inside. This dark dread was sitting heavily in the pit of my mind, strangling me with fear.

"It's the hardest part," she said, picking at the collar of my shirt. That's what she had said before.

"I can't tell them. Telling you is one thing, but it'll change everything. Nobody will even see me as the same person. Dad and John might think I'm gay or something. They know me as the guy who had sex with a man."

Siri was still.

"No way, no, don't even think that way. It doesn't matter who it was with. You were the victim, and you were a child! But even if you were older, he still forced you and you didn't have a choice. Besides, you didn't want him to touch you last night. How could they think you're gay?" She exclaimed, "If there is any common sense in this, the main concern will be about your mental well-being, not your sexuality."

"Are you sure about that?" I asked, not sure what to think.

"Look what you're cuddling with? You would ever even think about cuddling with a guy?" She asked, smiling. I frowned at her.

"No!"

"Okay, see?"

The main thing racing in my mind is how I am stuck with explaining what happened last night to my parents today. If I had the choice, I wouldn't tell them directly, but through my therapist. I have no way out today.

"I just can't. I. Can't. Tell. Them."

"When I told my mom, it was nerve-racking. I knew she would be upset. But I became scared when I began to learn how that kind of abuse can affect a person psychologically at school and through media. I even researched it. I felt like I was doomed for a hard future. Internally, I felt like I had been suffering by keeping it a secret. I never felt secure or safe, and it was horrific to me every time he did it. It then became a decision to tell for myself. I wanted help. I wanted to know that I could have a normal life, and that I could be an individual separate from his seductive, manipulative, incestuous control."

"It seems like a big sacrifice," I said.

"Yeah, you're right. It was. I sacrificed my parents' relationship, but also Dad's love and loyalty to me. That was the hardest part. I cried every night for a month after I told because I felt so selfish, but that I had also betrayed him. That guilt was just awful."

"Sounds terrible."

She nodded and sighed.

"Everyone supported me though. In fact, people were so proud of me for telling. Once I became commended to no end, I began feeling way better that I had told. For Ellie too. It was like I had become someone different. Before I had been a victim. I was told that I was no longer a victim. I was a survivor."

"A survivor, huh?" I said.

"Yes, that's what they call it," she smiled, "And you are too. I can promise you this, okay? When you talk about what had happened to you, it's when you heal. Once you begin, it'll become easier. You already told me. I know you can be brave enough to tell your parents."

"Legally I'm not even a child anymore. I mean, I'm not all innocent. What if the system doesn't even bother because it was so long ago and there's no more evidence?"

"Well, that's the tough part. He probably will not confess to it because the court may not find enough evidence but your word. And I know that he deserves to be convicted. But everything will eventually fall into place and work itself out."

Sure it will. She doesn't know that.

"Yeah. I just feel like I'll be burdening my family through the whole process. That's why it's almost worth it not to even say anything. I have no idea how Dad will react."

"I'm sure that they would rather know and deal with the process then to never know. The resentment won't fall on you. It'll fall on your uncle."

She seemed to know what she was talking about. I had good reason to listen because she had been through it. For the time after, we were silent. There was a lot going through our minds, and we both knew it. I continued to hold her. Very slightly I was shaken up inside still from what I had almost done earlier. I was like a maniac. Now, here I was, considering what I had ultimately feared most.

Exhausted, the two of us fell asleep together in the bare silence of my room.

Aldin

Sitting on the noisy bus ride home, I only hoped I would see Roy's truck parked in the driveway. I had tried calling him today at lunch to see where he was or what he was doing. Kade told me that he had stood up his sister last night. He asked me to kick Roy's butt for him. But that's not realistic. Roy had kicked Uncle Mark's butt last night, and Dad had kicked Roy's butt. I think he already has enough on his shoulders. Or, to phrase it better, his butt.

There it was, his canopied, blue and silver Bronco parked sloppily in front of the house. I wasn't sure what kind of state he would be in when I greet him. Would he be grumpy? Pissed? Wanting to be in solitude? My guess is that he would want nothing to do with me. I walked quickly to the house, noticing an unfamiliar, older Honda car in the driveway as well. When I walked in the door to the kitchen, I saw the mess of medicine bottles spewed on the counter and floor. What had he done? I didn't want to call his name. Instead, I made my way to the stairway, assuming he was in his room like usual.

I was in for a surprise. Opening the door to his bedroom slowly, I nearly stopped, not sure what to think. He and Siri were laying on his bed together, still in full clothing. They were facing each other, arms around the other, fast asleep. They hadn't even flinched to me opening the door. This was just too good. I pulled out my ipod touch and snapped a picture of the scene to Kade and John. That way, Kade knows my brother isn't a total blow off and John knows he's okay. Never have I seen Roy cuddling with anybody or anything like that. She must be a special girl, because I didn't think he would get a girlfriend any time soon. It was a first.

I closed the door, not wanting to disturb whatever was going on. I went downstairs to clean up the medicine bottle mess to avoid chaos.

Roy

"I'll hunt you down."

His revolting eyes narrowed at me, pushing me up against a wall, gripping my throat with a strong grasp.

"You're dead. Your life is over. I warned you not to tell you stupid kid."

His nose was bandaged and bruised. Yes. I was stronger than him, taller than he was. I tore his hands off of my neck, throwing him off into a round table. It buckled, and he fell to he fell to floor with a crash, moaning in pain.

"You're wrong. It's your life that's over."

Faint noises began taking place. I drifted away from a nightmare my uncle's presence to the creak of a door.

"Roy?"

It was Dad. I forced myself to open my eyes. I felt hot from being pressed against Siri. She was still breathing quietly, her forehead resting against my collar bone. I had no idea how long we have been asleep. I turned my attention to Dad standing in the doorway, looking like he didn't know what to say. I'm sure he wasn't expecting to see this. I didn't respond to him. He looked like he was waiting for me to wake her.

"Siri," I whispered calmly. She didn't react, so I shook her shoulder lightly.

"What's going on?" Dad asked, crossing his arms. That irritated me a bit. I wished he would give us some privacy. I watched her eyes open, looking confused for a second.

"What…oh yeah," she said lethargically, her cheeks rosy and hot. I sat her up, wanting the awkward situation to get over with. She looked at Dad.

"Hi," she smiled. There she goes, being her super friendly self. I don't think he even remembered who she was.

"Hi there." Dad shot her a smile to hide his uncertainty. Siri and I stood up.

"Roy," Dad began. I didn't look at him.

"We are going to talk, so, I don't want you going anywhere. Your mom will be here soon."

I gave a quick nod, and he left. Respectfully, he closed the door behind him. Siri and I looked at each other.

"I should go," she said, breaking eye contact.

"Yeah. But I wish you didn't have too."

She stuck out her lower lip, "I know."

"I didn't expect us to fall asleep. It kind of just happened."

She met my eyes and solemnly said, "I hope you will be able to tell them," her fingers brushed the top of my hand at my side, "Just…please. I really care about you."

Sighing, I took her hand to lead her out, blown away I even happen to have a girl who cares about me like this. As we hit the bottom of the stairs, the front door swung open to Mom. Immediately, she noticed Siri and me.

"Roy! And Siri," she exclaimed with relief, setting everything she had down on the table. Siri only smiled. Dad was on the other side of the room in the couch area, waiting patiently.

"C'mon," I directed Siri. Her hand still in mine, she stopped me in the kitchen. I was intending to walk to out to her car to avoid

224

the curiosity of my parents. Mom had joined Dad in the living room. I could feel their eyes on us.

"Hey, you don't have to walk me out, it's okay. They are waiting for you," Siri said quietly and thoughtfully. She saw my expression. I'm not even sure what I was ultimately feeling at that moment. It was a composure of dread, grief for seeing Siri leave, and nausea. God, it felt awful.

"Everything will be okay," she attempted to comfort me. Without much thought, I swooped down and pulled her into me. Standing on her tip-toes, she released a long breath. It was a nice, long hug. I had never felt so emotionally attached to a single person before. Spilling myself to her like I had come as an element of surprise. That hug was a thank you.

"Let me know what happens, k?" She whispered in my ear.

Nodding, I let her go. Before walking out the door, she shot me one last little comforting smile. Then she was gone.

The time was now. Like a weirdo, my feet stayed planted, staring ahead at the door where the one source of knowledge holding my secrets was walking out into the world. The adults waiting behind me were the next ones to know, reluctantly. Siri is right. It's the best thing I can do for myself. If Siri had the courage to do it, I know I have it too. I no longer feel so incredibly alone. I want them to know the truth about Mark. With the two of them burning holes in my back, I forced myself to turn around and face them. Mom and Dad both were situated on the couch.

"Come over here, Roy," Mom said firmly. My feet barely budged. Come on, just do it.

"Sit down," Dad ordered. I took a seat on the chair across from them. Immediately, Dad started as expected.

"So, I'm sure you understand why we are having this talk. Your problems with violence are getting out of hand. I hope you had time last night on your own to think about what you had done and what you have to say about," He folded his hands in his lap all serious like, "Now, based on what you tell us, your mother and

I will decide what needs to be done about you and your behavior, whether—,"

"What do you mean?" I asked.

Mom chimed in, "We have in mind an institution to help with your behavior."

Are they serious?

"What? But what if I refuse?"

Immediately, Dad said, "Well if you don't, then you will not be able to live in this house." He sounded very straight forward. One glance at Mom basically revealed she had a hard time agreeing to that result. Before I could say something, Dad continued.

"You broke Mark's nose. You assaulted him, Roy. You're lucky he chose not to press charges. He could have. That is absolutely… just completely insane. There couldn't have been anything that guy could have said or done to you to deserve that."

Wow. They think he's a Saint. It makes me want to puke. How will he believe me? I stared at the ground.

"Is there anything you have to say?" Dad said sternly, piercing me with his look.

"The resentment won't fall on you. It'll fall on your uncle."

Looking up at Dad, I said, "There are some things I have to say." I returned Dad's piercing stare. This was about me, not Dad. I am in control here.

"I want you to listen to me, okay? I punched Uncle Mark in the face last night. I don't regret it, and I never will," the both of the flinched, but I pretended not to notice, "The pieces in the puzzle don't seem to fit here. I get it. He seems like a nice guy. Why would I break his nose? Some things aren't easy to reveal. I know that because there are things here that I know I should tell you. I probably should have told you a long time ago, but I didn't. I was scared. I'm scared now. So scared, in fact, that I held a gun to my head today because I would rather have kept things secret than tell you."

I was wild eyed. Never have I felt so bold, saying it so straight out Mom's mouth dropped open.

"You didn't!" She shrieked. Dad had an oddly neutral face I couldn't read. I was going to continue, but Dad spoke up. Of course, Mom began crying. Ugh.

"So, you found my hand gun."

Pause. Mom stopped, looking at Dad.

"Why didn't you do it?" He asked me, staring at me directly in the eyes. Then came an intense moment of silence between the three of us. Mom seemed uncertain about Dad's reaction. I continued staring at Dad in the eyes, showing him my dominance.

"I didn't because Siri came. I couldn't do it with her here."

Mom's hands were over her mouth. She leaked out an "oh my God."

"She convinced me not to. At the same time, she convinced me to do something else; tell you why I had punched him."

"Roy—," Mom began.

I held out my hand to stop her.

"I will be ready right to go back upstairs and kill myself. I will. Don't even doubt it. If the two of you decide not to believe me but that creep instead, there will be no reason for me to be here anymore. Do you understand?" I said firmly. The two of them were still, both with astonished looks on their faces. I only half way meant that.

"You're mad, you are absolutely mad," Dad said, shaking his head. He buried his face in his hands.

"Excuse me, how can you talk like that to us?" Mom said, her eyes puffy, "I mean, oh my God! You are not going to go and kill yourself. That is absolutely stupid! And why do you think you can't trust us? Huh? It's offensive how you're acting."

"Mom, look, I need you to know that I'm serious, okay?"

"Well why would you call your uncle a creep?" Dad said, raising his voice a little.

Here goes. I began to feel my heart flutter with nervousness. I had to catch my words. Releasing a big sigh, I began at the best place I could think of, "Mom, do you remember when you got that job as a receptionist? It was during the time when Dad had that old job and we were hard on money?"

They both looked confused, as if what I was saying had nothing to do with anything.

"Okay, well, I was five or six. I had a.m. kindergarten and I needed a babysitter for when I would come from home from school. John was at school, and Aldin was in the daycare at your work, Mom. Do you remember where I would go two to three times a week after school?"

Mom thought for a second with a frown on her face. I think she realized it.

"You mean when Mark and Marie would watch you?"

"Yeah, well Aunt Marie would usually come home later, or sometimes after I would leave. It was mostly him."

"Right," she said.

"Okay, well…"

I stopped. The firmness in my voice was being replaced by shakiness. They noticed that.

"Roy, what?" Dad asked impatiently.

"Shh, let him take his time," Mom said, patting his shoulder. It became silent. I was doubting myself, and I wanted badly to retreat.

"When you talk about what had happened to you, it's when you heal. Once you begin, it'll become easier." I couldn't look at them anymore. Instead, I blew out a sharp sigh and covered my face with my hands.

"What are you going to say? Did…did something happen?" Mom asked with concern.

"C'mon, Roy," Dad said. Suddenly, Aldin comes thundering down the stairs. Irritation ripped through me. I think he noticed the tense conversation.

"Go away, Aldin," I said in a serious tone.

"Why?" He asked, frowning.

"Just go!" I said again. It was not for his ears.

"Okay, calm down. Aldin, for the time being, we need to talk to him alone," Mom said to him. He shrugged his shoulders and headed back up the stairs. I waited to speak until I heard his bedroom door close.

"I…he…"

I just can't do it. It's too humiliating. Their eyes were intently watching mine, and that added pressure.

"I'm…I'm afraid you won't believe me," I said straight out. They both seemed caught off guard.

"Believe what?" Dad urged.

With my face turning red, I had to go by impulse. It was the only way I could force it out of me.

"He used me. For sex." It didn't come out as shaky as I had thought. I avoided their eye contact, burning through me like a torch. I felt naked again, exposed. Everything at that moment in me was caving in with fear.

"What?!"

That came from Dad. It was a shrill exclamation.

"Roy, honey, what do you mean?' Mom said, covering her mouth. I continued. Does she really not get it?

"Every day, he forced me to touch him and do sexual things. In many instances, he forced me to….to…," I couldn't say it.

"Are you telling us that that man had sexually abused you while he was supposed to be taking care of you?" Dad asked, his face red.

"Yes. He abused me, okay?"

Mom's expression reflected her devastation.

"Oh no, no, no!" She cried, "It can't be! Why would I not have noticed?"

Geez. This was going to be chaotic.

"I mean, we trusted him! How could he have done that to you!?"

"Do you believe me?" I asked, unable to breathe fully. Mom

cocked her head.

"Oh honey, I would never believe that you would lie about something like that!"

She moved over to me and sat on the arm rest. Her arms went around me.

"Oh God, I'm so, so sorry! I'm so sorry I didn't see it." Drama.

"You never told us," Dad said, folding his hands in his lap.

"He threatened me. Told me that he would hurt me. Even Aldin. Not only that, but he said that you guys would disown me. Last night, he approached me again, even touched me. It brought back everything and I freaked out. Now that I am bigger than him and can actually fight back, it was just a defense mechanism I suppose."

Dad shook his head.

"Roy, what specifically did he do? Did he hurt you? Did he… did he rape you?" Dad demanded. His voice was intense.

I couldn't believe he was asking that. Was I not clear?

"He…he…"

Then it began. It was completely out of my control. A river load of tears pushed at my tear ducts, hot and fresh. They came out like an unstoppable wild fire. I couldn't stop. Mom's arms were tight around me, trying to rock me. That made me uncomfortable. My reality was being completely exposed, and I was vulnerable. Dad now knows. He knows I had done sexual things with a guy. It felt as if I was coming out of the closet, and the fear of them judging me was strong. There was no turning back. I had told my secret, and my tears were releasing it all. It was incredibly demeaning and embarrassing.

"Dad—," I managed to choke out. I wasn't sure what I wanted to say. After all, I couldn't speak. Mom was hugging me like Siri had been earlier. I couldn't believe that I hadn't been stronger. I wanted to be stronger, not a crier, especially in front of Dad. But I shouldn't have been too worried. With my surprise, Mom and I jumped to a loud crash against the wall. Dad had thrown his flip-phone and it broke apart across the floor. I tried to catch my breath and stop shaking to see what he was doing. He looked terribly angry, but different than usual. He was legitimately upset.

"Richard?" Mom asked, pressing her head against mine. I let her head stay there. I understood how hard this was for her. Dad paced across the room, his fists clenched.

"Just...just hang on!" He shouted, giving us the index finger. He lowered his head and shut his eyes.

"That bastard," I heard him mutter. Did he just call Uncle Mark a bastard? There were envelopes and junk mail sitting on the kitchen table. He thrashed it all off and beat his fist on the surface, making loud thudding noises. I was in disbelief. His next move was to the home phone in the kitchen. He stared at it for a second and then yelled "Dammit!" He came storming across the room with furious eyes to pick up his cell phone that had flew apart. Hastily, he puts it back together again, Mom and I unsure what to say or think. It took him a few moments to put in back together, and once he did, he held it to his ear.

"Richard? Who are you calling?"

Dad threw down his arm and turned away from us, "Just..."

Silence. Mom and I sat in anticipation. Was he calling him? My question was about to be answered.

"YOU! YOU SON-OF-A-BITCH! Shocked? Well yes, so am I you deceitful, disgusting, cowardly bastard! I heard what you did to my son! I hope you are scared out of your wits for what is to come! Do you have any idea what you have done to his life? Do you have any idea how much pain it has caused him, our family, and will continue to? How DARE you! You're done, you child molester!"

And he shoved the phone into his pocket, took one look at me for a moment of eye of uncertain contact, and he fled upstairs to his bedroom.

Holy shit.

Chapter Ten

John

I got a surprise call from Mom today. It was during a ruckus of my roommates playing air hockey, so I stepped out of the room to hear her speak. At first, I was expecting her to ask if I have heard from Roy. That is a definite no. I've tried contacting him these past couple of days. The kid wants to be left alone. I get it. So I gave up. Whether or not he's okay? I don't know. I was hoping she'd know.

"Hi honey, I just thought you should know what is going on right now. I ask for your sensitivity towards the situation."

What situation?

Well, she laid it out for me. I was pretty shocked. Roy had gone through some trauma with Uncle Mark molesting him? When we were little kids, and none of us had any idea? Does that explain all of his weird behavior from time to time?

I guess even the nicest people can be sick. God, poor Roy. Just the other night that guy was in our house. It even makes me a feel a little guilty for how I had been cold to him that day. That could have been me. Uncle Mark could have targeted me. But no, he didn't. It had to be him, my secretive, unique, playful, talented middle brother. I can't imagine going through something as awful as that, staying in your memory forever.

Must have been the most heart pounding experience of his life telling Mom and Dad what had happened. That's true bravery. I'm a little surprised he did. Roy better brace himself for Dad's fury, as loyal and protective as he is.

Me? I'm just plain livid at my uncle. He took away my brother's childhood. I feel so ignorant for thinking highly of Mark when he was hanging out with us. Now, I could kill him.

Roy

There was a different feeling in the house the next few days. We were anticipating the expulsion hearing, but at the same time, everyone was still trying to take in the news. It devastated Mom to have to hurt her sister and tell her what happened. Not only did Marie refuse to believe what Mark had done, but she was already appalled about Dad's haughty voicemail. At the time, Mark wasn't home. Mom had handed the phone to Dad, who basically told my aunt we had no choice but to contact the authorities and report him. I was sitting close by, able to hear her voice on the other end.

"This is crazy! Your son is lying. He's always been a trouble-maker, and now he's blaming my husband on his problems? What kind of sick twist is that?"

Mom began to cry. I genuinely felt terrible for her.

Aunt Marie continued, "You really want to do this? It'll be a hell of a process for us all. What chance do you think you have of trying to prove my husband is a child molester? Huh?"

"Marie—," Dad tried.

"No, Mark would never do anything like that. I know him, you and your son don't as much as me."

"We can't just leave this alone. That man traumatized one of my boys, and who knows if he tried anything with the other two, or any other kid in that fact. I don't see any possible reason why he would make this up. I'm sorry you are caught up in the middle of this, we are not trying to attack you Marie, okay? But I want him targeted for what he did," Dad said, relatively calm.

"We'll see," and she was gone. Dad sighed and hung up the phone. He looked at me, then at Mom.

"It'll be okay, you can't expect her not to be defensive, Cathy."

"I know, I just…I don't want this to come in between me and her."

I feel like this is all my fault.

"Mom, I'm sorry I—,"

"No, no way. Do not blame yourself for this, okay?" She said firmly, shooting me a look, "I know this won't be easy, but it's for the best."

I nodded, accepting.

"Dangit, Richard, I just wish you wouldn't have left that horrible message. I know you were mad, but for the sake of Marie, you know?" She sniffled.

"I know, I probably shouldn't have. I was out of hand."

Why did Dad's lashing out of anger remind me a lot of myself?

As for me? Well, I'm pretty complicated at the moment. At times, I feel like I've done a terrible thing. The reveal has been putting a big burden on my family, especially with other things going on right now like the expulsion and my Grandpa. So far, my parents have kept it on the down low for my sake. I know Mom told John, and I'm not sure how to feel about that either. I haven't talked to him or seen him yet. Then there is the enlightened portion of this situation. It feels like this cage around my heart has been broken down, releasing the secrets turning my flesh black. The pain is all there, hidden underneath, but the two-ton weights on my shoulders and chest are slowly lifting away.

What amazes me the most about the reveal was how easily Mom and Dad believed me. All of that time I had been so worried. Maybe it's wired in them because I'm their kid, or because I started crying, making it a little more convincing. But most of all, it's no longer me against him locked in a tiny shell, suffocating my life. I'm no longer that shy, defenseless little boy. I'm tall and I have a damage-causing fist. It's me, Siri, Mom, Dad, and John so far against him.

The day before the hearing, I asked Siri if she wanted to take a drive with me. We didn't really go anywhere in particular. I just wanted to tell her things. The vanilla-scented, freckle faced cutie sitting in my passenger seat chewing on a Milky Way made me feel clearer. Now that she knows, I feel different. We became closer, intricately connected. Increasingly, it became more and more relaxing.

"Do you feel good about it?" She had asked, referring to me telling.

"I'm not really sure yet. It's all still new. All this attention is on me, and it's weird."

The day Aldin was born, I was four years old. I remember that day. A transition was happening in my life, quite more significant than I had realized. No longer was I the baby. John was Dad's perfect boy, and Aldin was the adorable baby attracting everyone's looks. Where was I?

"Isn't it neat, Roy? You're a big brother now," Mom had said. I was excited. After the first year, I began to resent the little thing. As terrible as it sounds, I thought I hated him. When Uncle Mark began abusing me, I became increasingly secretive to shelter my inner demons. Along with that, I was aggressive and confusing for my family. One time I had pushed Aldin because I was annoyed at him. I hadn't anticipated him to fall and smack his five year old face on the corner of the kitchen table and start screaming because he bit through his tongue. As awfully sad and fearful as I felt, Dad whipped me several times with his belt on my front side and told me afterwards, "I don't wanna hear you cry."

As time passed by being the unnoticed one, the majority of the attention I seemed to receive was from negative behavior. John was gifted, Aldin was charismatic, and what was I? The pain in the butt. That curse followed me into my teen years. Look at everything? I still get noticed, primarily by Dad, for my negative behavior.

Right now, it's different. Sure, I might be getting expelled. I got into fights. My grades are bad. I got caught cutting. But I'm not being punished, ridiculed, or lectured for this. Nobody is disappointed in me. There's more attention on me than ever, and it's not negative.

"I know how you're feeling," she said, her ponytail swaying in my peripherals as she looked my way. We walked along the river for a while until the early November rain began to pour.

That night I had a four hour shift. Mom asked me if I would be okay before I left. I told her not to worry. Aldin has been lurking around, trying to figure out what the heck is going on. Mom hasn't gotten around to it. But he has been avoiding me. I'm not sure why, it's a little odd. Dad has been quiet. I think he doesn't really know how to be around me. There's a stiff energy distancing him, like he feels he should reach out to me, but his emotional barriers are building a wall. That's my theory at least. He doesn't want that sappy father-son moment. That awkwardness I feel around him by what he knows is the killer here. I've never been sure whether or not his relationship with me means much in his life, and this situation embraces that question most. Why did he react the way he did? Why did he care so much if our relationship is borderline superficial?

Josh and I tip-toed around each other again at work. We would be walking towards each other and both of our heads would go down, avoiding any contact. When he was in the back folding boxes, he went to the bathroom when I walked back there to get a case of ranch sauce. I'm honestly sick of it.

The next day, Friday, was the hearing. Gosh, I was dreading it. Mom and Dad both came to support or defend me or whatever. It wasn't too bad of a process at least. The hearing officer listened thoroughly to me as I told my story. Basically, I had followed Derek and Dion into the bathroom when I saw they were bullying a freshman. Derek was ripping off his clothes and shoving Michael's face in the toilet, exactly what he used to do to me. I pulled him off of Michael and began punching him in the face to make him stop. The administration member stating the situation mentioned the brutality of my punching, that Derek is suffering from a broken nose, one broken tooth, and swollen eyes. This had been unacceptable on school grounds. Then, Mom brought up the recent findings of the trauma I had went through, but that I am already enrolled in therapy and am getting treatment for my issues. I think the hearing officer could see the pleading very clearly in Mom's eyes. So badly I was hoping that helped. Furthermore, she mentioned how being in drumline helps me vent my emotions in a healthy way, and taking that away may disrupt me. In the end, it came down to a decision we would have to wait to hear.

Mom had squeezed my hand as we left the building, saying, "We did what we could. Let's just hope they agree that expelling you wouldn't be right."

Then, surprisingly, "Those punks who picked on you better not win," Dad said under his breath.

Mom nodded, "I know, it makes me so mad." I walked behind the two of them, hands in my pockets, unsure of what to say. I hadn't realized they were this much on my side. What, did the sympathy meter spike up when they found out I was abused?

We went out to lunch, just the three of us, which was a bit odd. I couldn't remember a time where Mom and Dad both had taken me alone somewhere with them, excluding the therapy sessions in middle school. Somehow, John and Aldin had always gotten that time. Me? Not that much. That thought was running through my head as we sat in a booth, the two of them across from me. We talked about the hearing mainly. Dad wanted to bring up reporting Mark, which he and Mom planned on doing this evening.

"Renee called me this morning. She asked what was going on, because apparently Marie called both her and our mom and vented, acting all upset," Mom said.

"What did she say?" Dad asked. Mom sighed.

"Oh gosh, that's what I'm upset about," and she then looked at me, "I didn't know whether or not I should tell you Roy because I want to protect you. I don't want you to worry, but...Renee and Jeff, Marie, and Grandma Helen are all questioning what you said."

"I knew this would happen. I'm just some 'rebellious,' 'troubled teenager' nobody will believe. That's what Mark told me, and he's right. It's true."

"No, don't believe that. You are a good-natured kid, and both of us believe in you."

Dad chimed in distantly, swallowing a bite of green beans, "It doesn't matter what they think. They just don't want to believe it."

"Do you even think reporting him will do any good? I mean, it's only my word," I asked. This question was arising in fear that all of my parent's efforts will go to waste because there is hardly any evidence. I don't want all of this family drama.

Dad gave me eye contact for a second, "Whatever happens, happens," he said plainly. I sighed.

"Okay."

Mom looked at me and reached across the table near my space, "I hope you know that you did a good thing, and none of this is your fault."

It's easy for her to say that. But I feel like it is.

There was a play-off game that night. Technically, because of my temporary suspension, I wasn't allowed to play with the band. I just didn't go. It's crummy that's I've missed so much rehearsal. I know Elliot isn't happy about it. Although, I'd rather have him be unhappy with me than knowing what I told my parents. Therefore, I said yes to working. Walking in Dominos and not seeing Josh was quite a relief. I made a couple deliveries and crafted some pizzas. During that duration, avoiding conversation with my co-workers, I thought. My drumming deprived hands are beginning to taste the hunger. I need to drum. I need that outlet. I don't know what to do with that stored anger I feel towards Dad taking my drums away. I want to cut, but I'm being monitored. Mom is checking my arms every day now. You would think I can refuse to let her, but that will only spark a fight with Dad. I'm eighteen years old and I feel like I'm trapped in my parent's basement.

The chime from the entrance door goes off, and I pause with the roasted peppers to turn around and greet the customer. But it's Josh in uniform, and I turn my head away before we could make eye contact. Dang. He clocks in and stands over by me to make another order. I don't breathe because it's so awkward. I want this to end, I just have nothing to say to him. But I guess he's the better man.

"Look, I know we're pissed at each other and all, but people around here are starting to notice, especially Harry."

After he ended his sentence, I pursed my lips and stopped what I was doing.

"So what?"

He shook his head and almost slammed the dough down onto the pan.

"C'mon, man," he tried. I turned to look at him, but froze at the sight of his eyes, bloodshot like candy cane.

I hissed quietly, "Are you serious? What…are you trying to get fired?" He'd be able to get away with it if his eyes weren't so obvious.

He looked around, suspicious someone was listening, but nobody was close at the moment.

"Who gives a fuck?"

"What?"

He sighed, rolled his eyes, and turned his back on me. This was bugging me.

"Why would—,"

He snapped back around, "Well how about you? You've been acting like a zombie here lately, not talking to anybody. You are even short with the customers."

Geez. I didn't think it was that noticeable.

"You're not the only one with problems around here, you know," he said with hostility.

"Obviously not. Geez."

"I just had a really shitty day today, so I would appreciate it if you just—,"

"Wait, I thought you wanted this intensity to end. Now you just don't want to talk to me anymore?"

It's not making sense to me. That had caught him, and he realized he had just contradicted himself. I was curious.

"What happened?"

He blew out his cheeks, "Well, sure isn't something I can just tell you."

"Why not?"

He paused and locked eyes with me, "Why do you want to know?"

I shrugged, "Forget it." He reminds me of myself.

Once again, we avoided talking throughout the rest of the shift. However, even though being incredibly annoyed, I still found the ability in me to deal with all the customers so that Josh's eyes wouldn't be exposed. He had jumped out and defended me against Derek and Dion that one time. I kind of owe him I suppose. We both were let go at the same time. He had beat me out the door after clocking out. When I went outside, I spotted him leaning against his car texting. He looked up and saw me walking across the small parking lot. Unexpectedly, he called me out.

"Hey, Roy, come here."

I frowned, wondering what he was going to say. If it was raunchy, I wasn't in the mood. I thought we were avoiding each other again anyway.

"Yeah?" I said, trotting over to where he was. He shoved his phone is his pocket and didn't speak for a moment.

"Look, I'm sorry about the whole Kendal thing. That text I sent you kind of topped it, and I feel bad."

I should apologize too.

"I put myself in that situation. I was just being stupid."

He gave me a half smile, "I know," and wacked my upper arm.

"I know you were only trying to give me a good time."

"Are we good, man? I'm really tired of not talking," he said.

"Yeah, I guess so," I agreed, nodding, "Just...never set me up with girls again, okay?"

He smirked, "Sure, whatever." It was silent for a moment as he looked at the ground. I was just about ready to walk off when he spoke, "Hey, thanks for you know, covering for me in there. I was kind of a cranky jerk, and I didn't expect that from you."

Wow, he managed not to cuss. Never heard him say "jerk."

"What could possibly make you want to smoke before work?

You know your eyes get bad."

He took off his cap, "Well, I kind of forgot I had work. I was having a rough go, and it was just an immediate action to go get high. Dang, I was so freaked out Harry would catch me."

"Got lucky."

He tucked his hands in his pockets and looked at the ground.

"I really want to know, bro. Why did you say no to Kendal? Like, why'd you freak out and everything?"

I sighed. I was hoping he wouldn't ask.

Shaking my head, I said, "I...I dunno. I don't get myself sometimes. It's not that I don't want to do sexual things, it's just..."

It felt a little awkward expressing this to him. But seeing his engaged expression, I could tell her was seriously curious.

"What?" He urged.

"Look, I don't know. It just reminds me of something I don't want to remember."

"What, like trauma or something?'

"Umm..."

"Like something in your past happened, a bad sexual experience that ruined it for you?"

I squeezed my eyes shut, blown away by how accurate that was, "Something like that." I turned away, not sure why he was going there or how he guessed it.

"Wait...seriously?" He asked again. I looked back at him.

"Just forget it."

"No, no way, man."

"What?" I frowned.

He then said, "This is really random, but do you think we can go somewhere and talk?"

Spontaneous.

"Umm...okay?"

"Here...just...get in my car."

This was odd, but I did it anyway. Getting situated in the passenger seat, I turned to him curiously. He began talking.

"I know you're probably thinking 'why is he reacting to what I said this way,' but you just remind me of this guy I met in NA."

"NA? What's that?"

"Narcotics Anonymous. It's like AA, Alcoholics Anonymous, but more about drug addiction."

"Why were you there?"

He explained nonchalantly, "I was depressed when I was about fifteen, mainly because of family shit. I started getting into cocaine and some other weird street stuff. I spent a lot of time out of the house, and I somehow became friends with this guy a couple years older who really got me into using. Oh man, let me tell you. It was like medicine from heaven. But I got busted. As a part of addiction rehabilitation, I went to NA for a short period of time."

"I had no idea."

"Yeah, most people don't. Most people don't even know I pierced my nipples."

Cringe, "What? Ow."

"Yeah, did it myself too, went through this whole self-punishment stage. So anyways, in an NA meeting, there was this guy who began telling his story to the group. He was this big, macho guy, which made it a little ironic. Basically, his step dad molested him and his older brother when they were kids. This went on for about…I don't know…five years?"

My God.

"During that time, his older brother started coming on to him as well. It was like a learned behavior, which seems so sick. The whole thing began to traumatize him. Like, he had bad problems with intimacy with girls, but he was afraid to be gay. So he just strayed completely away from sex. Long story short, he eventually turned to meth to try and escape his problems."

Turned off from sex completely?

"So when you said that sexual things bring back bad memories, it's like that with him."

I get what he's saying. At least I still want to have sex, just don't know how not to see Mark's face.

"You would think that would be me too," he added.

That came out of nowhere with surprise, "Wait, what?" I asked. What is he talking about?

"My mom. Well, she did it to me."

I was speechless.

"I know, it's crazy. It really was. Basically, her marriage was falling through. Dad was drinking and became distant. She got lonely and depressed. That's when she started turning to me...for... you know. I was thirteen and the only close male she had. I was so uncomfortable, so disgusted. It felt so wrong. But she pleaded me. If I didn't she would make me feel guilty for 'not loving her.' Then Dad would come home drunk and yell at me. It was scary how much he's swear and call me horrible things."

First Siri, now him?

"Wha...what?"

"I know, I know. I'm laying a lot on you and it seems shocking, but I'm not afraid to tell people anymore. When I heard Danny, that guy I was talking about who told his story, it kind of inspired me to tell mine. I'm glad for that now. I was put in extensive therapy after revealing, and I'm still in it."

"You are?"

"Yeah, there's still issues I know I have that are hard to work out. Like, I fricken have sex to feel better about myself. In my therapy, I've discovered that I turn to girls to have sex with in order to make up for my low self-esteem, which horribly enough, is what my mom did. But...with Danny, it was the opposite. He strayed away from sex. It's just odd how people cope so differently from that type of stuff, you know?"

"So...you were sexually abused," I confirmed. It's a familiar term now. It was an idiot question.

He gave one form nod, "Yep. Sure was. Worst damn years of my life. Since it's been a couple years, I am so glad I didn't wait to

243

tell. You have no idea how much it would have sucked to live with that in me. I mean yeah, the shit still lingers, but I'm getting closer to leaving it behind."

I played with my shirt seem.

"I'm sorry."

He looked at me with a frown as if I said something dumb, "Why? Don't be."

I didn't say anything to that. I was trying to fathom why he had told me all of this. Was he seeking for an understanding? It almost felt wrong not to tell him my story now that he spilled his. I felt the way I did after Siri told her story. Not only that, but a knot was seeding from within me, growing bigger to the moment with terrifying regret. Did I waste away my whole childhood? Because both Siri and Josh told early on and things got better.

"Hey, um, I know what it's like to have a secret, one so humiliating it eats you from the inside out."

"Tell me, man. I just told you my secret," he begged, resting his hands behind his head.

Sighing, I continued bluntly, "My uncle. Sex abuse. I was six....the thing is, that wasn't even the worst part of my life. At least then, I didn't really know what was going on. I was just scared. Now, it's a lot more complicated. Things get bad when certain things happen that make me remember it. I re-live it all the time."

"Oh my God, wow. Triggers. That's what you're talking about. Abused people all have their own triggers that regress them back to the abuse. Have you told anyone?"

"Of course…well…I did the other day for the first time."

During the silence, I watched his expression turn to shock.

"What? Literally just a few days ago?"

I nodded, "Yeah."

He whistled, "Wow, you waited all the way until eighteen? Man," he threw his head in the head rest, "but do you have good support and all?"

"Yeah, seems like it. It's still all new to me. I don't what what's going to happen next, you know?"

"Yeah, I hear ya. I was there…God, your uncle? Ugh."

I smirked, "I broke his nose earlier this week. That's what pretty much kicked off my reveal. I really had no choice but to tell."

He threw his head back and laughed before I finished, "No way! That's wicked, dude."

Things calmed down again, and he spoke in seriousness, "I used to fantasize killing my parents."

I lost my breath for a second in momentary shock.

"What? You serious?"

I never really thought about killing.

"Would have never done it though. Even though it seemed like it would have made everything stop, it would have made my life hell. No thanks, prison."

"You live with them? Your parents?"

He snorted, "Hah, no. God no. Dad left a long time ago, disappeared off the face of the earth. Even with all of her mental help, Mom still wasn't fit to keep me in the house. I live with my aunt. She's sane at least. She makes sure I get to my sessions, but she lets me roam free pretty much."

Josh is like a free man. However, he is still odd in some ways, and I'm beginning to understand why.

"So what made your day suck?"

He sighed, "Well, if you must know, Mom visited me today. We got in a fight about things…stupid, pointless, regressive shit. I told her to fuck off and she stormed away crying. My aunt got pissed at me, told me to grow up. She wasn't there years ago. She doesn't get it."

I wasn't sure how to respond, so I only nodded. He picked that up.

"Look, you don't have to say anything. I just appreciate you listening. It's cool to talk to someone about it who knows what it's like to be used. Most people just don't talk about it. Kids become

245

victims, grow up, and keep it locked up until they just die inside."

"I used to think it would destroy everything if I talked about it," I said, "He was never around after that time, so I never had a reason to tell." He looked at me directly in the eyes and smiled.

"You were right and you were wrong. At least you can get on with your life and get out of the painful, never ending rut. I'm working on it and I'm getting there. You can't lose when you're the victim, ya know?"

Never in a million years would I have thought that Josh and I would have had this conversation tonight.

The next day, Mom suggested to tell the therapist what I had told her and Dad. My claim was heard to DHS. I'm not sure whether they cared that much since I'm eighteen. As we speak, he is currently under investigation. I hope he's crapping in his pants right now. But telling the therapist could get me the type of treatment I need apparently for the childhood trauma. So I told Lydia everything. It was becoming easier to tell. Siri was right.

Lydia didn't act shocked or surprised. She was completely calm, as if she was expecting it. That's just a part of the professionalism I suppose. She listened to everything, even the part about me wanting to die. I decided to tell her that too. She had asked what inspired me to reveal. It was the messed up situation, really.

By keeping it a secret, I could have destroyed a lot more childhoods come to find out. That's my conclusion. She explained the likelihood of Mark targeting other children, and that I may not be the only one. I had asked if keeping it a secret for so long was a bad thing. She shook her head and only explained the normal tendencies in so many situations like mine. Hearing her talk about it made me see how it directly related to how I felt; threatened, embarrassed, and guilty. There's no blame.

When I arrived home that Monday evening, Mom greeted me at the door with an opened envelope in her hand. Seeing the smile on her face washed me with relief. Nothing bad this time?

"Roy, honey, you are going back to school tomorrow!" She threw herself into me, looking as though she was going to cry once again. So the judge pitied me after all.

"Seriously?" I asked, almost in disbelief. I was prepared for tutors or a community college GED.

Dad peered at me from across the room, nodding. He turned away and tuned back into the TV.

"Well, that's one less thing to worry about," I said.

"No more fights, you hear?" She said sternly but cheerfully.

"Okay."

We will have to see.

I almost went up to Dad to ask for my quads back. Something in me was telling me not to bother. I wasn't in the mood to associate with him really.

I laid in bed for a while staring up at my white ceiling. There were a lot of thoughts floating around in my head. Siri had texted me, asking how the session went. I gave her quick reply saying I'll tell her tomorrow at school. She nearly flipped, "Yeeeeeesssssss! This is one happy girl."

You don't deserve to be happy. After all you've done? You think you can just walk around with your cutsie little girlfriend and pretend everything is okay? You're a fool.

I shook out his spine-chilling voice, uninvitingly sickening. Then came a call I wasn't expecting. John.

"Hey," I answered.

"Hey man, what's up?"

I haven't talked to John since the day of the funeral.

"Umm, I don't know. Why, what are you doing?"

He paused, "Well, my friend Clay has a gig here at the Pine Lounge, and I want to go listen. I was wondering if you wanted to come hang."

"Really?"

Out of all his friends, he invites me? His weird brother?

"Yeah really, just get your butt over here at seven. I wanted to invite Kyle, but wasn't sure if you guys still aren't talking or what."

"Umm, I don't know. You can invite him I guess."

"All right, seeya later. Bring five bucks."

"Okay."

I put on a black t-shirt, slipped on some blue jeans, and covered myself with my worn out, cotton black jacket. The raggedy thing needs to be replaced. No doubt Mom will stick one in a box under the Christmas tree this year. I can tell her and Dad hold back from saying anything when I wear it.

Entering the place full of people, I saw both John and Kyle already sitting back and chatting away. Clay was up on the stage jamming it out on the acoustic guitar. I figured this would be awkward. I'm unsure why John is even getting us together. Either John is only inviting me so he doesn't feel guilty for last time, or they want me to talk. I'm not sure I'm comfortable with either. I caught Kyle's eye, and for a second, he only stared at me walking over.

"There you are," John greeted. I looked at him directly.

"Can I talk to you?"

He gave me a strange look, but he stood up and walked with me a few tables away from Kyle.

"What's up?"

"Does he know? You didn't tell him, did you?" I asked, fearing Kyle knows more than what I'm comfortable with. John shook his head.

"No, no. I wouldn't do that. That's up to you. The only thing I told him was that you went through something. He asked about you, so that's all I told him."

I nodded, "Okay. Thank you. If he doesn't have to know, I'd like to keep it that way for now."

"Yeah, I get it. It's cool."

There was a pause while he stared at the floor.

"Look, I...I couldn't believe that happened to you. I mean, I believe you, it's just hard to take in. I'm so, so sorry. I wish I knew what to do or what to say, but I don't. I just feel angry it happened. Our whole childhood went by and nobody ever knew."

248

I appreciated that.

"It's okay. You don't have to pity me. I'm glad it was me and not you or Al."

John set his fists on his hips and shook his head.

"C'mon," he emphasized, "don't. Don't say it like that. Don't be glad. Don't think that you had to sacrifice yourself for us, okay? You're not disposable. You're a person who didn't deserve that horrific abuse."

I broke eye contact, unsure of how to respond.

"Let's just…hang out and act like normal, okay?" He said, patting my shoulder. I nodded.

The three of us casually sat and listened to the music, munching on nachos. John and Kyle were talking together more than I was. It felt uncomfortable, but I pretended things were normal. Kyle turned to me and asked about DCI, surprisingly.

"I'm not sure anymore."

Kyle's expression held pure disappointment.

"No way," he said, "But that's all you ever wanted to do."

"Things change," I said bluntly. He didn't respond.

John eventually got up to leave when Clay was done playing. Kyle and I followed him outside. Before I climbed in my truck, Kyle hollered my name. He began to walk towards me.

"Yeah?" I said. He stood in front of me with his hand in his pockets, hunching his shoulders like he was uncomfortable.

"Im…uh…glad we get you back in the line. It hasn't been the same without you. You know, I'm not clear on everything that's been going on in your life right now, and I'm not saying you have to tell me. I just want us to be good."

I nodded, "Yeah. Me too."

He shrugged, "You know, you never thanked me or anything after I helped you get home from Cameron's. I was honestly a little mad about that."

Now that I think about it, I really didn't. Some friend I am.

"Yeah, um, I'm sorry. Really. I've been a pretty crappy person

249

lately. I was being stupid that night and I didn't deserve your and John's help. Like, at all."

"I know," he smirked.

There was a brief silence where I wasn't sure what to say, but he spoke.

"What is with giving up DCI? Huh? It's not your dad, is it?"

"No freakin' way. I'd do it in spite of him, you kidding? It's more about a loss of motivation. I probably wouldn't make it or fit in I guess. It just seems unrealistic."

He got wide eyed, "You serious? How many times do people have to tell you how good you are? Huh? If there was such thing as all-state rudimental drummer, it'd be you. Where the hell is this coming from?" He said, becoming passionate about it.

Kyle

Then I realized what it has to be. It's a self-esteem thing. I recall back to that night taking him home from Cameron's, "I'm a piece of shit."

Roy

"I don't know, man. Let's just drop it, okay?" I said.

He smoothed a hand through his short curls, "All right. See you at school." He turned around after giving me a short wave and got into his car.

Don't think this is over just because you ran to "Mommy and Daddy." I told you not to tell anybody, and you defied me. You can't prove anything. Once they let me go innocent, you will be scared as hell. I will be coming for you. You won't know how or when, but you will be sorry. Karma is a bitch. Stupid kid.

250

A little over a week went by. Saturday was marching band finals for the region. We placed third in our class. That was kind of cool. Elliot is already passing out music for the winter drumline indoor season. He's pretty much ordering me to write myself up a piece for the voluntary solo competition. Reluctantly, I went to another therapy session, and we talked about trust. I'm glad these things only run once a week. I don't like talking about myself so much.

It was this Tuesday evening that my family and I found out something shocking. A true table turner. Aldin and I were in the other room watching TV, Dad was in his room doing business work, and Mom was jabbering away on the phone in the kitchen.

"The same time you get a girlfriend, I get a girlfriend," I said to Aldin. He was texting the girl he calls his girlfriend.

Aldin ginned, "Took you long enough to get one. Who wants that face?"

I stood up and ruffled his hair to tease him. He slapped me in the back.

"Bad big brother. Mean big brother!" He said, smoothing it out.

"Roy! Richard! Come here, I have something to tell you!" Mom yelled loud enough for the neighbors to hear. In a few seconds, I heard Dad's business shoes thumping down the stairs. Mom had hung up the phone. Reading her expression was hard. I couldn't tell if it was good or bad, which made me curious. She had us sit down.

"Is there something wrong?" Dad asked. Mom looked at me.

"Renee called me. I know there has been a lot of talk on my side of the family about what Roy said. They are in denial, and we have no evidence."

"Well yeah, and Mark and Marie feel attacked," Dad added. She agreed.

"Yes. It has been getting to me that they aren't believing us, or you, Roy. It's making me angry, actually, because they are accusing my kid of lying. They think you are trying to justify punching him because you don't want to get into trouble, and Jeff even accused

251

you of being on drugs."

Okay, so I've done a bit of drugs here and there to ease my mind. I'm not an addict, though. It's not like it had anything to do with that. The irony is that his daughter is a drug user. I bit my lip.

"What did Renee say?" Dad asked, folding his hands on the table. Mom took a deep breath as Dad and I waited in anticipation.

"She said that Jessica came out today. Apparently, she claims Mark had touched her on numerous accounts."

Oh. My. God.

"What?!" Dad nearly shouted. He sighed and hid his face in his hands. Mom gave me eye contact, and I looked at her with shock.

"Jessica?" I said. Jessica had experienced similar things as me with that horrible man? After all this time, she had never told either?

"I just…feel so sad. Our children fell victim to this man, and he was obviously good at enforcing them to keep it inside. Renee was crying, going through the same thing I went through when you told me," she gestured a hand at me, "I just don't understand how he could have gotten away with it."

Dad put a hand on her back, "Well, thank God for Jessica. We have a team of evidence now. He won't get away with it."

She nodded, "I know."

Jessica is like my savior right now. I sat at the table quietly, still trying to take it in. That's when I felt the buzz in my pocket. Expecting it to be Siri, I was wrong.

Jessica texted, "So, idk if you have heard. My sobbing mother just got off the phone with yours, spilling my life story. I got so tired of hearing everybody calling you a liar. It made me down right sick, because I know you are telling the truth. When I heard what he had done to you, I thought about how brave you were to tell. I had a hard time being at that funeral. I'm beginning to wonder if you were even in the bathroom "throwing up." Good news is now we know we have each other. Thanks for giving me the courage, Rog."

Questions were being thrown around inside me. How long ago

did it occur? How far did it go? Did he threaten her like he did me? Is she an unusually sexual person like Josh as a subconscious way to cope with what's inside? Not only that, but it's like this whole reveal of my twelve year secret triggered a train-reaction of sexual abuse reveals. I feel like I'm being bombarded. Siri, Josh, and now Jessica? Who's next?

"Well, that's that. They can't call me a liar now," I said.

"Dang right they can't," Dad said, "The DA called today for you, Roy. They want to ask you questions. I wrote the number on a piece of paper on the counter for you. Make sure you do that tomorrow, got it?" He said sternly. I just nodded. He brushed a hand on Mom's shoulder before going back upstairs. Mom rested her cheek on her fist and sighed.

"You okay?"

I silently nodded.

"You're lucky to have a Dad who takes care of us the way he does. I'd have a harder time going through this if it wasn't for him."

"He's too much of a hard-ass," I said.

She blew out her cheeks, "Sure. He can be. But he's a good man. You know that, right?"

I wasn't sure how to respond. Dad is totally different with her than me. It's difficult to have such a high opinion of him when he's the way he is.

"I guess. I just want my drums back."

Mom rolled her eyes.

"I'll talk to him about it."

That following Friday, Siri finally convinced me to let her come over for dinner. John wasn't there, so she took that place of his lively personality. Siri wasn't shy like I had been with her parents. Mom was excited. She had made her most delicious spaghetti dinner and homemade rolls for the occasion. I had never brought home a girl before. Even Sophie never made it here. She sat by me, wearing a red dress shirt and dark blue skinny jeans. Her hair was down, a rare occasion, which tucked cutely behind her ears. I observed Dad through the duration. He seemed unusually dazzled by Siri and her charming charisma. I could see it in his quiet eyes and smile. Before I knew I was staring, Dad's eyes met mine. I darted away from the contact and focused on the noodles in my fork.

"Seems the two of you are getting to know each other well, then," Mom commented.

Siri and I gave each other a mutual look and I said, "Who are you again?"

That made Dad slightly chuckle and Aldin laugh, which gave me a good feeling.

"You sarcastic butt," Mom said in return. Siri hooked her ankle with mine, which made me uncomfortable at first near my family. But I warmed up to it.

"That wasn't so bad," she whispered in my ear. Back up in my room, she laid against my chest as we stared up at the ceiling.

"They love you," I said, "Then again, how could they not?"

She lifted herself up and cocked her head.

"You know, you're not the most affectionate guy ever. I guess it's a good things when you say sweet things to me on occasion. It makes it more special."

I scrunched my face and smiled, "Gag."

She slapped my chest, "Shut up." She sat up on top of me and randomly began to flap my ears.

"I hardly ever see these things. They're kind of big."

"You're kind of big."

"Big hearted!"

"Big weirded!"

"You're dumb," she said in an exaggerated voice. She stretched out my ears, "You're Dumbo!"

"You're done," I grinned, "And dumb."

She got up and lightly laughed, "Why am I here? Who wants to be with somebody so dumb?"

"Get out of my house," I joked.

In that moment, the girl who had saved me curled herself back into my side. Having the influence of a fellow survivor is something I wish I had a long time ago. I know I have had a hard time trusting people most of my life. Lydia and I had a long talk about this. My distance from intimacy has stunted the growth of relationships, and my hesitation of trust has caused fractures. The fear of girls hidden within me has always been a troubling hurdle. Little by little, I'm surprising myself with how far I have been able to get in my growing relationship with Siri. If there's anyone in my life right now who has earned the most trust, it's the person brushing the hair out of my eyes. She understands me.

"Your eyes make me want melted dark chocolate fudge with rich, hot, dark chocolate drizzle," she said with a sexy smile. She's cool like that.

"Well let's go get some."

This revealing process has just begun. I can't say I'm complete. I can't conclude at this moment that I'm entirely happy. Siri is like my temporary medication, but there is a lot I have coming ahead of me. My family and extended family are in a crisis due to the allegations against my uncle. I still have minor anxieties, fearing the worst. I can still get triggered. His voice is lingering inside me, like a nightmare I can't escape.

My world had been colorless for years. Maybe more so black, red, and shades of gray. It's like an overcast Monday repeating itself. Even a girl hasn't brought enough color. The sun has peeked out, but the blade is in my pocket, thirsty for just one more drop of blood. Everyone around me is promising that things will get better. I look forward to the days ahead when the haunting memories trickle out of my everyday living. The light is visible, and now I know there is hope.

I have told my story, but I'm only waiting for something better. I've got a lot of treatment to undergo, but I know it won't be so bad. I'm hungry for these blanks to be filled.

---10 months later----

Siri

It was a beautiful late summer day in the afternoon. I could tell it was going to be a good time. The whole gang of us, Roy's friends and family, gathered at the nearest DCI show. He might have an idea that we are here to see his show, but he certainly isn't expecting it. His mom wanted it to be a surprise for him.

"Listen to those bass splits. Sick!" Preston grinned, passing Santa Clara Vanguard's bass drum line practicing out in a grass area. Their horns were warming up as well in the distance. The place was filled with music already. The stadium was well-sized, and we chose seats in a decent spot after buying tickets. I had never seen an actual DCI show before. I know that it's pretty cool. Roy's dad seemed to be on another planet. It didn't seem like he was too thrilled to be watching band stuff. It's not his thing. I sat just below his parents and Aldin next to Fiona and Melony. Unfortunately, Preston was directly behind me by Kyle and John. I just know he will be his typical self. He leaned down closer to my ear, "Siri, your boyfriend is coming. In his pants. And other uniform items. Seeeexy."

I smiled, "Shut up." Krysten swiped his arm.

"Gross," John said without hesitation. We all laughed.

We watched the couple first groups perform. They weren't world class like Roy's band, but they were enjoyable. During the transition between two groups, a man squeezed through above me to take the open seat next to Roy's Dad. None of my friends were talking to me at the moment, so I overheard him starting a conversation with Mr. Sanders.

"So, you have a son or daughter in the program or are you just coming to enjoy?" He asked. He seemed like an uppity, friendly guy.

"Oh uh, son."

"Oh yeah?" My seventeen year old daughter is playing trumpet. She loves it."

Momentary silence.

"What does your son play, or what group?"

"Um, Blue Devils? He plays the...tenors? Yeah."

I heard the guy whistle.

"Wow! That is amazing. I mean, they are one of the best drumlines in the world. You must be so proud. How old is he?"

"Eighteen."

"Wow, that's great. Takes a lot of talent to be in a quad line like that. There are only what, four or five of them? He's gotta be pretty dang good. I believe they play next, right?"

I saw Mr. Sanders fumble with the program at the corner of my eye.

"Looks like it."

"God, I'm so jealous. I could never be good enough for this," Preston said, "Roy is like my hero. I hate him for it."

"Yeah, I do too," Kyle added.

"But Siri doesn't. She loves Roy sooo much. She's gonna cry when he walks on the field," Preston teased. He and Kyle laughed. I just shook my head.

"I won't cry."

"No, maybe not. I'll just take a picture of you dramatically running into his arms when we talk to him later. I'll post it and be like hash tag, 'missed your bod so much,' hash tag, 'so cute,'" he said in his funny voice.

"My God, quit picking on her you jerk," Fiona said grinning, thumping her fist on his knee, "hash tag 'you're a douche.'"

"Well said," I told Fiona.

Krysten said, "Can you believe the crap I have to put up with? Hash tag 'my boyfriend has special needs.'"

The rest of us laughed.

"Wow. You're so mean," Preston said in a girly voice, "you can't joke about people with disabilities. How dare you guys verbally abuse a person with special needs. Jerks."

"Okay Preston," I said. I had to laugh.

On the far side of the field, the band in blue began to appear. I smiled, excited as ever to see Roy perform. I felt so genuinely proud.

"Calm down Siri," Preston whispered in my ear. Oh geez. The band set up the production. As they did, the tenor line marched onto the field. Roy had told me he was on the far left of the four dudes. I could definitely tell it was him by his height. He looked so sharp in the uniform.

"There he is!" Roy's mom said enthusiastically, pulling out her video camera.

"Where?" Aldin asked.

"He's on the far left," I told him.

"See, she knows," Preston said, smiling widely.

The drum major started the performance, and already, the precision of the music was incredible. Fiona and I exchanged glances at the nice pit solo.

"Wow," I heard Roy's mom mumble.

I thought the music was cool. The show carried on, and my eyes followed Roy marching in the tenor line. I could imagine how hard he has worked all summer in the hot sun on this show. It takes dedication and conditioning, and this group is so professionally good. He has overcome so much, fought so hard to do this. Less than a year ago he almost killed himself. Now here he is, thriving, doing what he is so passionate about without holding back.

The drums marched to the front center of the field. It was the drum feature.

"Yes, yeeees," Kyle said enthusiastically. The snares played a feature, then the bass drums, and then came the tenors. They marched out in front of the other sections, halted, and played an intense solo so awesome that they tilted their drums forward to show it off. They slammed their sticks down after the last note, and the crowd erupted. Nice.

"YES! That was so sweet!" John said, standing up and clapping.

"YEAH ROY! YEEEEEAH!" Preston screamed, jumping out of his seat. The rest of us were cheering, but laughing at Preston's enthusiasm at the same time. The epic show came to an end, and we all sat with our faces blown off by the incredible drums and horns.

The evening set in. As the performances came to a close and the awards were being presented, I anticipated getting to the lot and seeing Roy. I couldn't wait to see his face. We walked as a group together to the back lot. It was a big place, and there were band members all around.

"Hey, everyone! Over there!" Kyle said, pointing to a semi-truck with The Blue Devil's logo. We followed him. The entire band was clumped together for a meeting. When we got close enough to hear voices, I could tell it was an intense staff to performer conversation. I stood in between Fiona and Preston, who I could tell were searching faces in the massive group to spot Roy.

And then I saw him. It had been over two months since I have associated with Roy in person. He's been on tour all summer around the country with his group. He stood tall compared to a lot of the people around him. His hair had been cut fairly short, which was the most noticeable difference. From the side, he almost looked like a whole new person. His skin was sun-soaked bronze, standing out by the white t-shirt he was wearing. My gosh, he looked good. Seeing all of the girls around him made me borderline jealous.

"Oh my God, I've never seen his hair that short," Fiona said, "Even in middle school. Not even kidding."

His family and friends stood in a group, watching him. He hadn't noticed us yet. When he just happened to look our way, he seemed to not notice. Then came the double take. His face read total surprise, but more than that. His smile held something I haven't seen very often since I've known him; overwhelming joy.

"HA! I got his face!" Preston hacked, showing us his iPhone. He had captured the picture of Roy smiling from noticing us. Looking back at Roy, he was shaking his head like he had saw Preston taking the picture. We all know he doesn't like pictures.

"Instagram," Krysten said to him.

"I'm going to zoom in on his face," Preston grinned mischievously.

The group took a few minutes longer to talk, and then all of the members were temporarily released. Roy knew what was coming. I could see it in his hesitant body language. We were going to bombard him. But there he came, walking straight at us with a smile on his face. Being in front, I got to him first.

"Hey," he greeted me, lifting me up with his super tan, toned arms. I wrapped my legs around him and gave him a squeeze.

"I miss you," I said in his ear.

"I know, I miss you too," he said in return, planting a quick kiss on my lips. I took a quick moment to study his exposed face up close, running my hands in his chopped hair. It was crazy different. He was different.

"Oh Roy, hi," Mrs. Sanders exclaimed. She hurried up to hug her son. Then came a Preston-lead group hug. We attacked him: Kyle, Preston, Krysten, Fiona, John, Nathan, Sean, Melony and I all in a mob. He grinned and put his hands up to block, but we caved him in.

"Help!" He said, laughing. Mrs. Sanders flashed pictures.

After a minute or two, the group of us stood around Roy, curious to hear about his summer adventures.

"My God, I just can't believe you all are here," he said, his face flushing red. That was new.

Roy

It was an incredible moment I had not foreseen. Here everyone was, gathered to support me in my show. Their enthusiasm was apparent, and the mood was great. Siri had greeted me like I was the most special person in the world, and seeing that sweet face was a privileging moment. Not seeing everyone all summer has been tougher than I thought. They're my support load.

"That was a sweet show, dude," Kyle said.

"Ha, yeah. Thanks. I would sure hope so, we've been working our butts off twelve hours a day."

"Oh it was incredible, you did a great job, hon," Mom said. I smiled to her overly proud, motherly comment.

"You guys should see this tan line," I said. Being out in the scorching sun for hours and hours with our shirts off gets quite overbearing. I pulled my shirt collar below my shoulder to expose the white stripe where it had darkly burned around the harness.

"Ohhhh! Look at that!" Krysten said, covering her mouth.

"Looks like pain," Aldin said. I patted his shoulder.

"It happened to a lot of the guys, so it's cool."

"No, it's hot!" Preston corrected. A bunch of us chuckled.

Mom wanted pictures. She gathered the group of us friends up revolving around me. Then more.

"One with the family," she insisted. I stood in the middle of my two brothers and gripped a shoulder on each. I couldn't have asked more than the two cool, supportive guys on either side of me. It was a great feeling to sink that in during that moment.

John patted my shoulder, "It may not be a sport, but seeing you in that drumline was pretty cool, man."

Responding to that sincere of a comment, I said, "Thanks. That means a lot." He smiled and gripped my hair.

"Ah! There's not enough to grab anymore!" He said, giving me a playful shove in the direction of Dad, who still hasn't said anything. He's been the man in the background, the one who told me previously, "You do this summer band, I won't help you pay for college. That's final." It hurt that he still didn't get it, especially when I found out I had made the Blue Devil's tenor line. Going on with the therapy at the time, Lydia had nearly prescribed the drum corps to me. My friends and Elliot had been increasingly diligent on convincing. I'm thankful every day they did. When you do what you love, there's always a way to make it through. I'll figure the community college situation out.

"Hi Dad," I greeted. My heart picked up speed seeing his surprised expression. Mom and John even turned their heads. If there's anything in the entire world I wish I could have at this time, it would be his acceptance. I knew if I asked for it, I'd fall short with predictable disappointment. He's the way he is, and he gives me what he gives me. Although internally I plead for his praise, the best I can do is be thankful he actually came. That's big in itself.

"Hi Roy," he responded, hiding his hands down in pockets.

"Thanks for coming."

He gave me a smug smile and quickly nodded his head. That's all I got, but it was better than nothing.

"Hey can I get a picture of you with Dad?" Mom piped up, holding her camera up without a chance for question. Dad and I made quick eye contact, and I awkwardly shifted myself to his side. I haven't posed in a picture personally with Dad for years and years. Taking a deep breath, I pulled my hand out of my shorts pocket and brought it around his shoulders. Being affectionately distant from Dad for so long now, it was a strange and daring feeling. He did the same thing and wrapped his arm around me, giving my side a small squeeze. I held my breath.

"Awe look at that!" Mom grinned, finally setting off the flash. My smile during that had definitely been genuine.

During the entire legal process of prosecuting Mark, Dad was determined to bring forth justice for me and what I had gone through. It was the most loyal, tough-skinned love I had ever seen him portray. Through some work in therapy, I was able to see him for a lot more than I had let myself before.

The case never made it to trial. I never had to give a testimony in court. Once Marie became increasingly frightened by what was coming forth, she threatened to leave him. That was a few months after a six year old boy was questioned. It came out Mark had lured him into a Sunday-school room at a church and took advantage of the kid. An eleven year old girl claimed he had fondled her a few times, then took it to sexual rape. That makes four of us, connected by unfathomable means, suffering the everlasting consequences of one man's obsessive crave. There could be more. He didn't bother hiring a defense attorney, and eventually confessed to his crimes after living under a layer of his own sweat for months. There were too many allegations against him. Whether he'll get successful treatment in the future or not? I'm not entirely sure. At least for me, I have so much anger stored inside towards him, it's easy to see him suffer. It's difficult to see Mark being a well-functioning person someday. I'm not sure there is capacity in me to ever forgive what he did, but a part of me hopes I can someday. Same goes for Derek and Dion, who showed me no mercy with the everyday pain they caused me. They put an extreme strain on my life, and it's tough to let go of.

Recently, towards the end of the school year, I overheard heard Dion talking to someone in the locker room regarding Derek. I never thought much of Derek's bruises he showed up to school with. Mainly, I figured he had just been street fighting or something of the nature. But no. Dion explained that Derek's abusive drunk of a father had recently been arrested for running a meth lab in their home. Neighbors had reported some loud yelling going on and that's when the cops recognized the smell at their doorstep. Apparently, Derek had been severely beaten by his dad and uncle for delving into some of the drugs. But Derek being beaten wasn't a rare occurrence. It was regular. I now understand that he had inflicted the suffering on me to feel the power he felt he lacked. I believe the way my father went about hitting me wasn't always right. However, compared to Derek's dad? It's quite different. I can't forgive him now for what he has done to me. But at least I know where his mind might have been during those times he kicked me on the floor repeatedly. Most likely, unless he gets help, he'll be another jail statistic.

Eventually, because all of the legal stuff going on, my closer friends found out about my past abuse. It became difficult to hide. Kyle had been incredibly understanding. In the back of my mind, I have always figured that we are only buddies because of drumline. Being two different guys, we wouldn't have been friends outside of this experience. I believe now that I was wrong. He has this understanding about me I feared he never would if he knew. But he was there. He is one person I made sure to receive a brotherly hug from before I had to load in the charter.

Giving Siri one last hug goodbye, she stuck a candy bar in my pocket.

"Here's your reward," Siri said, kissing me on the lips.

"Uh, for what? Picking the best girl ever as my girlfriend?"

"No! I'm so proud of you!"

"You're cheesy," I said, running my hand along her waist, happy this girl is mine, "But I accept your sweet compliment."

She smiled, "Oh so you've learned a thing or two about acceptance, huh?"

I shook my head vigorously to tease her, "Nope!"

They left a few minutes later. Although I love them, being away from the home situation this summer has been the relief of my life. Escaping the court system, the family drama, and all else that kept putting my mind in the realm Mark has kept me sane. I went through quite a bit of treatment already to help me move on with my life, but this summer drum corps program has been my empowerment medicine. Being around new people, working hard, and doing what I love is exactly what I needed after such a stressful process. Every minute of every hour now, I am thankful that my secret is out. Realizing now how I have been living all these years in an ongoing depression with low self-worth, repressed rage and fearing trust only put me lower. I could have never been happy, no matter what kind of romance I got to experience, what good of friends and family I had, or how much I loved drumming. I was drowning in issues I didn't fully realize I had. Siri had been the element of miracle I never saw coming. She gave me the courage. Josh gave me reassurance, Jessica gave me alliance, and as for the rest of the children out there who fell victim to such a saddening crime, I give them my word. There is always hope somewhere of some kind, and life is worth living at its best.

We are no longer victims when we choose to disclosure our abuse secrets. We are survivors. It gets better.

Chapter 10

Aldin

My brother is the same in so many of the good ways as he has changed over the course of ten months. There is that piece of him that's always been present, a darker entity in his person that refused to speak out but harmed the lives of others with hurt and confusion. That aspect is becoming distant now in Roy. I model him. He's my big brother, and seeing him hurt had always hurt me. Now that it's becoming apparent his life is gradually shifting into something preserved and genuinely optimistic, I feel our family has to worry about him less and less. Roy is a unique individual and always has been to me. Seeing him thrive in a way I had always wished lowers the burdens I have felt for so many years caring for such a troubled person. My uncle, or ex-uncle I can assume, is doing his time for the detriment he had caused for Roy. It's been a ride being caught in the middle of this.

As for my parents, they seemed emotional on the drive home from Roy's show. Seeing him doing so well after such rough times tear-jerked my mom.

"Did you see how happy he looked? I've never seen him glow like that," Mom had said.

If he would have committed suicide like he had planned, he wouldn't be in this grand place as a part of our lives. Dad was tougher to read. His quiet exterior is a sign to me that he was heavily thinking. At least, when Mom uploaded the photos from the evening into the computer, I interpreted Dad's extra-long look at the photo he took with Roy as taking things in.

I have always idolized John in ways I didn't Roy. They are two very different people, and it was said Roy lived under his shadow. But from the strength and passion Roy has exerted and proven to showcase, I can honestly say he is my hero.

Roy

A few days after my encounter with my loved ones, we were back in the summer sun again rehearsing show music. As a tenor line, we were having a sectional and working on some tough phrases we still could perfect better. My sun bathed, calloused hands have been through so much work.

I got a call during a momentary pause in playing. Pulling it out of my pocket and seeing it was Dad, the curiosity was killing me.

"I gotta take this guys," I said before walking off behind a building for privacy.

"Hello?"

Slight pause, "Hey son." His voice was neutral. He usually doesn't call me "son."

A little surprised, I said, "Hi Dad. What's up?"

"Well...um...I don't know, I want to see how you are doing."

He had just seen me three days ago. Why didn't he take the opportunity to talk to me then? I didn't bother bringing it up.

"Um, fine. It's hot today. We're in southern Cali."

"Yeah I know, actually. Your mom posted a tour date flier on the refrigerator."

"Right."

Momentary silence.

"So uh, I wanted to tell you that I wasn't expecting what we saw on Saturday. You know it's not my thing. But it's obvious you worked really hard to do this, and I could see that."

Is he really saying this?

He continued, "I also underestimated how much talent you actually have. I never really realized it. It's pretty...cool what you can do."

Another silence, longer this time. I couldn't speak because I was in shock.

"Look Roy, I know I have been hard on you. I know it. I also saw how hard you have worked to do this, and I know it really means a lot to you. I know I haven't said it too much, but…you know…I'm proud of you. For all that you are doing and what you overcame. Even if it seems like I'm not. I really am."

It took me a moment to gather my words as he waited on the other line. He has been hard on me, and it has been years since he's told me that. It was sappy, but so overdue and deeply desired that I could have cried.

"That means a lot," was what I managed to say in return.

I can picture him nodding.

"Okay well, I'll let you get back to your stuff. Have a good time."

"All right, Dad."

Then he was gone. I guess in moments like this, where just about everything in your entire world falls into place, you get to that mountain peak point of fulfillment you feel you've never reached. I have been craving my dad's acceptance more than I've felt comfortable with. It's been a battle for years. He just gave it to me. I wish there were other ways to express happiness other than tears at this moment. My eyes watered up, but only because I couldn't help it. It wasn't only that Dad had just told me what I wanted to hear. We have laid out a foundation for the beginning of a better relationship. I have the ability now to seek healthy relationships, but starting now, one with my father.

The truth is, I am a worthy person worthy of good relationships. Hearing Dad's encouragement not only magnified my sense of self in less than just a minute of time, but led me to a place where I am closer to feeling complete with him as my father. Realizing this along with what I have worked on already, I know I have a good life ahead of me. This was only an addition to my now continuing strive to find empowerment. Perhaps in the future, I can help other lost kids find theirs too.

Made in the USA
Lexington, KY
27 November 2015